"What was with all of the flirting and the looks?"

Anthony's eyes flashed in anger. "You said you're bad at this. I'm bad at this too! I may not be handling this attraction between us well, but at least I'm trying!"

Maggie's eyes widened in surprise. Both at the words, and the blurted nature of them. Captain Moretti struck her as the type of man who was always in control, but he didn't look in control now.

"I should go." He backed away.

"Wait!"

He paused and she went to him.

"About the . . . attraction," she continued before she could lose her nerve. "I don't know what to do about it either. But I feel it. Like I've never felt anything before."

He closed his eyes. "You shouldn't have said that."

"Why not?" she asked.

He made a low growling noise. "Because now I won't be able to stop myself from doing *this*."

He pushed her backward into the wall. His eyes were wild as they looked down on her, and the last thought Maggie had before his mouth slammed against hers was that Anthony Moretti completely out of control was the sexiest thing she'd ever seen . . .

STEAL ME

LAUREN LAYNE

FOREVER

NEW YORK BOSTON

Copyright © 2015 by Lauren Layne
Excerpt from *Cuff Me* copyright © 2015 by Lauren Layne
All rights reserved. In accordance with the U.S. Copyright Act of 1976, the scanning, uploading, and electronic sharing of any part of this book without the permission of the publisher constitute unlawful piracy and theft of the author's intellectual property. If you would like to use material from the book (other than for review purposes), prior written permission must be obtained by contacting the publisher at permissions@hbgusa.com. Thank you for your support of the author's rights.

Forever
Hachette Book Group
1290 Avenue of the Americas
New York, NY 10104

www.HachetteBookGroup.com

Printed in the United States of America

First Edition: November 2015
10 9 8 7 6 5 4 3 2 1

OPM

Forever is an imprint of Grand Central Publishing.
The Forever name and logo are trademarks of Hachette Book Group, Inc.

The Hachette Speakers Bureau provides a wide range of authors for speaking events. To find out more, go to www.hachettespeakersbureau.com or call (866) 376-6591.

The publisher is not responsible for websites (or their content) that are not owned by the publisher.

ATTENTION CORPORATIONS AND ORGANIZATIONS:

Most Hachette Book Group books are available at quantity discounts with bulk purchase for educational, business, or sales promotional use. For information, please call or write:

Special Markets Department, Hachette Book Group
1290 Avenue of the Americas, New York, NY 10104
Telephone: 1-800-222-6747 Fax: 1-800-477-5925

To Anthony—for use of your name, and maybe one or two other things as well. And for Tony and Patty. Couldn't have made this journey without you.

ACKNOWLEDGMENTS

A huge thank-you to all the usual suspects:

Nicole Resciniti, my fabulous agent, for always being there to talk me off the ledge.

For Lauren Plude, for gently nudging me back on track when my story ideas go in all the wrong directions.

For the entire Grand Central team, for the fabulous cover, the marketing support, and, of course, the production process that turns this from messy manuscript into beautiful book.

For my husband, for being understanding when I speak only "grunt and tantrums" when knee-deep in a story, and for my family and friends for understanding when I drop off the edge of the earth.

Lastly, for my super-secret NYPD source (and brother of one of my most darling readers), who helped me keep the "cop stuff" grounded.

STEAL ME

CHAPTER ONE

For Captain Anthony Moretti, three things in life were sacred:

(1) Family.

(2) The NYPD.

(3) The New York Yankees.

And on this breezy, September Sunday morning, two out of these three things were making him crazy. Not in the good way.

"What do you mean, you don't want to talk about it?" his father barked, leaning across the table to help himself to one of Anthony's pieces of bacon.

Maria Moretti's hand was deft and practiced—the mark of a mother of five—as she swiftly swatted the bacon out of her husband's fingers. "The doctor said you were supposed to take it easy on the bacon!"

"I *am* taking it easy. This is Anthony's bacon," Tony clarified, rubbing the back of his hand.

"Is it?" Anthony muttered, glancing at the now empty plate. "I don't seem to remember actually getting to eat any of it."

His youngest brother and fellow cop stabbed a piece of fruit with his fork and waved it in Anthony's face. "Cantaloupe?"

Anthony gave Luc a withering look. He could appreciate that his baby brother felt man enough to get a side of fruit with his Sunday brunch, but Anth would stick to potatoes and fatty pig products, thanks very much.

"I think I'm going to hurl," his other brother, Vincent, said to no one. "Shouldn't have gotten the side of pancakes. Too old for this shit."

Anthony felt the beginnings of a headache.

Item number one on his priority list (family) was also the number one cause of his frequent *Please, God, take me away to a deserted tropical island* prayers.

But there was no tropical island. Just the same old shit.

For every one of Anthony's thirty-six years, Sundays had looked exactly the same. All Morettis filed obediently into their pew at St. Ignatius Loyola Church on the Upper East Side of Manhattan for ten o'clock Mass.

Breakfast always followed, always at the same diner, although the name had changed a handful of times over the years.

The sign out front currently read *The Darby Diner*, named after...nobody knew.

But the Morettis had never cared what it was called. Or why it was called that. As long as the coffee was hot, the hash browns crispy, and the breakfast meats plentiful, they were happy.

Granted, the greasy-spoon food of the Darby Diner was

a far cry from the Morettis' usual fare of home-cooked Italian meals, but Anthony was pretty sure they all secretly loved the weekly foray into pure Americana cuisine. Even his mother didn't seem to mind (much) so long as her family was all together.

"So what did you mean, you don't want to talk about it?" Tony Moretti repeated, glancing down at Anthony's plate and scowling to see the bacon supply completely depleted.

Anthony scooped a mouthful of Swiss cheese omelet into his mouth before sitting back and reaching for his coffee. "It means that Ma doesn't like cop talk at the table."

"*Riiiiight,*" Elena Moretti said from Anthony's left side. "Because you guys *always* respect Mom's no-cop-talk rule."

Anth took another sip of coffee and exchanged a look and a shrug with Luc across the table.

Their sister made a good point.

In a family where four out of five siblings were living in New York, and three out of *those* four were with the NYPD, cop talk was likely.

And when the family patriarch was the recently retired police commissioner?

Cop talk wasn't just probable, it was *inevitable*.

Still, it was worth a shot to throw up his mother's token rule of "no cop talk." Especially when he didn't want to talk.

About any of it.

It had been a long time since he'd been the one in the hot seat, and he wasn't at all sure that he cared for it.

Scratch that. He was sure.

He *hated* it.

But his father could be like a dog with a bone when it came to his sons' careers. And today, like it or not, it was Anthony under the microscope.

He surrendered to the inevitable.

"Dad, I told you. It'll get handled." He went for another cup of coffee, only to find it was empty. Diner *fail*.

He scanned the dining room for the waitress, partially because he wanted more coffee, partially because he wanted a distraction. Partially because—

"You've been saying it'll get *handled* for weeks," Tony said, refusing to let the matter drop.

"Yeah, *Captain*. You've been saying that for weeks." This from Anthony's other brother Vincent. Two years younger than Anth, Vin was a homicide detective and the most irritable and irreverent member of the family. And the one least likely to kiss Anth's ass.

If Anthony was totally honest, he was pretty sure that most of his younger siblings respected him, not only because he was the highest-ranking family member, but simply because he was the oldest. He was the one they'd come to when they needed to hide that broken vase from Mom, or when they were scared to death to tell Dad about that D in chemistry, or in the case of his brothers, when it was time to learn their way around the female anatomy.

But Vincent had authority issues and was always the first to jump at the chance to gently mock Anthony's status as captain.

A title that had been hard earned and still felt new. As though it could be ripped away at any time.

Which was *exactly* the reason his father was on his ass right now. Anthony had passed his captain's test three months ago, and his father had every intention of him climbing the ladder all the way to the top. The *very* top.

It was a path Anth had never questioned. A path that, up until recently, had been remarkably smooth.

And then...

And then *Smiley* had happened.

"Well surely you've got a couple leads to go on," Tony said, leaning forward and fixing Anthony with a steady look.

Anthony looked right back, hoping the bold gaze would counteract the hard truth. *That Anth didn't have a damn clue who or where Smiley was.*

For the past two months—the majority of Anthony's tenure as captain of the Twentieth Precinct—the Upper West Side had been plagued by a smug and relentless burglar.

Nickname? *Smiley.* Courtesy of the idiotic, yellow smiley-face sticker he left at each of his hits.

The plus side, if there was one, was that Smiley hadn't proven dangerous. If it had been a *violent* criminal on the loose, Anth's ass would have been on the line weeks ago.

But still. It had been eight weeks since Smiley's first hit, and the man was getting bolder with each passing week, hitting three brownstones last week alone.

And Anth wasn't even close to catching him. Neither was anyone else in the department. Hence why number two on his life priorities (the NYPD) was making him crazy.

"We'll get him," Anthony said curtly, referring to Smiley.

"You'd better," Tony said. "The press has gotten ahold of it. It'll only get bigger from here."

"Yeah, thanks for the reminder," Anthony muttered.

His phone buzzed, and a quick glance showed it was a text message from his grandmother, letting him know that she'd self-diagnosed herself with tuberculosis, but that whiskey might help and could he bring some by when he was done with breakfast.

Anth put the phone away without responding, picking up his coffee cup again. Still empty. "Damn it. Where the *hell* is what's-her-name? Is it too much to ask to get some damn coffee around here?"

"Now there's a good plan," his sister mused. "Blame poor Maggie because you can't catch a pip-squeak cat burglar."

As if on cue, *poor Maggie* appeared at their table, coffeepot in hand.

"I'm so sorry," the waitress said, a little breathless. "You all must have been waiting ages for more coffee."

Anthony rolled his eyes, even as he snuck a glance at her. Her friendly smile was meant to hide the fact that she was frazzled, and for most of her customers, that apologetic, dimpled smile probably worked.

It *was* a damn good look on any woman, but especially her.

Maggie Walker had become their default waitress at the diner back when their old waitress, Helen, had retired a couple months ago. And while Anthony missed Helen and her too-strong floral perfume, he had to admit that Maggie was better to look at.

She had a wholesome, girl-next-door look that appealed to him mightily. Brown hair that was always on the verge of slipping out of its ponytail. Wide, compelling green eyes that made you want to unload all your darkest secrets.

Curvy. Hips that were exactly right; breasts that were even better.

And then there was that smile. It managed to be both shy and friendly, which was handy because he was betting it was very hard for even the most impatient customers to get annoyed at her.

But Anth didn't buy the doing-my-best routine, and seeing as she was dealing with an entire table of observant cops, he was betting the rest of his family wouldn't buy it either.

Then Luc leaned forward and gave Maggie an easy grin.

"Don't even worry about it, Mags. Didn't even notice I was running low!"

Luc's girlfriend, Ava, smoothly reached up one hand and swatted him on the back of the head, the gesture so graceful, so practiced, that she never once sloshed her coffee. Anthony nearly smiled.

To say that Ava Sims was good for his little brother would be an understatement. The big brother in Anthony would be forever grateful that the gorgeous reporter had helped Luc vanquish his demons. But the big brother in Anth was also grateful that Ava helped keep his younger brother in line. Or at least tried to.

He rolled his eyes as Luc shot a guilty smile at his girlfriend, even as he slid his mug toward the edge of the table so Maggie wouldn't have to reach as far.

Then Anth watched in utter dismay as Vincent did the same.

Vincent. The guy who'd practically devoted his life to being perverse was trying to make life easier for their inept waitress.

Un-fucking-believable.

Anthony was so busy trying to figure out what about the frazzled waitress turned his brothers into a bunch of softies that he didn't think to move his own mug to be more convenient, and Maggie had to lean all the way in to top off his cup.

It was a feat that their *old* waitress could have handled readily, but for reasons that Anth didn't understand, the rest of the Moretti family had embraced Maggie as Helen's replacement.

Anthony didn't realize that his mug had overflowed until scalding coffee dripped onto his thigh.

"Son of a—"

He caught himself before he could finish the expletive, grabbing a large handful of napkins from the silver dispenser and trying to soak up the puddle of coffee on his jeans before it burned his skin.

"Nice, Anth," Elena said, tossing another bunch of napkins at him. Like this was *his* fault.

"Oh my God," Maggie said, her voice horrified. "I'm *so* sorry, Officer..."

"It's Captain," he snapped, his eyes flicking up and meeting hers.

Silence descended over the table until Vincent muttered *douchebag* around a coughing fit.

But Anthony refused to feel chagrined. The woman had waited on the family every Sunday for weeks; one would think she could get his title right. To say nothing of mastering the art of pouring coffee.

Her green eyes flicked downward before turning away with promises to bring back a rag.

He watched her trim figure for only a second before glancing down at his lap. A rag wouldn't do shit. He now had a huge brown stain on his jeans.

And this wasn't the first time.

Last week, it had been ketchup on his shirt. Maggie had been clearing plates, and a chunk of ketchup-covered hash browns from Vin's plate had found its way onto Anth.

The week before *that*, it was a grease stain from a rogue piece of bacon that his father had somehow missed.

And it was always the same oh-my-gosh-I'm-so-sorry routine, and his family would lament the unfortunate "accident" and tell Maggie not to worry about it, even though none of *them* had basically tripled their laundry efforts since Maggie had taken over their Sunday brunch routine.

"I don't know why you always have to do that," Elena snapped at him.

He gave his little sister a dark look. Elena was basically a female version of Luc. Dark brown hair, perfectly proportioned features, and bright blue eyes. His siblings' good looks had worked very well for them with the opposite sex, but with their brother? Not so much.

"I didn't do anything," he snapped.

His mother—his own *mother*—gave him a scolding look. "You make Maggie nervous, dear. All that glowering."

"Wait, sorry, hold up," Anth said, abandoning the futile effort of blotting coffee from his crotch. "It's *my* fault that the incompetent woman can't do even the most basic requirements of her job?"

A startled gasp came from the head of the table, and too late—*way* too late—Anth realized that Maggie had reappeared with a clean white rag and what seemed to be a full cup of ice.

"I thought...I wanted to make sure it didn't burn your skin," she told him brightly.

To her credit, her voice didn't wobble, and her eyes didn't water, but damned if she didn't look like she wanted to cry just a little.

Shit.

"I'm fine," he muttered.

"Thank you, sweetie," Tony said kindly, taking the rag and ice from Maggie. "Maybe just the check when you get a chance."

"Of course. And really, I'm so sorry," she said, not quite glancing at Anthony. "You'll send me the dry-cleaning bill, right?"

"He'll do no such thing," his mother said firmly, reaching

across her husband to grab Maggie's hand. "I can get any stain out of any fabric. I'll take care of it."

"You hear that, Anth?" Luc said. "Mommy's going to wash your pants for you!"

Anth shot his brother the bird.

"I just can't believe Mags called you *Officer*," Vincent said in a sham reverent tone. "I don't know how she missed the nine hundred and forty-two reminders that you're a captain now."

"Well she damn well should remember," he muttered. "Is anyone else remembering that she spilled iced tea all over me at my coronation party?"

"She spilled it on your *shoes*," Elena said. "Which were black."

"Still," Anth said, glancing around the room this time to make sure she wasn't within earshot. "I don't know why we have to act like she's a new member of the family when she can't seem to go a single Sunday without spilling somebody's breakfast on me. It can't be an accident *every* time."

"Maybe she wants to get your attention. Your humble, pleasant personality is *so* charming," Ava said quietly into her coffee mug.

Anth looked at Luc's girlfriend. "*Et tu, Brute?*"

Ava winked.

And then his dad leaned back in the booth, folded his arms, and glared at his oldest son. "So tell me again what you're doing to close in on this Smiley character."

"Oh my God, he's like a dog with a bone!" Elena said, throwing her arms up in exasperation before turning her attention back to her cell phone. "Also, is Nonna texting anyone else? I've been getting mucus every five minutes."

"Yes," everyone replied at once.

"She just sent me a Wikipedia link on phlegm," Vincent grumbled.

To say that his grandmother had been upset to miss brunch because of a lingering head cold was an understatement. She'd been punishing them all with updates on her illness.

Anthony glanced at his watch and mentally counted the minutes until he could relax with a beer and watch the Yankees game.

Of the three sacred things in his life, the New York Yankees had always been a *very* distant third to family and the department.

Now he was seriously rethinking his priorities.

CHAPTER TWO

A little-known fact about life in New York City: the subway gods rarely had your back.

In fact, it was a pretty sure bet that there *were* no subway gods, much as one might pray to them when running late or *really* wanting a seat, or just plain hoping for a BO-free subway experience.

But when Maggie stepped onto the Q train after the *mother* of all horrific shifts at the Darby Diner, the subway gods, or maybe just *The God*, smiled down on her.

There were only a handful of other people on her car, so she got not only a seat, but an entire *row* to herself. Having a spot to set her enormous handbag, and another to set the box of day-old lemon meringue pie that her manager had kindly bestowed on her, was a small luxury she wasn't going to take for granted.

Not after yet another day when she'd managed to spill all over Anthony Moretti. No, wait...

"*Captain* Moretti," she muttered out loud to herself. "It's *Captain* Moretti."

Maggie fell silent, because the city didn't need any more weirdos talking to themselves on public transportation, but it didn't stop her from *thinking* about him.

For the life of her, she couldn't figure out how two people as warm and friendly as Tony and Maria Moretti had produced someone as uptight and conceited as the *captain*.

Their oldest son was a rotten seed in a family full of charmers.

Maggie *adored* the rest of the Morettis. She had ever since they'd been ridiculously kind to her on her first day, despite the fact that she'd dropped iced tea on the guest of honor. Yes. *Him.*

She and Elena had clicked almost immediately. Probably because Elena always seemed slightly desperate for female company in the midst of all her brothers, and Maggie very desperate to make a friend.

But the brothers were sweet too, Anthony excluded, of course.

Maggie thought she could *almost* have a crush on Luc if it weren't for the fact that he was dating the gorgeous, super-smart Ava. Still, a girl could look. And admire. It was impossible *not* to. Luc Moretti looked like a freaking movie star, with his perfectly styled dark hair, laughing blue eyes, and the way he filled out his uniform *just* right.

And yet, despite the fact that the man was every woman's fantasy, Luc was also refreshingly down to earth, even after his whole brush-with-media fame a few months back.

Vincent wasn't nearly as friendly as Luc. In fact, he wasn't friendly at all. But there was a blunt honesty about the detective that Maggie found comforting.

One always knew where they stood with Vincent Moretti. And luckily, he seemed to like her.

There was another brother...Matt or Marc or something, whom she'd never met since he lived in California.

But of the East Coast Morettis, Maggie could say without hesitation that they were lovely.

They were the kind of family that she used to think only existed in after-school TV specials. Lord knew she hadn't seen a whole lot of that growing up in her hometown of Torrence, New Jersey.

She *certainly* hadn't seen much in the way of family togetherness in her own home.

Still, even with all their perfection, the Morettis had a blight. A big pockmark on an otherwise flawless visage:

The oldest sibling had *such* a stick up the butt.

What made Anthony Moretti's personality disorder even *more* of a bummer was the fact that the man was really, truly gorgeous.

At least to her.

All of the Moretti men were good looking, from Tony with his sage, silver fox appeal down to Luc with all of that blue-eyed charm.

But it was Anthony who appealed to Maggie the most. He was pure fantasy material.

All of the Moretti men were tall, but Anthony was *tall*. Like, six-four, at least. And then there were the ridiculously broad shoulders that tapered into a narrow waist, giving his upper body that beguiling inverted triangle look that all but begged a woman to cuddle up close and be held.

His dark hair was shorter than his brothers', not quite a crew cut, but it was definitely a no-nonsense style that perfectly framed his harsh jawline, serious brown eyes, and olive skin.

And if she were to *really* get into it, it would have to be said that Anthony's features were too broad to be classically handsome, and yet too symmetrical to be completely rugged. The resulting in-between was almost unbearably *him*.

Not that she'd been studying him.

Well, okay, maybe just a little. And only out of the corner of her eye. And *only* when he wasn't paying attention. Which was pretty much always since the man *never* paid attention to her.

The only time he even seemed to know she existed was when she dropped a buttered biscuit on his sleeve or scalding hot coffee on his crotch...

Maggie's eyes went wide. Oh *God*.

What if he thought she was doing it on purpose to get his attention? Women had done crazier things to get a man to look at them. And a man that looked like him had probably had all sorts of crazy admirers.

Or worse... what if subconsciously, she really *was* doing it to get his attention?

She discarded that last thought almost immediately. Maggie Walker had never been the type to want to get noticed. Blending into the background was easier. Safer. Plus, flying under the radar had the added benefit of turning her into a top-notch observer over the years. A handy skill for an aspiring author.

Maggie winced as she realized she was almost to her subway stop and instead of spending the commute thinking about the upcoming scene she was writing tonight, she'd spent the whole time thinking about *him*.

She'd read somewhere that J.K. Rowling had come up with the main premise of Harry Potter while sitting on a train. Most days she tried to duplicate this, and some days she was semi-successful.

But Sundays were harder. Sundays were Moretti days.

Maggie sighed at the wasted time daydreaming when she should have been plotting her story, and gathered her bags, waiting for the train to pull up to the Seventh Avenue station in Park Slope, Brooklyn, where she lived in a cozy (translation: *tiny*) studio.

Maggie knew that for most women moving to "the city," it was all about Manhattan, but although she loved Manhattan in all its high-rise glamour, she'd been drawn almost immediately to Brooklyn.

Not only for the (slightly) more affordable rental rates, but also for the neighborhood feel that was harder to come by in Manhattan.

Maggie mentally cataloged through the contents of her fridge and pantry and decided that between eggs, dried pasta, and a *probably*-still-good loaf of bread, she could get by without a stop at the store. Plus there was the pie. Surely having pie for dinner once a week (or twice, maybe twice) wasn't the worst thing in the world. There were worse vices, right?

One of these days, Maggie thought, she'd be one of those super *together* women who threw together a healthy dinner for one with all the food groups. But for now, she was pretty dang content with eating whatever the heck she felt like.

Sometimes that was a nice salad with chicken breast and veggies, and other days it was, well…lemon meringue pie. Either way, it was the *freedom* that was wonderful.

There was nobody to sneer that she'd overcooked the

meat. Nobody to wrinkle their nose at the pasta sauce because they "didn't feel like it." Nobody to remind her "again" that they didn't like spinach in any form.

For a woman who'd spent her teens and early twenties hearing those comments from her father and brother, and her late twenties hearing them from her husband, the ability to have whatever the heck she wanted for dinner was the ultimate luxury.

Sure, she was a thirty-two-year-old divorcée living in an itty-bitty studio and contemplating scrambled eggs and pie for dinner again, but it was *her* apartment. Her eggs. Her pie.

Her *choice*.

It wasn't until she'd finally gotten the courage to divorce Eddie that she'd realized the sheer power in making a decision and acting on it. Any decision.

Maggie rummaged around in her purse until her fingers found the Tiffany key chain her best friend had gotten her for Christmas a couple years earlier.

It was easily the nicest thing she owned. And it made missing Gabby a *little* easier, although not much. Her best friend had moved to Denver, and though they still talked on the phone occasionally, it wasn't the same as when they'd been twelve and Maggie could be at Gabby's house in two minutes for the homemade chocolate chip cookies that she'd never get at home.

Nor were their long phone chats the same as when they'd gotten married within six months of each other at twenty-four and had set up their respective newlywed homes just minutes away from the other.

Still, much as she missed Gabby, leaving Torrence had been the best thing. For both of them.

Sure, only one of their marriages was still intact, but at

least both women had managed to escape their childhood town, with all its toxic gossip and small-town thinking.

Maggie only wished her best friend hadn't had to move *quite* so far. Gabby's husband was a middle-school principal who'd gotten a job offer at a prestigious Denver prep school, and they'd moved two years earlier, along with their adorable twins.

Now Gabby had her own interior design company, the twins had finally gotten the dog they'd always wanted, and though Maggie hadn't been able to afford a visit out there, their Christmas cards showed the perfect suburban home that Gabby had always longed for.

Maggie's own retreat from their New Jersey hometown had been a lot less glorious.

When she'd filed for divorce, she hadn't expected the process to be pretty, but she *definitely* hadn't counted on the fight to keep the house (she lost) or the fact that all of her "friends" would listen to Eddie's lies that she'd been unfaithful.

Still, silver lining? She'd gotten *out*.

Her Park Slope studio might be tiny, but there was no Eddie.

There was, however, Duchess.

"Hello, baby," Maggie said, shoving the front door open with her hip and immediately collapsing to the ground to greet her dog.

It said a lot about Duchess's loyalty to her owner that the poodle-mystery mix showed more interest in Maggie than she did the lemon meringue pie. Maggie happily accepted every last messy dog kiss on her chin before landing a kiss of her own on top of Duchess's scratchy brown head.

On paper, it was Maggie who'd rescued Duchess a few

months earlier from the animal shelter. But she and Duchess knew the truth: they'd rescued each other.

"Does Her Grace need to go out to the ladies' room?" Maggie asked, giving the dog one last smooch before climbing to her feet and grabbing the dog leash off the hook by the door.

Duchess did three fast three-sixty spins before planting her little butt on the ground and all but vibrating in excitement while she waited for Maggie to clip on the leash.

"Okay, remember, ladies don't poop in the middle of the sidewalk," Maggie said as they stepped outside. Duchess wagged her tail rapidly to indicate she understood.

A long walk around a nearby grassy patch later, it was clear that Duchess had *not* understood, because she held her "business" until they got back to the sidewalk. Maggie smiled an apology at the grumpy-looking elderly couple as she tried to open one of the stupid pink doggie bags she'd bought online because they were cheaper than the ones in the pet store.

Three defective bags later, she found a bag without a hole in it and picked up Duchess's mess.

Maggie frowned at the dog. "Why do I bother walking you to the park when you insist on poo-ing on the pavement, hmm?"

Duchess barked twice at a leaf.

"Good talk, baby. Okay, let's go get some pie."

Back at home, Maggie pulled a bag of carrots out of the fridge and munched on a handful while she changed out of her orange diner uniform into a pair of pj's.

It was just barely getting dark, but since she worked the breakfast shift again tomorrow, her four a.m. wake-up call came around fast. Her frequent early mornings were just one of the *many* things Eddie had found to complain about, although back then it had been Denny's in Torrence.

And her paltry waitress income had been supporting *two* people.

Eddie hadn't "liked" to work.

Maggie bit a carrot with more force than necessary and gave the other half to Duchess, who nipped it out of her fingers and leaped onto the bed.

"I better not find that under my pillow later," Maggie said with a warning finger.

Duchess wagged her tail. Maggie was *so* going to find the carrot under her pillow later.

Then Maggie cut herself a big ole slice of pie and settled down with her secondhand laptop at the tiny table that doubled as desk, kitchen table, and ironing board when needed.

Maggie opened her manuscript and settled her fingers on the keyboard. Then changed her mind and took a bite of pie instead.

It was a tricky scene she was working on. The *almost* first kiss between the teen hero and heroine. Mood and tension were everything. She had to make the readers want it as much as the characters wanted it.

Tricky indeed.

But scenes like this were part of the reason Maggie wrote books for teens, or "YA" as it was known in the publishing world. Because *nobody* knew how to long like a teenager. Sure, adults felt longing too, but it was different, because on some level, adults knew that the reality was never as great as the buildup. Which in turn made the buildup *less* somehow.

But fifteen-year-olds...man, their yearning was the real deal. They weren't jaded by knowledge that sex was inevitably a letdown, or that Prince Charming didn't exist, or that when people said *I love you* what they really meant was *I need you to do something for me.*

The characters in teen fiction didn't know any of that stuff. At least not in Maggie's story. Her book-world was kinder, softer, sweeter. And so with one last fortifying bite of pie, Maggie put her fingers to the keyboard and started writing.

It used to be harder. Early on when she'd first tried to turn the images in her head into words on a page, it had been harder to block out the rest of the world and lose herself inside the story.

But she'd been writing nearly every day for eight months now, ever since she moved into her little Brooklyn apartment, and now that it was routine, it was easier to ignore her upstairs neighbor's thumping bass.

Easier to ignore the bottoms of her feet, which hurt from standing all day.

Easier, even, to ignore the fact that Duchess was burying and then reburying the carrot amid Maggie's white pillows.

Maggie heard and saw none of that.

There were only the characters. Only the story.

Only the *want.*

Colin shifted closer to Jenny, his hand lifting and then hesitating, as though afraid she'd move away. But she didn't move away, and his fingers touched her cheek. Questioningly at first, and then surer, his palm cradling her face as he moved closer still. Jenny wanted both to close her eyes and feel, but also to keep them locked on his, to watch the way they darkened when her fingers touched his waist...

It took Maggie several moments to come out of the zone and realize what she was hearing: the steady vibrations of her cell phone.

She nibbled her lip and tried to block it out the way she blocked out everything else, but...

Maggie reluctantly tore herself away from Jenny and Colin's almost-kiss and dug her phone out of her purse.

If she felt a small stab of dread at the name on the screen, she ignored it as she swiped her thumb to accept the phone call.

Family was family, after all.

"Hey, Dad."

"Buggie."

She winced. It was a *terrible* nickname. Left over from Maggie's childhood fondness for bringing bugs into the house. Back when her dad had still been sober enough to marvel at her latest six-legged find. And when her mom had been, well, *present* enough to screech and demand that the "nasty creatures" get out of her house.

"How's it going?" Maggie asked her father, looking wistfully at the open document on her laptop and immediately feeling guilty. She turned her back on the computer.

Her dad was silent for a few moments. "Not so great, Bugs."

No surprise there. Her dad only ever bothered to call when things were "not so great."

"What's going on?"

She asked the question because it was expected, not because it was necessary. She already knew exactly what was going on. He needed something.

"I'm ready to get better, Maggie."

She closed her eyes. Didn't have to ask what he meant

by "better." The words *should* have filled her with joy. And they *had*, the first, second, and fifth time that she'd heard them.

"How's AA going?" she asked, opening the fridge and staring blindly into it.

Her dad made a derisive sound. "They don't know shit, Bugs. A bunch of self-righteous assholes yammering on about God and steps. I need *real* help, Buggie. I found a place..."

Maggie closed the fridge door without taking anything out. Even another slice of pie didn't appeal. Her appetite was gone.

Her dad was still rambling on. "...it's up in Vermont. Gets great reviews. Doc said he can probably get me a referral, but..."

Maggie already knew what the *but* was. It would be expensive. The fancy rehab centers always were.

There were, of course, cheaper paths toward sobriety. Cheaper options that her father had tried (at her insistence) and failed at.

She turned, leaning back against her tiny kitchen counter, and looked up at the ceiling.

"Is there any sort of financial aid?" Maggie asked.

"Sure, sure, of course I'm going to try, but Bugs... this place is the best. I'll send you the info; they've got some great success rates."

Maggie opened her mouth to argue that all the other places had been "the best." They *all* had great success rates. It was just her father who continued to count among their few failures.

But she couldn't bring herself to say it. Everything she'd read said that an addict taking initiative was a big step. That she should be supportive and enthusiastic of his desire to get help.

The thing that the books hadn't told her was what to do when the enthusiasm led to treatment that led to temporary improvement that led to crushing relapses.

Again, and again, and again.

"That's great, Dad," she said, meaning it. Nobody wanted Charlie Walker to get clean more than his only daughter.

It was just…

"So whadya say, Bugs? You think you could spare some money for your old dad? Just enough to put a deposit down."

Maggie swallowed, thinking of the tiny, slowly growing fund she'd been saving up for school, or for a break between jobs so she could work on her book…

That would just have to wait. Everything else would have to wait.

She'd been waiting over a decade. What were a few more months if it meant seeing her father finally get clean?

"Sure, Dad," Maggie said, forcing a brightness into her voice. "I've got a little bit."

Her dad's relief was palpable. "Thanks, Bugs. I'd ask Cory, but he's been having trouble finding work. He keeps getting screwed over…"

Maggie tucked the phone under her chin and picked at a cuticle. She couldn't muster even a sympathetic grunt for her brother's "plight." The guy was twenty-seven but hadn't held a single job for longer than a few months. He couldn't afford his own cell phone bill, much less rehab for their father.

"I'll come out next weekend," Maggie said. "We can talk details."

There was a too-long beat of silence. "I'd like to get

started as soon as possible. I don't want to waste another second on the bottle. Maybe you could just send a check…"

Maggie swallowed. *It's for a good cause*, she reminded herself. *It's for a great cause*

"Sure, Dad. I'll mail a check."

"Bugs. I owe you one."

Actually, you owe me thousands *of ones.*

"Maybe I can drive you out there," she said, hating her voice for sounding so needy. "Help get you settled?"

"No need. Cory already said he'd give me a lift. Look, Bugs, I gotta run, but I appreciate it. Thanks for taking care of your old man. Love ya."

"Of course," she said softly. "I love you too."

But he was already gone.

Maggie let the phone drop to her side before walking numbly to the bed and sitting down.

Duchess propped two paws on her shoulder and licked her ear.

"It'll work this time, right, baby?" she said, absently rubbing a hand over her dog's little body. "He's going to get sober? Be a real dad? Maybe even pay me back someday?"

Duchess dropped to her belly on the bed and rested her snout on Maggie's thigh, her big brown eyes mournful and sympathetic.

Maggie pressed her lips together and hoped like hell her dog was wrong.

CHAPTER THREE

At thirty-six years old, after thirteen years in the NYPD, Anthony had seen some pretty gnarly shit. The kind of stuff that kept a man up at night. Haunted his dreams. Things that could destroy a soul if you let them.

Anth had heard stories of seasoned officers throwing up on the scene of a crime. Hardened sergeants retiring after a particularly rough case. Cops on every side of the NYPD food chain just *losing it* after seeing some of the city's worst horrors.

So in the grand scheme of things, Anthony's current case was nothing. A PG crime through and through.

It's not that the crimes were insignificant. More serious than jaywalking, certainly; home invasion was a serious of-fense. But Smiley wasn't *dangerous*. And in a city that could turn vicious on a dime, that was something.

Oddly enough, it was Smiley's relative harmlessness that made his elusiveness all the more annoying. That, and the fact that the guy left a *literal* calling card with every place he robbed. It was cocky, obnoxious, and stupid.

And yet, Anth hadn't caught him yet. He had all his best people working on it, but nobody knew when Smiley would strike next; nobody knew how he targeted his victims.

The cards he left were standard-issue card stock, the simple, yellow smiley-face stickers you could buy at any drugstore.

No fingerprints. No hair at the scene.

He was both consistent, and yet not at all.

Best as they could tell, he struck within minutes of his well-to-do victims leaving their house. Which meant he watched them leave; knew whether or not they had an alarm system (he never struck if they did, which told Anth he wasn't experienced enough in home invasion to disarm one).

Smiley's loot varied. Laptops and other small electronics were common. Jewelry, although he didn't discriminate between costume jewelry and precious gemstones, so he either didn't know the difference or didn't care.

Wine and booze were also high on his wish list, but again, there was no method to which bottles he took. Sometimes it was a thousand-dollar bottle of champagne, other times it was an eight-dollar Merlot.

But one thing was always constant: He helped himself to something from the pantry or fridge, whether it was a glass of Chardonnay from the fridge, a slice of cake from the counter, a portion of leftover takeout. And next to the used wineglass or carton, he left the note.

Thank you written plainly across the front. Inside was always the same play on an old idiom:

Su casa es mi casa.

Your house is my house.

They were dealing with an asshole with an entitlement complex, clearly. Someone who thought that other people's belongings were his for the taking.

The case just plain pissed Anth off on every level.

But...

They'd had a break. Sort of.

An elderly neighbor of one of the more recent break-ins had come forward claiming to have seen a man "loitering" on the street the evening of the break-in.

Thank God for nosy neighbors.

Granted, they had no way of connecting the man to the crime, but it was telling that he'd stayed on the street for nearly an hour, walking back and forth. No dog, no destination...

"More coffee?"

Startled at the interruption, Anth glanced up into a pair of pretty green eyes.

Maggie.

"Please," he said gruffly. On instinct he moved all papers to the far side of the table from the slim hand holding the coffee, but he promptly regretted it when he heard her exhale in embarrassed dismay.

Still, he refused to feel guilty. The woman did seem to have a remarkable knack for spilling on him. All of the documents he was working with were copies, but still...

"Meeting someone?" she asked. "I can bring another mug."

He knew why she asked. The Morettis came as a family every Sunday, and he and one or more of his brothers had been known to stop for a late-night dinner or early-morning breakfast. Hell, he and Luc had come at least a couple times a *week* before his little brother had met Ava

and started spending most of his time at her place down-
town.

But rarely did Anth come alone. Not because he didn't
like the solitude; he relished time alone to think.

But in recent months he hadn't come here.

Because of *her*.

Back before Helen had retired, he'd come here all the
time to catch up on things, to think, or just to read the damn
newspaper in peace.

But whereas Helen's presence had been as soothing as
his own mother's—perhaps even more so, since Helen never
pried—Maggie's presence was distinctly . . .

Well, *not* soothing.

In fact, truth be told, he'd been half-hoping that she
wouldn't be working when he'd stopped in today. She was
too damn distracting.

"No, it's just me," he said, his voice more curt than he intended.

She nodded and gave a smile. Forced, if he was reading
it correctly. "Okay, no problem! Just coffee? Or I can bring
you a menu if you're hungry."

"Don't need a menu."

Her smile disappeared altogether.

Damn it. You ass.

"I just mean, I've got the thing memorized. Been coming
here for years," he said, his voice even more gravelly than
before.

"Is that supposed to be an apology?"

The question was as tart as it was direct, and definitely
not expected.

Well, well, well, he thought, leaning back in the booth.
The pretty kitten had claws.

He studied Maggie curiously, and although she blushed, he gave her credit for not looking away. Nor did she apologize for the little burst of sass.

"Do you think I owe you an apology?" he asked, keeping his tone mild.

She pressed her lips together and took a step back. "Never mind. I was out of line."

He reached out and grabbed her wrist before she could move away, startling both himself and her with the unexpected contact. He dropped her arm immediately, but not before he registered that the pale skin was impossibly smooth against his rougher fingertips.

"You think I'm an ass," he said.

She laughed delightedly at his statement, and that response too was unexpected.

Anthony frowned. He didn't like surprises.

"Do you actually think you're *not* an ass?" she asked. She had a low, melodic voice.

His frown deepened. "It's hardly my fault that you're always spilling all over me, and that you've ingratiated yourself to my family."

She crossed her arms, the effort surprisingly graceful considering one hand still held a coffeepot. "Ingratiated myself?"

He waved a hand awkwardly. "You know. Smiling, flitting around them, making them think you're so wonderful just by being nearly competent at your job."

Her mouth opened, but instead of responding, she merely touched the tip of her tongue to her upper lip for a split second before narrowing her eyes.

"My answer to your previous question is yes, *Captain*. I *absolutely* think you're an ass."

Anthony didn't even flinch. It was nothing he hadn't heard before. From his brothers. His sister. Ex-girlfriends. Even his mother, although Maria Moretti had never used the word "ass" in Anth's hearing.

And God knew he'd heard *plenty* of it from Vannah over the course of their doomed relationship. He took a sip of coffee to avoid the memories. To avoid the guilt over a woman he'd neglected too often. Until it was too late.

"That was probably uncalled for," Maggie muttered when he didn't respond. "I apologize."

He nodded, knowing full well that an apology on *his* part wouldn't exactly be out of line, but *sorry* had never been an easy word for him. Not for an oldest sibling who'd grown up with the heavy expectation that he be right at all times.

She gave him a bright smile he didn't deserve, as though she hadn't just called a customer an ass to his face. "Well, I'll let you get back to work. I'll check back in a few. Or just flag me down if you need me."

If you need me.

The words caused an inconveniently sexy mental image. Anthony couldn't help his gaze from drifting over her figure, the ugly orange uniform doing nothing to detract from enticing curves.

It was probably long past time Anthony accepted the real reason he was so irritated by the mere existence of Maggie Walker.

Awareness.

A highly inconvenient *sexual* awareness.

Maggie didn't roll her eyes at his complete lack of verbal response, but he got the sense she wanted to. Instead she walked away without ever losing that falsely bright smile.

"Just say the word. *Captain.*"

He forced himself not to watch her walk away.

Anthony knew nobody would ever describe him as charming, but he'd never hurt for female companionship. Much to his sister's proclaimed confusion, women seemed to *enjoy* his brusqueness.

Most of them didn't even seem to mind that he started every date with a very blunt proclamation that he had no intention of entering a long-term relationship. Ever.

Hell, most of them seemed to get off on the fact that the only relationship he *did* have was with the NYPD.

How many times had he seen the worshipping gleam in a woman's eye before she all but licked her lips and informed him that she loved a man in uniform... and out of one.

Truth be told, Anth wouldn't mind, just once, being seen as a man instead of a cop. Wouldn't mind skipping the frisking puns, the handcuff jokes, the only-half-joking suggestions of role-playing.

His eyes flitted around the diner until he saw Maggie slip into a booth across from an elderly couple and laugh heartily at whatever story they were telling.

He jerked his gaze back to his papers. No need to worry about *that* one having a case of hero worship. The woman had managed to pack a shit-ton of disdain into the single utterance of the word "captain."

Anth ran a hand over his face and picked up the case file on Smiley's most recent hit. He practically had the Smiley case files memorized, but he still pored over them on a daily basis, desperate for that one detail they were missing... the one connection that would lead them to motive, or some sort of pattern that would help them catch the damn guy.

So he read them all. Start to finish.

His coffee cup emptied, and he vaguely registered the

smell of…oranges?…as Maggie drifted by to refill his mug. Vaguely remembered saying *thank you*. Or maybe not.

When he finally glanced at his watch—an expensive gift from his family after passing his captain's exam—he was surprised to see that over an hour and a half had passed.

He was beyond hungry.

Anth set his pen aside, rubbing his eyes briefly before looking around for a waitress. He half-hoped that Maggie's shift had ended, but no, there she was. She'd pulled her hair back into a messy bun thing that was annoyingly cute, and seemed to sense that he was finally ready to eat because she lifted her eyebrows and headed his way.

"Captain?" she said. Her smile and tone were deferential, but there was a slight gleam in her eye.

He probably should tell her to just call him Anthony. She called the rest of the Moretti family by their first names. And Helen had always called him *Anth*. Or *Antonio*. Or *Baby*.

Somehow he thought *baby* coming out of Maggie's mouth would be quite a different thing altogether.

He put a hand over his cup when she went to refill it, grateful she stopped before dumping scalding liquid all over the back of his hand.

"I've had plenty of caffeine," he said gruffly. "Can I get a sandwich? Turkey or ham is fine. Whatever's back there."

"White? Wheat?"

His gaze had drifted down to a copy of one of Smiley's mocking thank-you notes.

"Captain?" Her tone was gentler this time.

"Hmm?" He glanced up.

"White or wheat for that sandwich? And do you want fries?"

"Whatever is fine," he muttered. Like he'd taste any of it anyway.

Narrow, unpainted fingertips touched his sleeve. "Hey, you okay?"

He let out a little laugh.

Was he okay?

Hell no, he wasn't okay.

He hadn't slept in weeks, and he was likely on the verge of losing the confidence of his superiors, and even worse, the men and women who worked for him.

Adding to the sting was the fact that he had nobody to talk to about it.

Vincent was too wrapped up in his own homicide caseload to care about mild home invasions, and Luc, who'd been his roommate for the past six years, was all but moved into his girlfriend's place.

Even Nonna, his meddlesome grandmother with whom he shared the Upper West Side home, was gone more often than not, either with his parents on Staten Island, or with her latest "beau."

He felt … *alone.*

"Yeah, I'm fine," he said in response to Maggie's question.

She gave him a little smile shadowed with sadness. "Sure. I know all about that kind of *fine.*"

They exchanged a look that felt too personal for two strangers in a crowded diner, and Anth was surprised by the sudden urge to ask her if *she* was okay.

"I'll get your sandwich order in," she said, stepping away and ruining the moment.

Anthony began gathering up his various folders. Organization didn't come naturally to him, but his father had warned him that it was a necessary skill if he hoped to move up the NYPD food chain.

So he'd done his best to develop a system. The files went into piles by category. Then by date. Then he put big rubber bands around each of them and lined them up neatly in his briefcase. Then—

"*Motherf*—"

Anthony caught himself before the full gust of profanity could burst out of his mouth, but the swearing continued in his head as he picked up half a piece of turkey that had just been dumped unceremoniously in his lap, the mayo leaving little oily splatters all over his uniform pants.

"How the *hell* am I supposed to believe you're not doing this on purpose?" he asked, glancing up angrily at Maggie.

But to his surprise, the pretty waitress didn't look appalled, embarrassed, or apologetic. Nor smug. Her expression was completely *wrong* for a woman who'd just dumped a customer's order all over them for what had to be the twelfth time in three months.

She looked horrified. And scared.

"Hey," he asked, forgetting all about the sandwich as his fingers touched her arm. An arm that shook as it reached out for one of his papers.

"You okay?" he asked. Stupid question. She obviously wasn't okay.

Her fingers closed on a piece of paper. Evidence he really shouldn't have had out on the table in the first place, much less let a civilian touch.

But Anthony hadn't gotten to where he was by following the rules exactly; he'd gotten where he was by following his instinct. And instinct told him that whatever Maggie Walker was thinking and feeling at this moment was important.

Vital, even.

So he let her pick up the paper.

"Maggie?" he asked as gently as he could, the name feeling strange on his tongue. For as often as he thought it, he couldn't remember ever saying it aloud directly to her.

"How do you have this?" she asked, her voice small.

He glanced at the paper held between her fingers. It was the police sketch of Smiley. Or what they thought might be him. Hoped.

When Anthony looked at it, he saw an average, nondescript, thirty-something white dude. A guy that could have been one of a million people walking Manhattan sidewalks every day.

But Maggie saw something different.

"You recognize him?" Anthony asked, his voice losing all gentleness in its urgency.

Her green eyes never strayed from the piece of paper.

"You could say that." She blew out a long, slow breath, as though steadying herself. "Seeing as I was *married* to him."

CHAPTER FOUR

Women that had tried as hard to be *good* as Maggie had weren't supposed to know what the inside of a police station looked like.

Unfortunately, good girls didn't always have good families, and between her father's DUIs and her brother's MIPs, she was more familiar with law enforcement than she'd like.

But this? *This* was a whole other ball game.

She cupped her hands around the ugly, generic coffee cup to keep her hands from shaking. "Do we have to do this in here?" she asked.

Detective Browning smiled gently at her. "I know it's not the most comfortable room, but bright side...at least we didn't have to cuff you."

Maggie knew the other woman meant it as a joke, but she could barely muster a fake smile at the stout brunette woman.

Detective Browning's partner seemed to sense this and

leaned forward with a kind smile. "You're in no way a suspect, Ms. Walker. I'm sure Captain made that very clear."

Maggie all but rolled her eyes at Detective Poyner. Actually, *Captain* hadn't done much other than pepper her with a half dozen questions in the diner yesterday, only to growl in irritation when she was too flustered to answer them coherently.

Then he'd *ordered* her to the precinct today, on her day off, to answer some questions about Eddie. *Her* Eddie.

Or the man who *used* to be her Eddie.

"We could have come to your house, but Captain said you didn't want that," the male detective said, his voice kind.

Maggie nibbled her bottom lip. It was true. Anthony Moretti had asked her (gruffly) if detectives could come by her place, but she'd immediately said no.

She'd worked so hard to remove Eddie from her life...she didn't want him anywhere near her home, even in discussion.

So here she was, sitting in a hard metal chair in a dark, intimidating room with two cops who were perfectly nice but also increasingly impatient, if she was reading them correctly.

Meanwhile *he* was nowhere to be found.

A tiny part of Maggie—the selfish part of her—wished that she'd never seen that picture at the diner. Never opened her mouth.

But of course she had to. Because if Eddie was really doing something illegal...

She took a deep breath. "Okay. Okay, let's talk. But first...can you tell me what exactly it is that Eddie's done?"

Captain Moretti had said burglary, which sounded pretty

damn bad, but it also didn't seem like Eddie. Her ex-husband had always lacked...guts.

And frankly, he'd also lacked motivation and energy. The thought of him going through all that effort didn't line up with what she knew of the man.

Maybe she'd been wrong.

"Can I see the picture again?" she blurted out, just as Detective Browning was about to answer her question.

Detective Poyner opened the folder in front of him and slid a piece of paper toward her.

Maggie couldn't hide the wince as she looked at it again. If it wasn't Eddie, it was a darn close likeness, and seeing those familiar features again brought up a part of her life that she'd been deliberately putting behind her for the past eighteen months.

"Is this your ex-husband?"

Maggie lifted a shoulder. "It looks just like him, but it's hard to be one hundred percent sure in a drawing, you know?"

Detective Poyner nodded slowly. "But based on what you know of Mr. Walker—"

"Hansen," Maggie interrupted. "Eddie's last name is Hansen. I took my last name back when we divorced."

"My apologies," he said. "I shouldn't have assumed—"

Detective Browning leaned forward. "Ms. Walker, why don't you just tell us whatever you feel like telling us about Eddie? What he's like, where he is, the type of man he is—"

"The type of man he is?" Maggie interrupted again, her voice going just slightly higher than normal. "Detective Browning, have you ever been married?"

The woman gave a quick nod, her thick chin-length hair bobbing at the gesture.

"Divorced?" Maggie asked, noticing there was no ring but not wanting to assume.

Detective Browning hesitated, then nodded again. She wasn't conventionally attractive. Her cheeks were round and smattered in freckles, her forehead broad, and her body gave the impression of being ill-suited toward exercise. But Maggie prided herself in recognizing kindness, and this woman had it, even around her impatient bluster.

Maggie met her eyes and hoped to reach a kindred spirit. "I don't know what kind of divorce you had. Maybe it was the quiet, irreconcilable differences kind. But mine was..." Maggie pursed her lips and searched for the right word. "*Eruptive.*"

"Your divorce was eruptive?" Poyner asked.

Maggie flicked her gaze to his. To his silver wedding band. "Yes, it was."

So was the marriage.

But they didn't need to know that part.

"So you and Mr. Hansen aren't on good terms."

"We're not on *any* terms," Maggie said a little desperately.

"So you haven't seen him since the divorce?"

Maggie shook her head. "Well, I guess *technically* I saw him at the grocery store when I was still living in New Jersey, right after the paperwork was finalized, but we didn't speak."

Not for Eddie's lack of trying.

Browning glanced at her notes. "Captain said you've been divorced about a year and a half. No contact whatsoever in that time?"

Maggie hesitated, and they both sat up imperceptibly straighter. No dummies, these detectives.

She fiddled with her coffee cup. "The divorce was my idea."

There was a world of meaning in those words, and she saw immediately that Detective Browning recognized it, either because of her status as a woman or fellow divorcée label.

"He didn't take it well," Browning said.

Understatement. Such an understatement.

Maggie shook her head. "No."

Poyner's eyes narrowed. "Has he been harassing you?"

"No," Maggie said quickly. "Not recently, anyway. But for a while there he called a lot. Texted. E-mailed. Facebook messages, the whole deal. I tried to just ignore it, thinking he needed time to come to grips with the fact that we were over…"

"He didn't stop?"

Maggie's lips twisted in a half smile. "For a man who couldn't keep a job for more than a couple months, he was surprisingly persistent."

Poyner folded his hands on the table and leaned in. "So he's still contacting you."

"No. I changed my phone number."

And my e-mail. And got off Facebook and quit talking to all of our mutual friends who might give him my address…

"Ah," Browning said, as though she understood perfectly. And perhaps she did. "How long exactly since he last contacted you?"

Maggie took a sip of now cold coffee, thinking back. "I changed my number about eight months ago when I moved to the city. There's been nothing since then."

"What about his last known address?"

"He got the house in Jersey when we divorced. I can give you the address, but I have no idea if he still lives there or not."

Both detectives nodded, and she didn't think she imagined their look of disappointment. No doubt they were hoping that they'd be able to get to Eddie through her.

Maggie set her cup aside. "Look, I've answered all your questions, I'm helping as best I can, but at least tell me why I'm here . . . what he's done."

They exchanged a look before Poyner cleared his throat and spoke. "The picture you've identified as your ex-husband is a suspect in a series of burglaries on the Upper West Side. So far there have been eight break-ins, and this sketch is the closest thing to a clue that we have."

"Eight break-ins," Maggie said, jaw dropping slowly. "Are you saying that Eddie is *Smiley*?"

Browning flinched. "Gotta love when the media turns a crime into entertainment."

Maggie hardly heard the detective. Her mind was racing. Between work and writing, she hardly paid attention to the news these days, but there was a TV at the diner that was set to the local news more often than not. It was impossible to miss mention of the celebrity criminal known as Smiley, apparently so dubbed because of cheeky notes left at the scene of the crime.

The details on the guy were sparse, probably because the cops wanted them to be, but even still, that couldn't be Eddie. Not her Eddie.

Could it?

Doubt gnawed at the back of her mind. The man was lazy as crap, but he was also smart, in a wily sort of way. And she could totally imagine him getting an absolute kick out of earning a name like Smiley while evading the police.

"Ms. Walker, I understand that you haven't heard from your husband in a while, but if there's anything you can tell us about him—the way he operates, the way he thinks, you'd be helping us out."

Her fingers picked up the police sketch again and she studied it. "You really think my ex-husband is breaking into people's homes and stealing . . . what, exactly?"

They shrugged. "His MO's not consistent. Sometimes he takes a computer, sometimes it's jewelry, other times it's nothing more than a crystal decanter. Best as we can tell, he seems to be in it for the thrill more than for the money."

Maggie didn't take her eyes off the picture. "Oh, trust me, if Eddie really is Smiley, he's in it for the money. At least partially."

"What does Mr. Hansen do for a living?"

Maggie snorted. "Drink beer? Eddie was unemployed more often than not, but to hear him tell it, that was never his fault."

Eddie had always gotten along well with her brother. Eddie and Cory could rant for hours about how The Man was working against them.

"We pulled up his record," Browning said. "A half dozen unpaid parking tickets, numerous traffic citations, and an altercation at an O'Malley's pub a few years back, although all charges were dropped?"

There was a question there.

"He'd had too much to drink," Maggie said quietly, remembering that night all too well. "Got into it with one of his friends."

Eddie's "friend" had been Jonah Morton, one of the few decent guys that Eddie hung out with and the only one of Eddie's crew that Maggie had been able to tolerate. Over beers, she and Jonah, who'd just remodeled his house, had gotten into a discussion about the best method of removing wallpaper—quite possibly the *least* sexy topic in the history of conversation—and Eddie had lost it. He'd accused Jonah of making a move on his woman about five seconds before launching himself across the pub table.

Jonah hadn't bothered to fight back, but the rest of Eddie's crew had thrown themselves into the mix. The night ended with four of them in handcuffs.

Luckily, Maggie had had plenty of experience with the whole bail process thanks to an alcoholic father and a delinquent brother. By midnight the same night she'd been driving Eddie home, and he spent the entire next day sleeping it off.

He never acknowledged the incident. Not to apologize. Not to thank her. Nothing.

Maggie told the detectives none of this. She was happy to fill them in on Eddie's history, but not her own.

"Ms. Walker, it would be extremely helpful if you could put together a list of any way we might be able to get in contact with Mr. Hansen. Family members, mutual friends, favorite hangouts…"

Maggie shrugged. "I can try, but it's been awhile. I'd like to think Eddie's moved on from his life with me."

"All the same, Mr. Hansen is the closest thing we have to a suspect, and you're the closest thing we have to *him*. The captain wouldn't have asked you to come down here if he didn't think you had something useful to share."

Maggie's eyes flicked to the mirrored window behind the

detectives' heads, which every cop TV show she'd ever seen told her was likely to be a one-way window.

"Yeah?" she asked, barely keeping the ire out of her voice. "Is that why your *captain* has been staring at me through a one-way window for the past hour instead of having the courtesy to talk or even say hello?"

CHAPTER FIVE

Anthony crossed his arms over his chest and continued to glare into the interrogation room. He made eye contact with a very annoyed, very angry Maggie Walker, although she wouldn't *know* they were actually making eye contact.

Then her eyes narrowed slightly, and Anth had the strangest sense that maybe she *did* know, even though common sense told him that all she was seeing was a reflection of herself.

"Hey, this just in: you're an ass."

Anth didn't even turn around to look at his brother. "What the hell are you doing here?"

Luc came up behind him until they were standing shoulder to shoulder looking into the interrogation room where Maggie was writing down anything she could remember about her ex-husband's old haunts.

Her ex-husband.

For some reason, it was strange to think of Maggie

Walker having been married. And divorced. Although he knew from the contact form she'd filled out today that she was thirty-two, she seemed younger somehow. Her light brown hair was pulled into a girlish ponytail; she was dressed in jeans, basic brown leather boots, and a long-sleeved white shirt that was just fitted enough to be… interesting.

"I repeat. You're an ass," Luc said.

Anth finally turned his head to look at his younger brother. "And *I'll* repeat: What the hell are you doing here?"

Luc turned to face him, the anger on his face catching Anthony by surprise.

"I'm here because Mags called me."

Mags?

"What do you mean, she called you? When?"

And *why*?

Maggie had called Luc. It shouldn't have bothered him so much. It was probably nothing…and yet, for reasons he didn't understand, the fact made him want to punch his brother's too-good-looking face.

If she'd needed to talk, why hadn't she called *him*?

Luc's blue eyes were exasperated as he glared at Anth. "She called me, wanting to know if she needed a lawyer."

"What the fuck would she need a lawyer for?"

"Exactly!" Luc said, throwing his hands up. "Did you bother to explain to her that she wasn't a suspect before you dragged her down here and stuck her in an interrogation room?"

Anth felt a little sting of guilt. He hadn't really told her much of anything. No wonder she hadn't called him. Still, to call his *brother*…

Too frustrated to sort out his thoughts, and too caught off

guard by the unexpected sting of jealousy, Anthony lashed out in the way of older siblings everywhere. He straightened his shoulders and glared.

But Luc was having none of it. "Puff up all you want, big brother. You handled this badly, and you know it. Get her out of there."

Anthony dimly registered that his brother was absolutely right, which made him fight back all the more.

"This isn't your case, *bambino*. Hell, it's not even your *precinct*."

A throat cleared from near the door, and Anthony glanced over to see Luc's partner standing there, looking half-fascinated, half-nervous.

Anth glanced back at Luc. "You dragged Lopez with you?"

Sawyer Lopez lifted a finger in agreement. "Dragged is the correct word there, Captain. If it were up to me, we'd be dutifully patrolling Broadway for jaywalkers."

"Shut it, Lopez," Luc shot over his shoulder. "Broadway is *crawling* with jaywalkers, and you hate Times Square."

Luc's partner grinned, his teeth white against his tanned skin. Anthony all but rolled his eyes. Between his baby brother's movie-star good looks and Lopez's exotic, dark-haired charm, the two younger men looked like a TV version of cops, not the real thing.

And Maggie had called Luc.

"Get her out of there," Luc repeated, his voice quieter as he jerked his head in the direction of the interrogation room.

"Don't you already have a girlfriend to worry about?"

"Ooh, I know the answer to this one," Lopez said, raising his hand.

"We *all* know this one," Anth ground out. His brother was head over heels in love with Ava Sims. So why had he dashed over here the second a diner waitress called him?

And come to think of it...

"How did Maggie even have your phone number?" Anthony asked.

Luc shrugged. "I gave it to her awhile back. She needed someone to go pick up a table she'd bought, and Vin and I helped her out."

Okay *that*...that didn't even make sense.

"*Vincent*. You're telling me that Vincent, the city's—no, the *state*'s—biggest grump, willingly helped some broad move furniture?"

Luc's eyes narrowed. "Not some broad. *Maggie*. Good God, man, we see her every Sunday, and Vin and I see her a hell of a lot more than that when we drop in once or twice a week."

"Mags always talks the chef into adding extra cheese to my sandwich," Lopez said. "Gotta love her."

Both Morettis ignored him.

Anthony stayed focused on his brother. "Is Vin interested in her or something?"

Luc's brows lifted.

"Don't," Anth snapped. "I know that look. I invented that look."

Luc's only response was to grin.

"I hate brothers," Anthony muttered, turning back to see that Maggie was still writing dutifully on the paper, her teeth nibbling at the corner of her lip as she thought.

God, had she really thought she needed a lawyer?

He knew he'd been a little intense at the diner yesterday when she'd recognized the sketch of Smiley—or *thought* she recognized—time would tell how accurate the sketch was...or how accurate Maggie's memory was.

But he thought he'd made it perfectly clear that she didn't have anything to worry about...that she'd be doing them a favor.

"I offered to send detectives to her house," Anthony muttered.

"Yeah, because that's probably a dream of hers. To have a bunch of strangers come invade her personal space on her day off and talk about her ex-husband."

"Well, what would you have done, Luca?" Anth asked, his tone surly. "She has potentially vital information to my case. I can't treat her differently just because—"

"Because why?" Luc prompted.

"Because she's hot," Lopez said, coming all the way into the room to join the Morettis at the window.

Anthony's hand fisted at Lopez's casual comment. "Have some respect, Officer; she's a witness."

Lopez and Luc exchanged a glance and Anthony realized he'd walked into a classic trap.

"She's not *actually* a witness," Luc said casually.

"Well, she's an informant," Anthony said, grasping at straws.

"I apologize for admiring the *informant*," Lopez said. "I was out of line."

Anthony scowled at the other man, looking for just the smallest amount of cheek or insolence to reprimand, but Officer Lopez's face was all respectful deference.

Luc's expression, on the other hand, was knowing, and Anthony decided to cut right through the bullshit and get it all out on the table.

"Why do I get the feeling that you two second graders

have gotten it into your head that I have an attachment to Ms. Walker?" Anth asked.

"Why would we think that? You don't have an attachment to *anybody*."

Luc's words were said in a jesting, younger-brother tone, but they caused a pang of…something. But instead of giving into the forbidden emotion, Anthony clung to an easier one:

Resentment.

Resentment that Luc could be cavalier about romantic relationships when he'd met his perfect match in an ambitious career woman who understood a cop's long hours.

Plus, Luc was an officer, who, for reasons Anthony didn't understand, seemed to be perfectly content staying at that rank for the time being. By the time Anthony was Luc's age, he was already a sergeant, but Luc had always been blissfully unburdened by titles. Blissfully unburdened by the crushing legacy of following in Tony Moretti's footsteps…

And then there was Vannah. That beautiful tragedy of a woman had taught Anthony one very important lesson:

He could be a cop…

…or a boyfriend.

Or was the operative word.

He couldn't be both.

And he sure as *hell* couldn't be a husband. Some cops, perhaps, were cut out for the double life. His father had made it work. Luc was making it work. His brother Marco had actually put the relationship *first*, moving to godforsaken Los Angeles for the sake of his girlfriend.

But guys like Anth and Vincent…they had the sort of single-minded dedication that didn't allow them luxuries like relationships.

Not that Luc and Marc weren't dedicated to the force. They'd die for the PD. Literally.

But...

Anthony's wandering mind snapped to attention at the realization that there was movement in the interrogation room. Maggie had handed over her notes to his two detectives and was shaking their hands, a friendly smile in place even though her face looked tired... nervous.

Nervous because he'd made a complete mess of things, because for reasons that made no sense, Maggie Walker made him act like a complete moron.

Luc was moving toward the door, Lopez on his heels, and Anthony frowned. "Where are you going?"

His younger brother's tone was suspiciously patient. "I'm going to check on Maggie. See how she's holding up."

"She's holding up fine," Anth said. "For God's sake, you guys act like I cuffed her and read her her rights. I just asked her some questions. And yes, I put her in the interrogation room, but she chose not to do it in her own apartment—"

"Why'd you have Browning and Poyner ask the questions?" Luc interrupted.

Anthony paused, annoyed at being interrupted, even more annoyed at the speculative look on his brother's face. "They're the leads on the case."

"And you're the boss. You found the 'informant.' You *know* the informant. And you know this case every bit as well as they do. Perhaps better. Why didn't you ask the questions?"

"It's not protocol," Anth responded.

He could have sworn the look on his brother's face was akin to disgust, but then Luc had turned away, shaking his head and heading out the door. "Lopez, whadya say we give Mags a ride to wherever she needs to go?"

It was on the tip of Anthony's tongue to remind Luc that that wasn't his job.

And that as an on-duty officer, he couldn't just be driving off to Park Slope to give a waitress a ride home.

But he stopped himself before he could issue the order.

Anth told himself it was because it wasn't his place; he may outrank Luc, but he wasn't his brother's captain. Luc and Lopez were in a different precinct. He didn't issue their orders.

But when his eyes caught on the weary features of Maggie Walker as his detectives led her from the room, he knew his reasons had nothing to do with the chain of command, and everything to do with the fact that Maggie Walker looked like she needed a friend.

Something that Anth could never be for her.

He didn't even know *how*. But he wanted to be there. Wanted to be the one she called—turned to.

And that bothered him more that he'd ever admit to his brother.

Or himself.

CHAPTER SIX

Saturdays were usually Maggie's day off, but every now and then she filled in for a co-worker. The extra shift meant extra cash.

And every time, she regretted it.

Saturdays at the Darby Diner always meant a weird combination of lost tourists, tired locals, and the hungover twenty-somethings who rolled in still smelling like vodka and stale cologne.

Maggie pulled one plate from the warming lamp even as she returned another. "Carlos, can I get fresh hash browns on this one?"

A dark, round face with a slight sheen from the heat of the fryer appeared with narrowed eyes. "Who didn't like my potatoes?"

"Table nineteen. The lady said they weren't evenly cooked," Maggie said, looking at the ticket for her pancakes, trying to remember who they were for. Usually she kept the details all in her head, writing things down more for habit than necessity, but her head wasn't in the game today.

"I'll show her evenly cooked," the fry chef said with an irritated glance in the direction of table nineteen. "I'll evenly cook *her*."

"Please?" Maggie said, giving Carlos her best smile.

Her friend must have heard something in her tone, because his dark eyes flicked back to her. "Someone give you trouble, *carina*? You want Carlos to take care of them?"

She winked. "How about Carlos just takes care of those hash browns?"

He blew her a kiss. "Anything for you."

Maggie deposited the pancakes in front of the sweet elderly man sitting at the counter, refilled his coffee, and delivered a fresh batch of perfectly golden hash browns to table nineteen, only to be informed that the patron was no longer hungry.

She got a seven-cent tip for her troubles.

"A nickel and two pennies," Maggie said into a glass of orange juice during a rare lull in the rush. "Why even bother?"

Her fellow waitress Kim came up beside her to inspect the haul. "Could be worse," she said. "Yesterday I got a condom."

Maggie's orange juice halted halfway to her mouth. "Please tell me it wasn't used."

"No," the flashy blonde said. "But I've gotten one of them before too."

"Gross," Maggie muttered.

Kim winked. "That's nothing. Stick with me, kid, you'll learn things about this business that will literally make your skin crawl."

"Oh stop," Maggie told her friend, setting her glass aside

and scanning the diner to make sure none of her patrons were looking distressed. "You're all of, what, three years older than me? Quit acting like an oh-so-wise mama bear."

"But I *am* an oh-so-wise mama bear. I have two kids and a dozen stretch marks to prove it. And you may match me in age, but *experience...*"

"Yeah, yeah," Maggie said, patting her friend on the cheek. "You've been waiting tables since you were sixteen. I remember."

"And a good thing too," Kim said, running a hand over her fluffy platinum blond bangs. "Twenty years' experience is exactly what's preventing me from 'accidentally' spilling coffee over the jerk at table two that keeps calling me Baby Slam."

"Baby Slam? That's a thing now?"

"Dunno," Kim said. "But whether or not Urban Dictionary deems it legit, I'm still about to dump coffee all over him."

Maggie groaned. "Don't even talk to me about spilling coffee."

"Oh right," Kim said, leaning back against the counter and putting her hands in her apron pockets. "The *captain.*"

Maggie winced. "Can we not talk about him?"

"*You* brought him up."

Maggie gave her friend a suspicious look. "What's that tone? There's something in that tone I don't like one bit."

Her friend merely smiled, her slightly crooked front teeth only adding to her allure. Kim Bowers had the hair of a *Baywatch* extra, the body of a Playboy bunny, the mouth of a trucker, and the type of fierce loyalty and friendship that Maggie wasn't at all sure that she'd earned, but was more than willing to accept.

"I heard about the sandwich incident the other day," Kim said sympathetically. "The man really makes you nervous, huh?"

Maggie poured more orange juice from the machine even though she didn't want it. "He doesn't make me nervous. He's just..."

She broke off, not really knowing how to continue. She hadn't told anyone about why she'd dumped Captain Moretti's sandwich on him that day.

One of the benefits of getting a fresh start, with a new job in a new town, was the new friends. And the perk of the new friends was that they didn't know your ex-husband. Didn't know what abysmal taste you had in men, or know that you'd spent the better part of your twenties letting said men tear you down.

"He's so cocky," Maggie said, tapping her nails on her cup. "He's—"

"Gorgeous, domineering, and sexy as hell?"

Yes. "Not what I was going to say. I don't get how a guy from such a wonderful family can end up such a jerk."

Kim wiggled her winged eyebrows. "Why don't you go find out?"

"Huh?"

Kim jerked her chin over Maggie's shoulder. "Table seven."

Maggie spun around, her heart pounding at the thought of seeing *him*.

It wasn't Anthony Moretti at table seven. It *was*, however, his mother and sister.

"Too bad," Kim mused. "Today's berry cobbler would have looked really good all over his uniform."

"Ha. Ha."

"You want me to take the Moretti ladies?" Kim asked.

"Nah, I got it," Maggie said, already moving toward them. *These* Morettis, she liked. *These* Morettis didn't keep her up at night.

Maria and Elena Moretti saw her coming, their faces lighting up with broad smiles. Maggie smiled back.

"You're looking pretty today, Maggie," the older Moretti woman said, standing to give her a hug and a kiss on the cheek.

Maggie accepted the hug and had to remind herself not to linger too long, not to cling too desperately.

What would it be like to have a mother like this? One who was warm and soft and smelled like almond and sugar?

"You *are* looking pretty," Elena said, holding out her arms and wiggling her fingers for her chance at a hug.

Maggie laughed and complied. "If by 'pretty' you mean tired."

"I don't, but I don't blame you one second for being exhausted. Luca told us what happened. How Anth dragged you by your hair like a caveman into the interrogation room—"

"It wasn't quite like that," Maggie said with a little smile as both women sat back down in their chairs. "It was more like—"

"More like my son forgot that you weren't one of his crack-whore-off-the-street informants?" Maria supplied.

"*Mother*," Elena said in mock horror. "Crack whore? My delicate ears."

"You don't raise four cops and stay married to another for most of your life and not pick up a few things," the Moretti matron said, primly fluttering a paper napkin to her lap as though it were fine linen.

"Anyway. We apologize on Anth's behalf," Elena said.

Anth. It was a strange sort of nickname, but she supposed it made sense considering *Tony* was already taken by his father.

"He was just doing his job," Maggie said with more magnanimity than she actually felt.

She wasn't so much mad that the man had expected her to answer questions. If it really was Eddie committing these crimes, she was more than happy to help.

It was that he hadn't even bothered to show up.

Not even to say hello, and *certainly* not to say thanks.

"So what brings you ladies out this way?" Maggie asked, pulling her little notebook out of her apron to keep her hands busy. It was important to remember that she was their waitress, not a friend or family member joining them for a ladies' lunch.

"A little shopping," Maria said. "Tony's birthday is next week, so it's about the only time of the year I can leave the house without him asking a million questions about what I'm doing, where I'm going, and so forth."

"Ah," Maggie said knowingly. "And did we find the perfect gift?"

Maria waved her hand. "Please. I found it months ago. Ordered it online."

Maggie tapped her nose. "Brilliant. So the birthday was merely the *excuse* for a shopping expedition."

Elena gestured to the half dozen bags at her feet. "Can we help the fact that there were fabulous stores all over the place? It was terrible. Just *terrible*."

"You poor things," Maggie cooed, playing along.

"Wanna see my new shoes?" Elena's blue eyes twinkled up at her.

Both Luc and Elena had their mother's blue eyes, while

the rest of the kids had their father's dark brown gaze. Although Anthony's eyes were just slightly lighter than Vincent's, almost a sultry gold color...

Don't go there.

"I'd love to see your new shoes," Maggie said, knowing that she should probably make the rounds at her other tables, but also not wanting to turn down this rare gift of female friendship.

She'd missed this. She had Kim of course, but she and Kim commiserated mostly about work. It was nice to enjoy female company without the added spice of *you'll never guess what table four just did*.

And with Gabby in Colorado, and the rest of her "friends" having taken Eddie's side during the divorce, well...

Let's just say Maggie was happy to gobble up every bit of kindness the Moretti women threw her way.

Elena proudly displayed a high-heeled patent leather stiletto that Maggie cooed over, even as she acknowledged that even if the gorgeous designer shoes had been in her price range, she'd never have a place to wear them.

Elena was an attorney; both her income *and* her work wardrobe were better suited to stilettos than Maggie's dingy diner income.

"I'll check back on you ladies in a couple minutes," Maggie said after confirming that, yes, Elena's shoes were bound to land her a promotion and, no, Maggie really couldn't consider borrowing them. Although the offer was tempting. Especially since she and Elena were the same shoe size.

After clearing two of her tables, getting yelled at by a third about a "skimpy portion of sausage," Maggie finally returned to the Moretti women with iced tea for Elena and water for Maria.

"What can I get for you ladies?"

"Are we too early for lunch?"

Maggie checked her watch—a cheap, plastic affair she'd picked up for herself at the drugstore.

She tried hard not to look at the dainty gold band on Elena's wrist with delicate diamonds encircling the face. She'd always been a sucker for watches. Eddie had bought her one for their first anniversary; she'd been over the moon until she'd learned he'd won it at a poker game, and that its original intended recipient had been the loser's sixteen-year-old daughter.

"The kitchen will switch over in a couple minutes, if you don't mind waiting?"

"Not at all." Maria glanced around. "I'll take the turkey sandwich please...the special. With salad."

"I'll have a club," Elena said, handing Maggie her menu. "Hold the salad, extra fries."

Maggie smiled. Her kind of woman.

She started to back away to put their order in when Maria reached out and touched her hand. "Maggie..."

Maggie met the older woman's eyes.

Maria smiled softly as she searched her face. "You know, if you ever need someone to talk to..."

Maggie's gaze shifted between the two women, and everything clicked into place. "You guys came into the diner on purpose, didn't you?"

"Well, of course," Elena said. "Because we were hungry."

Maggie gave the woman a steady look and Elena pursed her lips. "Okay, and maybe we wanted to check up on you. It can't have been easy learning..."

Maria made a quick clucking noise, and Elena glanced around before lowering her voice. "It can't have been easy learning that your ex-husband is suspected of... *you know*."

Maggie swallowed. "Eddie hasn't been a part of my life for nearly two years."

Maria touched her hand again. "But you loved him once. Didn't you?"

"Of course," Maggie said automatically, even though she wasn't at all sure it was true.

Had she loved Eddie?

Or had she been so desperate to escape her father's and brother's constant neediness that she'd walked right into an even worse situation?

"Well, regardless of what kind of tool your ex was, we just came to tell you that Anthony's an ass," Elena said.

"Elena," her mother murmured softly.

"He put her in the interrogation room, Mom."

"It wasn't so bad," Maggie said. "Really. And it's over now, so no harm done."

Elena and Maria exchanged a glance... a sort of unspoken mother/daughter communication that Maggie was fairly certain she wouldn't have been able to crack even if her own mother hadn't disappeared into the night before Maggie even reached puberty.

"What?" she said warily.

Elena leaned forward, elbows on the table, looking every bit a beautiful, confident woman who knew what she wanted... and more alarming, who *got* what she wanted.

It was Maria who spoke up, her facial expression all the more effective for its subtlety. "Maggie, sweetie, we're probably overstepping our bounds here..."

"*Definitely* overstepping," Elena said unapologetically.

"Are you seeing anyone?" Maria asked, dropping her tone just slightly to avoid eavesdroppers.

Maggie's eyes went wide as she realized the real reason that these two women had gone out of their way to come to the diner.

A setup.

"Um." It was all Maggie could manage.

Maria reached forward to pat her hand. "What I mean, is there a special man in your life?"

"Yeah, Mom, I think she probably knows that's what you meant," Elena said with a little wink at Maggie.

"No. And no," Maggie said. "Not seeing anyone. No special man."

Maria sucked in her cheeks, looking thoughtful. "Would you *like* there to be a special someone?"

"Oh. Well. Sure. Someday. I mean, everyone wants...I don't know," she said finally.

"I get it," Elena said, taking a sip of her iced tea. "I've never been married...or divorced. But I've dated some real pigs. It's hard to want to put yourself out there again."

Her mother gave her a look. "When have you *ever* put yourself out there?"

Elena ignored her mom. "Look, Maggie, we like you. A lot. And with the exception of Luc who somehow managed to snag Ava, the rest of them have horrible taste in women..."

"Only because they need a little help in seeing what's right in front of them," Maria said. "Say, a pretty waitress with a nice smile..."

Maggie blew out a long breath, wondering how the heck she was going to dodge this situation. "I'm flattered. So flattered. And I adore you two...your whole family is amazing, but..."

"But...?" Maria prompted when she didn't continue. "You don't like my boys?"

Uh-oh.

Luckily, Elena jumped to her rescue.

"Easy, mama bear," Elena soothed. "You have to admit, they're all a bit overdosed on testosterone and a little lacking in romantic charm. Can you blame Maggie for wanting someone a little more refined?"

"It's not that," Maggie broke in, even as her brain begged her to be quiet. "I actually like the...testosterone."

She winced at Elena's smirk, but it was true. She always wanted to like a nice guy with pretty manners, maybe a soft sense of humor, but when it came to who caught her eye...who she thought about on restless nights, well...

Then Maggie made it worse because she kept talking. Rambling, actually. "It's just, I don't think Anthony and I could ever work. He's so, um, rigid, and I can't seem to look at him without dumping coffee in his lap, and he's so—"

She broke off when she realized,

(a) she was babbling

(b) Maria and Elena were both looking at her in amusement and confusion.

"Who said anything about Anthony?" Elena said, sitting back in her chair with a puzzled expression.

"We thought you might be a good fit for *Vincent*, honey," Maria said. "He's always so standoffish, but we've noticed that he talks to you. Even smiles at you from time to time."

"In other words, he *likes* you," Elena said. "Trust me *that* is a rare phenomenon indeed."

Oh. *Oh*.

They weren't trying to set her up with the captain.

Of course not.

As if their precious captain would go for a waitress.

And Vincent was...nice.

She liked Vin. He wasn't as friendly as Luc, but there was something about him that was steady. Reliable. Honest.

Vincent Moretti was a good man.

She should *absolutely* be interested, especially if *he* was interested.

And yet...

She bit her lip.

"Mags," Elena chided. "Do you have a thing for Anth?"

"No!"

"Good."

Both Maggie and Elena glanced at Maria in surprise, and the older woman shrugged. "It's not that my Anthony isn't a good man. It's just that he's not...he's not suitor material. Not yet, anyway."

Suitor. Maggie nearly smiled. "What do you mean?" she asked, unable to stop herself.

Elena let out a sigh. "Mom's right. Anthony's a good guy. The best. But he's um...cautious."

Maria nodded in agreement, looking a little sad.

"Has he always been that way?" Maggie asked, even as she ordered herself not to act so interested.

"Yes, somewhat," Maria hedged. "But it's gotten much worse since that horrible experience with that poor girl who died..."

Don't ask. Don't pry...

Someone had *died*?

"Vannah," Elena said with a touch of snark. "Who was—"

"Elena." Maria's tone was soft but rife with meaning. *Don't go there.*

To Maggie's surprise, Elena listened to her mother and didn't finish her sentence.

"So that's a no on Vincent then?" Elena asked, changing the subject.

Maggie opened her mouth, wanting to say no...that she couldn't possibly date one brother while dreaming about another.

But then she remembered the way Anthony hardly spoke to her...the way he hadn't even come to see her when she'd stopped by the precinct at his request.

"That's a *maybe*," she said with a small smile.

"Good girl," Elena said happily. "I know Vincent's a little rough around the edges, but believe it or not, he's the least emotionally damaged of the bunch. And since it's obvious he's never going to make a move on Jill—"

"Jill, as in his partner?" Maggie asked curiously. She'd only met Jill a handful of times when she tagged along with the Morettis, but she had the impression of a bright, bubbly blonde who was the polar opposite of quiet, serious Vincent.

"Yup," Elena confirmed, her voice all happy-gossip. "For the longest time, we all thought...Mags? Maggie, are you okay?"

No.

No, Maggie wasn't okay.

Her entire world was tilting.

Maggie heard Elena's voice from a mile away and was distantly aware of Maria touching her arm softly.

Someone cried out, and she felt Kim's arm go around her waist as her friend lowered her into the chair Elena had just vacated, while Maria pushed a water glass into her hand.

"Maggie, talk to me," Kim said, crouching down in front of her and taking both hands. "You look ready to faint. Aren't you supposed to put your face between your knees or something? Or maybe—"

"I'm fine," Maggie said, finally tearing her eyes away from the window.

He was gone. Or maybe he had never been there at all. Or maybe...

It was Maria Moretti's no-nonsense, motherly voice that finally got through as she cupped Maggie's face in her hands and stared down at her face with a gentle but stern gaze. "Maggie. Talk."

Maggie licked her lips and blinked away the sudden sting of tears.

And then she talked.

"I'm pretty sure I just saw my ex-husband watching me through the window."

CHAPTER SEVEN

On the Moretti *Scale of Tempers*, Anthony fell somewhere in the middle.

Elena, Vincent, and their father were the hotheads.

Luc, Marc, and their mother were more the peacemakers.

Anth was in between. He may not be as mellow as Marc, who could probably coax a skittish horse onto a sinking *Titanic*, but neither was he as prone to bursts of fury as Vincent when a killer got off easy, or as fiery as Elena when she lost a case.

But at this moment, as he stood outside in the rain in the alley waiting for a stubborn, foolhardy waitress to finish up her shift, he was mad. *Good* and mad.

And by the time Maggie Walker finally slipped out the back door of the diner, he'd moved beyond mad.

He was well on his way to pissed.

"Ms. Walker."

She jumped so suddenly that she dropped the container

of whatever she was carrying. The sight of meat loaf and mashed potatoes splattered all over the pavement in front of her wasn't enough to take the edge off Anthony's anger.

But the expression of bewildered dismay as she looked down at the now inedible food was.

"Well, there goes dinner."

The quietly uttered statement was made all the more impactful from the lack of moping in it. She was just stating the sad fact as though it was her lot in life... to have strange men sneaking up on her and to have her dinner turned upside down in a dark alley.

And for that matter, it was nearly two a.m. She hadn't had dinner yet?

He didn't realize he'd spoken aloud until she cut him with an irritated look. "Surely you've worked a double in your day, Captain. Did *you* always find time to eat?"

He bit the inside of his cheek as he moved closer to her, ignoring the fact that it had started to rain harder. "Actually, it doesn't really matter how many hours captains work. We don't get paid overtime."

Now why had he gone and said that? What was *wrong* with him?

She rolled her eyes. "Fine. What about before your illustrious *captain* title? Did you get overtime then?"

"Yes," he said quietly, watching in annoyance as she knelt to pick up the food. "God, Maggie, you can't eat that now."

She glanced up, startled, perhaps by the use of her first name, before annoyance resettled on her pretty features. "I'm not *that* hard up, Captain. I was just going to clean it up and put it in the Dumpster so Carlos doesn't step in my mess when he leaves."

"Who's Carlos?" He knelt beside her, taking the two ends

of the plastic takeout container from her and using it to scoop the still warm leftovers onto one side.

"My fry chef," she replied, letting him clean up. "Well, not *my* fry chef. But he's my friend. He worked a double as well, so he'll be leaving soon."

"You should have waited for him to walk you." He walked the couple steps to the Dumpster and tossed the leftovers over the edge, careful not to let anything splatter onto his rain jacket.

"Well, what do you know, this just might mark our first meeting when I managed not to spill on you," she said with a bright smile that was totally out of place, given the increasing rain, her lack of a jacket, and the fact that her dinner was now food for the rats.

And for some reason, that too-bright grin was exactly the impetus he needed to remember his anger.

"You saw your ex-husband."

Her smile vanished and she turned as though to walk away, but he grabbed her arm and pulled her around to face him.

Her hazel eyes were a mossy green in the dim light near the back door of the restaurant, but there was nothing soft in them as she glared up at him. "That's why you're here? Because I thought I saw my ex-husband?"

"No, I'm here because you thought you saw your ex-husband, who you know full well is the prime suspect in a string of high-profile burglary cases, *and you didn't fucking call me.*"

She didn't even flinch at his outrage. "You're acting like I withheld information. I *did* call the cops! Right away."

"Yeah. My little brother."

"Who also goes by *Officer* Moretti," she spat back. "He's a cop, just like you."

He ran a hand through his hair. "This isn't Luc's case."

"Who was I supposed to call?" she asked incredulously. *"You?"*

The bafflement in her voice nagged at him, even though it shouldn't have. "Yes, me! It's my case!"

She spread her hands out to the side as though to indicate there was no problem. "Obviously all the minions beneath you gave you the update. Isn't that the way it's supposed to work?"

"You should have called me," he repeated, taking a step closer.

She rolled her eyes and cupped her hands over her elbows, as though trying to physically prevent herself from shivering.

Anthony swore softly and shrugged off his jacket, draping it around her shoulders, being careful not to touch her.

She glanced up at him, her eyes big and shocked. Jesus, what did she think of him? He wasn't a total animal.

"You'll ruin your uniform," she said, glancing down at his shirt, which was already getting damp.

"It'll dry," he said roughly. "It's not like it's Armani."

Damn it, he thought, watching as she seemed to cuddle into his jacket. Damn it to hell, because Anthony wanted nothing more than to tug her to him.

To drop his mouth to hers and *taste* her.

Damn this woman.

CHAPTER EIGHT

Cuddling in Anthony Moretti's coat was the best thing that had happened to her all week.

It didn't matter what brand it was, or whether it was designer, because it smelled...amazing.

It was a cliché, and she knew it, but she couldn't help turning her head just the slightest bit to inhale the scent of *man*. It had been so long—*too* long.

And even before things had turned really awful between her and Eddie, he'd mostly smelled like beer and Doritos.

Captain Moretti's coat smelled like rain and soap.

But the stab of longing dissipated the second her eyes returned to his and saw the harsh edge of irritation as well as the fact that he was staring at her mouth. Hard.

He shook his head, and she wondered if she imagined the flare of heat in his eyes. Especially since his next words emerged as an all-out bark.

"You're *sure* it was Eddie Hansen you saw yesterday?"

Maggie lifted her chin. "I'm sure it's all in the report. I told Luc what happened, and then when he called detectives Browning and Poyner, I told them as well."

Anthony swore and ran a hand through his hair, the gesture having virtually no effect because it was cut so short. Probably to avoid such nuisances as styling it.

If she knew anything about this man it was that he didn't like nuisances and that he *definitely* had put her into that category. It was written all over the hard line of his jaw, the flat, unsmiling mouth and unreadable eyes.

"I read the damn report," he said. "What I don't understand is why you called my brother instead of me."

"You're sounding like a broken record, Captain Moretti."

"And you're dodging the question, Ms. Walker."

Maggie licked her lips nervously and flicked a glance at the back door of the diner, wondering where the heck Carlos was. She could use a distraction right about now before she started sniffing this man's jacket again.

"Ms. Walker—" he prompted.

Okay. Enough was enough.

"You want to know why I didn't call you?" She took a step forward and jabbed a finger at his chest.

He didn't take a step back, but his eyes did widen slightly in surprise, and she felt a little thrill at having an advantage with this man—for once.

"I didn't call you because you're an unfeeling *jerk*," she said, jabbing a finger at his chest again.

The diva gesture was oddly satisfying.

And yet, the man didn't show any reaction—not so much as a blink.

"A jerk," he said finally, after they both let the silence stretch on.

Maggie licked her lips, already regretting her choice of words. "I called Luc, because he's...*nice*."

"And I'm not?"

"I don't know you well," she said, choosing her words carefully, "but that day at the station when you asked me to come down to answer questions...you weren't even there."

"I was there." His voice was gruff.

"I don't mean watching me through a one-way mirror, Captain."

He glanced down at his feet, his chin dipping down to his chest, and the gesture was so boyishly appealing that she started to soften.

Then he looked up. "I'm just doing my job, Ms. Walker. I don't have time to hold the hand of every potential informant or witness."

All encroaching warm thoughts she'd had evaporated.

She shrugged out of his coat and shoved it at him, not caring that her uniform was getting soaked and was probably clinging a little too snugly. It had been sunny and unseasonably warm when she'd left home yesterday, and she hadn't planned on leaving the diner at two in the morning...

"You want me to tell you that I'll call you next time I see Eddie?" she asked. "Well I won't. One, because Eddie Hansen is the biggest coward I've had the displeasure of knowing. If he knows I saw him, he'll be long gone by now. And two...two, I won't be calling you, because *I don't owe you anything*."

She spun on her heel, a gesture less sexy than it could have been thanks to the black utilitarian shoes she wore while working, but as with before, he grabbed her arm, pulling her back around before she could storm off.

Except this time, his grip was a bit firmer, his tug a bit

harder, and she came up abruptly against his chest, the coat she'd rejected sandwiched between them.

"You'll call me," he said, his eyes simmering with temper.

"I won't," she said again, stubbornly. "So you can drop the caveman routine."

"I could charge you with obstruction of justice—"

"Oh, stuff it," she said. "I didn't say I wouldn't call the *cops*; I just said I wasn't going to call you personally. Because there's nothing *personal* about you. You're overbearing and grumpy and—"

"I'm not Luc. I get it," he snapped. "But he's taken, so get over the crush."

Her eyes narrowed. "I have absolutely no interest in Luc. But while we're speaking of me and your brothers, did you know that when your mom and sister were in the Darby Diner yesterday they were trying to set me up?"

Moretti's eyes dropped briefly to her mouth. "You and me? That's preposterous."

Maggie ignored the sting at his incredulous reaction.

She leaned in just slightly, the heat in his gaze making her bold. "They weren't trying to set me up with you, Captain. With *Vincent*."

Moretti visibly recoiled. "Vin?" Then he laughed. "That's . . . There is no way he'd be interested."

Maggie blinked. Blinked again. The burn of his disbelief that someone might be interested in her was a bit too much to take.

She slowly eased away from him, averting her eyes so he couldn't see the hurt, only to realize she probably needn't bother. The man was an insensitive ass—he wouldn't recognize hurt feelings if they bit him in the balls.

"I'll be going home now, Captain."

"Ms. Walker . . . Maggie . . ." He reached out a hand again as she stepped backward, but this time Maggie was ready and she dodged.

"Quit manhandling me," she cried, her voice a little desperate. "I haven't done anything wrong and you know it."

His hand dropped to his side, his face the picture of masculine frustration. Their eyes locked for a few seconds, something complicated passing between them before the door beside them flew open.

"Maggie?" It was Carlos. *Finally.* "What are you still doing here?"

Her friend gave Anthony a suspicious look, and the taller man rolled his eyes. "Relax. I'm a cop. And if you're really her friend, you shouldn't let her walk to the subway alone."

Carlos frowned. "Hey! I've offered to walk her every day for months. She always says no."

Captain Moretti transferred his annoyed gaze back to Maggie, but she held up a weary hand. "Save it. Or add it to my list of sins. I don't really care. I'm going home. If either or both of you want to walk me to the subway station out of some macho display of chivalry, go for it, but under no circumstance do I want to chat. Got it?"

She walked away then, ignoring the rain, ignoring the hurt, and *definitely* ignoring the men behind her.

But she couldn't help but glance over her shoulder, just once before heading down the stairs to the train platform, and somehow she wasn't at all surprised to see that Captain Anthony Moretti had followed her, hands shoved in his coat pockets as he watched her from several feet away.

And despite her bad mood, Maggie might have smiled. Just a little bit.

CHAPTER NINE

Maggie had writer's block.

She *never* had writer's block. A little stumped on a plot twist, sure. Perplexed by what the heck her characters were thinking, definitely.

But this bone-deep inability to put words—*any* words—on the page was new. And unwelcome.

"What's the point of a day off if I can't write more than a crappy sentence about the weather?" Maggie asked her dog.

Duchess placed her snout on Maggie's leg, and Maggie absently handed the dog the other half of the chip she'd been nibbling on.

She glared at the blank screen. Grabbed another corn chip and nibbled the corner as she waited for her heroine to tell her all the ways in which she was devastated because Colin had asked Stacey to the prom instead of her.

Duchess's snout returned to Maggie's knee and Maggie

glanced down, happy for the distraction. "No more chips, sweetie. You have kibble in your bowl."

The dog's brown eyes were mournful. *Kibble sucks.*

Maggie rubbed Duchess's ear. "Okay fine, one more… but no salsa. Mostly because I forgot to buy any."

She *could* have been having cheesy scrambled eggs for dinner, but she'd finished off her egg supply last night instead of the yummy leftovers she'd been counting on.

Leftovers that had been delivered straight to the Dumpster after a certain tall, dark-haired police captain had scared the crap out of her and made her drop everything.

Of course, losing last night's dinner to the Dumpster wasn't really what was bothering her.

You and me? That's preposterous.

Maggie slumped back in her chair, annoyed that Anthony's words kept circling around and around in her head.

"You know what's annoying as heck?" she asked, running a finger down Duchess's snout. "That a cop born and raised in Staten Island throws around words like *preposterous*. Like he's freaking Sherlock Holmes or something."

The next words in the captain's vicious little put-down blindsided her, because she'd been trying all day to block it out.

Vin?… There is no way he'd be interested.

Ouch. *Ouch.*

Maggie blinked against the sudden sting of tears. It's not like she even *wanted* to date Vincent Moretti. Or any Moretti.

But that disdain on Anthony's face… the combination of shock and revulsion that his exalted family would ever lower themselves to the likes of her…

She couldn't get his expression out of her head. It was as though he *saw* her. Not the Maggie she tried so hard to be; the smiling, sweet, ever-cheerful diner waitress. It was like he saw the Maggie Walker she'd been before she'd met Eddie—pathetic, timid, and weak.

Even worse, she feared Anthony Moretti could see her as she'd been while she was *with* Eddie—submissive and gullible, a mere shadow of a person.

Why else was he so disgusted with her simply for *existing*?

Maggie gave Duchess's head one last pet and then forced her fingers to the keyboard, realizing that maybe she could get in her character's head after all.

Jenny, her teenage heroine, was feeling rejected.

And Maggie knew a little something about that...

An hour later, Maggie had added twelve hundred words. "Not bad, Duchess. Not bad at all. Shall we head to the freezer? The writing muse is demanding cookie dough."

Living alone could get lonely, but it had its benefits.

Say, like eating ice cream straight out of the carton with nobody to judge.

From her nightstand, Maggie's phone chirped with a text message. She leaned against the counter, crossing her ankles as she eyed the device across the room and slurped a chunk of cookie dough off her spoon.

Ignoring the phone was tempting. These days, it was bound to be one of three people, and Gabby was the only one of the three she wanted to hear from.

The others were her father and brother. Her father wasn't supposed to have access to his cell while in rehab, so if he was texting, it meant that he'd failed to see it through...again.

It was also likely to be her brother, whose texts tended to revolve around one topic: money.

As in, him *needing* money. From her.

And considering that she'd just talked to Gabby yesterday, it was unlikely that it was her friend calling again.

The phone had fallen silent.

Just that one text message, and the urge to ignore it was fierce, knowing that it would likely put her in a bad mood.

Once—just once—she wished her broken little family would need her for something other than money. Or better yet, to not need her at all. To contact her just to say freaking *hi*. Or *I miss you*.

Or heaven forbid, maybe an *I love you*, something she hadn't heard since the semi-tolerable years of her marriage, save for Gabby's ever casual *love ya*.

She glanced down at Duchess who was patiently waiting for the ice cream she wouldn't get.

"We're going to ignore the phone, baby," she told her dog. Duchess tilted her head.

"No. No dairy. It gives you gas."

Duchess tilted her head the other way, and Maggie scooped another spoonful of ice cream into her mouth. "What's that? You think I *should* check the phone?"

The dog lay on the ground, resting her snout on her front paws and looking mournful. Maggie pulled the spoon out of her mouth and pointed it at Duchess. "You're so right, Your Grace. It *could* be an emergency, and then I'd forever regret not checking it."

Maggie pushed away from the counter, moving across her tiny studio toward her nightstand where she picked up the phone, bracing herself for Cory's innocuous "Hey, Sis," or her father's "Bug, you around?"

But it wasn't from Cory. Or her dad. Not Gabby either.

Maggie sat on the bed, still clenching her ice-cream shovel in one hand as she reread the text.

It's Anthony. I realize contacting you via text is inappropriate given your connection to my case, but I can't stop thinking about last night. My behavior was inexcusable, and I owe you an apology.

Maggie chewed her lip as she read it again. Then she held up her phone to the dog who was still staring longingly at the ice-cream container on the counter. "Hey, get over here. What do we think of this?"

Duchess didn't even turn her head. Dogs had no appreciation for the ways in which technology had complicated modern relationships.

Not that she had a relationship—of any kind—with Captain Moretti. No, *Anthony*. He'd specifically used his name in the text.

She wanted to be annoyed at the message. In any other circumstance, she would have dismissed an apology via text as the coward's way out.

But an apology in any form coming from this man…

Maggie flopped back on the pillow, wondering how to respond. *If* she should respond. She felt a bit like her teen characters, totally overanalyzing things that probably weren't meant to be analyzed at all.

Her phone vibrated in her hand with another message, and Maggie hated the fact that her stomach flipped when she saw it was from him.

Yep, definitely as bad as her teen characters.

And in case you're wondering, I got your number the old-fashioned way…from my brother. Not from abusing police resources.

Maggie rolled her eyes. As if she would *ever* think that he'd put his precious career at risk. She didn't know the man well—or at all—but she was definitely getting the impression that Anthony Moretti was the badge first, the man second.

And yet, *he was apologizing…*

Stalling for time before she had to respond, she added the number to her contacts, hesitating over which name to go with, before settling on CAPTAIN, in all caps. Mainly because she figured it would annoy him. If her phone allowed italics, she totally would have added those too.

Duchess gave up hope on the ice cream and trotted over to the bed, jumping up and settling beside Maggie.

"Did you think of a response yet?"

The dog wagged her tail.

"Yeah, me neither," Maggie muttered.

Annoyed with herself for overthinking it, she forced herself to send a polite acknowledgment of his text, without making a *thing* out of it. It's not like the text held even a trace of emotion. And it wasn't the least bit flirty.

Apology accepted, she texted back. And then, because cookie dough made her brave, she added *Anthony* to the end.

His response was immediate.

Why do I get the feeling there was a fair amount of sass in that response?

Maggie grinned, then grinned wider when he sent another text immediately to follow. *How you've convinced my family you're this mild-mannered, sweet creature is beyond me.*

She bit her lip. *You don't think I'm sweet?*

His response was slower this time. *I think you're complicated.*

Stop, Captain. I might swoon.

Back to captain, are we?

Oh God. She was giggling now. Not that it stopped her from responding. *Seems appropriate, considering you only ever call me Ms. Walker.*

What do you want me to call you?

"Oh boy," Maggie muttered, blowing out a long breath, alarmed to realize she was grinning like a fool. "What am I doing here, Duchess?"

The dog gave her a baleful look.

"I know, I know, I'm *flirting* with the heinous man," Maggie said, flinging an arm over her eyes, resolving to put her phone aside before she could do anything stupid.

But instead, she texted back. *I think you should call me Maggie.*

Several minutes passed before his next response, and Maggie wondered if she'd scared him off. When her phone buzzed again, she sat up.

I probably shouldn't.

Why not?

You're an informant in my case.

She rolled her eyes. *Trust me, I know. But I thought this was Anthony I was talking to . . . the man, not the cop.*

I have a hard time separating the two sometimes. Maggie.

She swallowed, her mouth suddenly dry. Strange how that simple use of her name did dangerous things to her emotional stability.

His last text wasn't sexy. Or flirty. But it was revelatory. And somehow she sensed that he was confiding something important in her, even if he didn't mean to. And knowing him, he probably hadn't meant to.

Her response was slower. Careful. *How about you be*

Captain Moretti when we need to talk about Eddie. And be Anthony the rest of the time?

She held her breath until his response came. *Does right now count as "the rest of the time"?*

Yes.

Then I need to tell you something.

Her dry mouth went drier. *Ok.*

Yesterday when I laughed at the idea of you and Vin together...

She winced at the memory.

...It's because he's not good enough for you.

Maggie's breath whooshed out. *That's a fine thing to say about your brother.*

His response was slower this time. *I love my brother. But he'd be a horrible boyfriend. Plus there's this thing with his partner.*

Jill, Maggie replied, letting him know that she was following.

Yeah. They're...Let's just say I wouldn't wish any other woman into that situation. Not until the two of them deal with each other.

"Deal with each other." Nice.

She stroked Duchess's belly as she waited for his response.

Jill's not the only reason I didn't like the idea of you and Vin together.

Maggie's brows lifted. *No?* she asked, knowing she was playing with fire. Sexy fire.

No.

What's the other reason?

You know damn well the other reason.

"Oh crappers," she whispered to her dog, putting a hand

to her fluttering belly. "To play coy, or not to play coy, Duchess? I'm bad at these kinds of games."

In the end, she didn't have to choose. Because a man like Anthony Moretti apparently didn't play games. His next text said it all.

I didn't want you to date Vin, because the very idea of another man's hands on you, even my brother's, made me jealous as hell.

CHAPTER TEN

You did something. I know you did something."

Anthony gritted his teeth and let out a small grunt as he pushed through another bench press. *Eight.*

"You either showed her your wang, or didn't show her your wang. And whichever choice you made was obviously the wrong one."

He blocked out the voice of his grandmother and pushed through another. *Nine.*

"Big biceps won't help you with that girl. Do they have exercises for personality? You should do those."

"Bench presses aren't for biceps, Nonna. They're shoulders. Pecs." This from Luca, who was sprawled on the couch with a beer.

"Pecs, huh? Maybe I should give the weights a shot. Then again my push-up bras do the trick just fine."

Ten. Anth scooted down on the bench, grabbing a towel

from the ground as he glared at his grandmother. "We talked about this. No reference to your lingerie. Ever."

"He's right," Luc added, glancing over at them. "We did talk about it."

"I remember," she said. "But the way I remember it is you two boys doing a lot of yapping and me doing a lot of ignoring, because it's my name on the lease of this place."

Anth rubbed the towel over the back of his neck. Their grandmother had them there. Teresa Moretti had been living in this apartment longer than he'd been alive. She and Anthony's grandfather had moved into the three-bedroom brownstone back in the 1950s, back before the Upper West Side had become one of the most desirable neighborhoods in Manhattan.

The beauty of rent control meant that she could still afford it, even after losing the salary of her cop husband, although nowadays Luc and Anth split the cost of rent between the two of them. Nonna was hardly around anyway, and no way was Anthony going to let his elderly grandmother pay for his room and board.

He did, however, let her cook for him whenever she got the urge, which thankfully, was often.

Nonna might be the only living Moretti without Italian blood running through her veins, but she liked to inform everybody—often—that she was Italian by marriage.

And since Anthony's paternal great-grandmother had lived with them for the first months after the wedding, she'd taught Nonna the ins and outs of Italian cooking.

It was enough for Nonna to deem herself an expert, much to the chagrin of Anth's mother who thought being born in Italy made *her* the expert. The two women managed to fight about everything from garlic to how to store basil, and had been known to argue about pasta cooking time down to the second.

Nonna put hands on her slim hips and scowled at him. "Don't give me that sweaty, hungry look. I'm not feeding you."

"Why's that?" Anth asked. Nonna loved to feed her grandsons, and they all knew it.

"She's mad at you," Luca said from the couch.

"Yeah, I got that," Anth grumbled. "Observant of you, though. You should be a cop."

Luc gave him the finger without looking away from the game.

"Did you show her your wang?" Nonna asked again.

Anth stood up, rolling his shoulders as he stepped around the makeshift gym he and Luc had set up in the living room. "Okay fine, I'll bite. Did I show who my wang? Also, that word is hereby banned."

"*Maggie*," Nonna said, with no small amount of impatience.

Anthony grabbed a clean towel and wiped down the equipment while he rather deliberately ignored his grandmother.

He'd actually known perfectly well who she'd been talking about. He'd figured it was only a matter of time until one of his family members laid into him about the fact that everybody's favorite waitress hadn't been at the diner this morning.

The first Sunday since she'd started at the diner that she hadn't been there. Not that he'd been keeping track or anything.

"Anthony Franco Moretti Junior, did you—"

"For God's sake, I didn't show Maggie Walker my wang," he said.

Nonna scowled, unperturbed by his outburst. It took a lot
to perturb his grandmother. In fact, only his mother really
had any skill at it.

"Well then why didn't she show up today?" she demanded.

"Maybe because he didn't show her his wang," Luc muttered into the mouth of his beer bottle.

Anthony chucked his towel at his brother's head. "The
woman's allowed a day off."

"But Sundays aren't her days off. Thursdays and Saturdays are," Nonna said matter-of-factly.

Anth threw his arms up in the air. "How could you possibly know that?"

Luc glanced over. "*I* knew that."

Anthony glared. "Don't you have somewhere else to be?
We've barely seen you for weeks, and you choose *now* to be
here?"

Luc shrugged. "Ava's out of town. Covering some political rally in D.C."

Nonna pointed at her youngest grandson. "See, *he* has a
nice girl. Luca, at what point did you show Ava your wang?"

"Not answering that," Luc muttered. "Also, I'm with
Anth. Can we stop using the word 'wang'?"

"Penis?" Nonna suggested. "Appendage? Or in *my* day,
we called it—"

"Please don't finish that sentence," Anth muttered, heading toward the fridge for a beer. Only there wasn't any,
because his damn brother apparently took the last one, so
Anthony grabbed an ever-present bottle of red wine off the
counter and poured a hefty glass.

He turned around in time to see Nonna and Luc exchange
a knowing glance. "No," he said, shaking his head and tak-

ing a healthy swallow of the Chianti. "Whatever you're thinking, just stop it now."

"I wasn't thinking anything," Nonna said, laying a hand across her chest and looking scandalized.

"Good. Keep it that way."

"It's just..."

Anth closed his eyes as his grandma got that speculative look in her eyes.

"It's weird, isn't it, Luca?" she mused. "That Maggie wasn't there today?"

"It is," Luc said agreeably, attention still on the game, although the smirk on his face showed that not only was he fully engaged in his grandmother's pestering of Anthony, but also highly entertained by it.

"Hey," Anth called across the room to his brother. "Remember just a few months ago when our darling grandmother was meddling in *your* love life?"

Nonna pounced. "You said *love* life. Which means that—"

"That you should mind your own business," Anth said.

Luc caught his eye and lifted an eyebrow, and Anth knew his baby brother had caught the fact that he hadn't exactly denied that Maggie Walker had anything to do with his love life.

He *should* have denied it, because there was absolutely nothing between them. Not since the other night when he'd had one too many glasses of whiskey while home alone and crossed a line he absolutely should not have crossed via *text* of all things.

His grandmother let out a long-suffering sigh and lowered herself to the kitchen chair with a fragility that he knew was entirely faked. His grandmother was eighty-something, but she did yoga and walked daily, and, according to her, engaged in "enthusiastic sex."

So any time she pulled the "little old woman" routine, it was definitely an angle.

Anthony braced for it.

"Hey, *bambino*," she said, looking over her shoulder at Luc. "You have Maggie's number, right? Won't you give her a call, make sure she's okay? That business with her ex-husband is just awful, and—"

Anthony had to take another sip of wine to keep from telling Luca in disturbing detail exactly what would happen to him if he dared to call Maggie.

And yet if anyone should be checking in on her, it should be Luc. It was *Luc* who she'd given her phone number to in the first place. Luc who'd had to give Anthony her number...

Too late, Anthony saw his brother's face. Luc's grin was positively shit-eating.

"Why don't you have Anth text her?" Luc asked innocently.

"Oh?" Nonna said, her face the picture of sham confusion. "Anthony, you have her phone number?"

"He asked me for it the other day," Luc provided before Anth could intervene.

"Damn whiskey," he muttered.

"Yup," Luc confirmed, pushing up off the couch to put his beer bottle in the recycling bin and helping himself to a glass of the open wine. "Anth here spent a good half an hour texting back and forth with Mags, a fool smile on his face."

"You weren't even here," Anth snapped.

Luc looked at his glass. "But am I wrong?"

Anthony took another sip of wine. "She's an informant."

"So you texted her about work stuff?" Nonna asked.

"I—"

"Because if that *were* the case, you probably should have just gotten her number from the case file, right?" Luc asked. "I mean why go through me? Unless it was personal..."

Anthony put his glass on the counter with more force than necessary, grateful that their wineglasses were of the cheap, heavy variety and didn't easily shatter.

"And you wonder why I don't share my personal life with you," he snapped.

Luc looked at him blankly. "Actually, no. I never wonder that."

Nonna's hand shot up in the air. "I do! I always wonder. And your mother too. And your father, although he'd never admit it, and Elena sometimes asks Vin about the logistics of phone taps so she can verify you're not dating any skanks."

Anthony stared at his grandmother.

Nonna pursed her lips. "Okay fine, I may have added the *skank* part. But you could substitute whatever word you wanted. Say, like—"

Luc held up a hand to stop Nonna's endless supply of synonyms for *hookers*. "Dude, Anth. We're just giving you a hard time. I'm sure Maggie was just taking a sick day or a personal day. Nobody's blaming you for it."

Anth inhaled before running a hand tiredly over his hair.

They might not be blaming him. But he was certainly blaming himself.

He'd crossed a serious line with the texts. Came on too strong.

He'd meant to just apologize and leave it at that. Had wanted to undo any hurt he'd caused, because he knew first-hand how a couple offhand comments could have far more impact than one realized.

Maggie wasn't Vannah.

Objectively, he knew that, and Anthony thrived on objectivity.

Maggie and Vannah weren't even similar.

Vannah had been a compelling combination of waifish and glamorous, confident and fragile, all pale hair and exotic cat eyes. And cool...there had been an untouchable element to Vannah, when she wasn't being clingy.

Maggie was...warm. Beautiful but wholesome, damaged but sassy.

Luc was studying Anthony. "Dude. What's going on with you?"

He shot his brother a glare. *Don't.*

But Luca's gaze merely sharpened. "You know, if you really wanted us to fuck off, you can just go into your room."

"No, he can't!" Nonna chirped. "Don't put ideas in his head, Luca. He'll stay right here and tell us why—"

"I don't know why Maggie didn't come to work!" His voice echoed off the kitchen walls. "Okay? I have no fucking idea."

Nonna didn't even flinch at his language. She never did. Being married to a New York cop, raising one who went on to be police commissioner, and being grandmother to four cops did that to a woman.

"Well, why don't you ask her?"

"She won't respond to me," he muttered.

Luc looked confused. "Really? She didn't respond to your texts?"

"She did, at first," Anth replied grudgingly.

"Well, what did you do to make her stop?" Nonna barked.

"Nonna," Luc chided in a mild tone.

Anth was grateful for the moment of brotherly solidarity.

He and Luc didn't have the type of brotherly conversations that involved cozy fireside chats and discussions of feelings, but they were close. Being roommates did that. So did their shared status as cops.

They *got* each other. He understood that it had taken Luc months to admit his feelings for Ava because of what happened with his partner two years earlier.

And judging from the quiet understanding in Luc's blue gaze at the moment, his brother understood that Anthony couldn't be the type of man that a woman like Maggie Walker needed.

The type of man that *any* woman needed.

But just now, he wasn't thinking about any woman. He was thinking of wide hazel eyes and a mouth that could deliver the sweetest smiles and the sharpest setdowns.

And yet, it didn't matter that he couldn't give himself to a woman like her. Because she didn't even want him. She'd made that abundantly clear after her silence to his last text.

I didn't want you to date Vin, because the very idea of another man's hands on you, even my brother's, made me jealous as hell.

Oh Good Lord he was an idiot.

"You wanna talk about it?" Luc asked casually, taking a sip.

Anth's response was a glare. He started to storm toward his bedroom before stopping, doing a one-eighty, and planting a dutiful kiss on his grandmother's cheek. "Love you," he muttered.

She cupped his cheek. "You're a good boy, Anth. The very best."

He pulled away without responding.

He wasn't good. And he sure as *hell* wasn't the best.

CHAPTER ELEVEN

There were thousands of damn good cops in the NYPD. Men and women who were proud to serve one of the best law enforcement agencies in the country.

But only a handful of them ever went on to be a captain, or even take the captain's test.

Anthony had never understood that. He'd never been able to figure out why so many exceptionally skilled officers didn't have the interest in even trying for the higher rank.

But now, over three months into his time as Captain Moretti, he was starting to get it.

For starters, there was the lack of overtime. He got a salary, and the salary stayed the same no matter how many hours he worked. And it was good money...plenty of money for Anth's lifestyle.

But he'd be lying if he said he didn't miss the surge of gratification after working long hours and knowing it would result in a higher paycheck.

Now, he worked the long hours...but the paycheck stayed the same.

Still, even that didn't bother him. Much. He wasn't in it for the money.

And then there was the tricky leadership aspect. It was hard enough to work in law enforcement in New York City and take care of *yourself*, much less feel responsible for an entire team of people.

But this aspect of the job, he was learning. Enjoying, even. Must be the big brother in him, because Anthony sort of loved bossing people around.

But there was one aspect of Captain that was really starting to piss him off: bureaucracy. The politics were *killing* him.

He'd known it was coming, of course. His father had warned him that the higher you went, the more ass-kissing, the more red tape, and the more seemingly pointless meetings and paperwork awaited.

But what his father hadn't warned him was just how *thick* the bullshit level was. There were times when meeting with the higher-ups felt a lot less *protect and serve* and a lot more *whose dick is bigger*.

Today's meeting was made worse by its spontaneity. Anthony's direct supervisor, while overall a stand-up guy, had a penchant for making "unannounced drop-bys."

Initially Anth had figured this was a leadership approach...always keep the subordinates on their toes.

But the more he got to know Ray Mandela, the more Anthony realized that these little impromptu meetings were more about Ray's penchant for hearing himself talk than anything else.

Not that the man was all bluster; he had a good head

on his shoulders, was fair and surprisingly patient. But if there was a point that could be expressed in eight words, the deputy chief would find a way to explain it in fifty.

"So anyway, I guess you could say that we'll be sitting in the back of the church until Ana grows up!" Ray finished with a chuckle.

Anthony forced a laugh in return, although truthfully, he had no idea what the hell his boss was talking about.

He'd tuned out somewhere between the story about Ray Junior's soccer practice and how expensive Tessa's ballet costume was. Which one was Ana? His youngest? Or his oldest? He could never keep all of Ray's kids straight.

"Things are good with you?" Ray asked, leaning forward and resting his arms on his legs as he studied Anthony.

Anth knew that he shouldn't feel ill at ease.

Ray was in *Anth*'s office, sitting in *Anth*'s guest chair.

It was Anthony's domain, and normally the people who came into this office knew it. But with Ray looking at him with that shrewd gaze of his, Anthony resisted the urge to squirm.

Ray couldn't have been more than five years older than Anthony—maybe early forties at the most—but he had a quiet command about him.

"Things are good," Anth said cautiously.

I mean, minus the fact that I haven't caught Smiley, the one woman I've been even remotely interested in in months may or may not be avoiding me, and I haven't eaten my leftover lasagna for lunch yet because you've been running your mouth for forty-five minutes.

"Good, good," Ray said, oblivious to Anth's inner rant. "I hate to ask, but you know I've got to . . . any update on

Smiley? I know it's a run-of-the-mill burglar, but ever since the press picked it up, the bosses have picked it up, all the way to the very top."

Anthony was careful not to show a shred of emotion at mention of the current commissioner. He knew he was biased, but Tony Moretti's successor was a grandstanding asshole who cared a lot more about looking good on TV than he did about the people of the city.

"We've got a lead," Anthony said. "A good one."

"Right, the wife."

"Ex-wife," Anthony corrected.

"Remind me how she came into the picture?"

Anthony stayed resolutely relaxed in his chair. "She's a waitress at the Darby Diner. I was doing some off-hours work there and she saw the sketch."

He was braced for the deputy chief to ride his ass for taking potentially sensitive documents out of the precinct, but luckily Ray was more about results than he was strict adherence to the rules.

"Lucky break," Ray said, leaning back and tapping his fingers against the arm of the chair. "You trust her? Or think she's looking for attention?"

"She provided a handful of pictures of Eddie Hansen. The resemblance is there. If anyone's off base here, it's the witness who provided the description of our guy. If that's even our guy."

"Hell of a thing," Ray said. "A criminal savvy or lucky enough to evade us a half dozen times, and he doesn't even take anything worth stealing."

"He takes people's sense of privacy...their right to safety," Anthony said, barely managing to keep the lecture out of his mouth.

"Right, right," Ray said distractedly. "Well, I guess this wife…"

"Ex-wife."

"Ex-wife," Ray continued, "won't be much use if she's not in touch with the guy. You said in your last report they hadn't had any contact?"

Anthony shook his head. "No. Since then she thinks she might have seen him outside the diner where she works, but she won't swear it's him, and I can't justify putting a watch on the place based on a hesitant *maybe*."

Ray pursed his lips. "What if—"

There was a loud knock on Anthony's door, but it opened before he could utter his usual gruff *come in.*

Vincent stormed in. "Anth, for God's sake, would you answer your motherfucking— *Oh.* You've got company."

Anthony inhaled. Leave it to his clueless brother to refer to Anthony's superior as *company*, complete with a dark scowl.

"Vin, this is Deputy Chief Mandela."

He waited for his brother to show some sort of deference, but Vin merely jerked his chin in greeting. "Hey."

Luckily, Ray seemed more amused than he did offended, although he did look at Anthony for an explanation as to why uninvited visitors were barging into his office.

"Sir, this is Detective Moretti."

"Ah, the other brother," Ray said, standing and extending a hand. "I've met Luca a handful of times, but I don't think you and I have met in person. Homicide, right?"

"Yup," Vin said before turning back to Anth. "Dude, seriously, you haven't been answering your phone."

"Because I turn it off when I'm in a meeting," Anthony said. *To avoid interruptions like this.*

But his irritation faded quickly into a sliver of fear as he realized that his younger brother wasn't often disposed toward phone calls, much less drop-bys.

"Is everything okay?" Anthony was already pulling his phone out of the desk drawer where he'd placed it after Ray had shown up. "Mom, Dad—"

"They're fine. It's Maggie."

Anth's head shot up, his eyes pinning his brother with a lethal stare. "What's wrong? Is she okay? What—"

Vin held up a hand, his eyes narrowing slightly, perhaps in puzzlement over Anthony's fiercer than usual reaction.

"She's okay."

Anthony blew out a breath of relief.

"Who's Maggie?" Ray asked.

"Smiley's ex-wife," Anthony muttered.

Upon realizing this was police business, and not family business, Ray's gaze sharpened on Vincent. "There's been a development?"

Vin nodded once, then held up a plastic bag containing a single envelope.

Anth held out his hand.

There was no return address. There rarely was, not when you actually wished for one.

"Margaret Hansen," he read aloud. His eyes lifted to Vin. "Maggie."

His brother's expression was grim. "Keep reading."

Anthony did and saw a name even more familiar, "c/o Captain Moretti."

"What the hell," he muttered.

"It came to my home address," Vincent said. "Either the guy got the wrong Moretti or he's fucking with us in an even bigger way; letting us know he knows about our little family cop legacy. I dunno."

"How do you know it has anything to do with Smiley?" Ray asked.

Vin jerked his chin in the direction of the bag, just as Anthony flipped the envelope over. Sealing the envelope was a single, simple, yellow smiley-face sticker.

"What is wrong with this fucker?" Ray asked. "What's with the creepy sticker? I used to get one of those on the top of my long division homework."

"Could be a copycat," Vin said.

"Could be," Anthony said as Ray gave a halfhearted shrug. The silence in the room spoke volumes though... nobody thought it was a copycat. Copycats rarely cared this much unless money was at stake. This wasn't about money. It was personal.

It was about *Margaret*.

"Why not just send it straight to her?" Ray asked.

"Maybe he doesn't know where she lives," Vin added.

Anthony gave him a look. "He's gone through the trouble of finding *your* address. Best we can tell, he figured out where she works. He could have followed her home."

The men were silent again. If Smiley—*Eddie*—had gone this far, he probably had followed her home. The thought made Anthony's stomach turn, not just with anger, but with something far worse: *fear*.

Smiley hadn't proved dangerous, but Eddie Hansen very well could be if he wasn't over his ex-wife. Even the most harmless of men could turn lethal over a woman. The stats about your spouse being the most likely to kill you were sadly true.

Anthony rubbed a hand over his face. "You brought this straight here?"

Vin nodded.

"We'll need to send it to evidence, but anything going through the postal system…"

"We'll find dozens of prints," Ray concluded. "What about the postmark?"

"Eighty-third and Columbus," Vin said. "I checked."

"Think he lives around there, or think he's sticking with the same neighborhood where his hits are?"

"Probably the latter," Anthony said, opening his desk drawer and pulling out a pair of gloves so he could handle the letter without adding his own prints to the mix.

He carefully opened the bag and pulled out the letter, mentally willing it to give up any clues as to what the hell sort of game Smiley was playing.

"We'll need Ms. Walker to open it," Ray said, sounding annoyed. "The bastard sent it first-class, which means we can't open the damn thing without a warrant."

"I can go get her," Vin volunteered.

Ray shook his head. "She might be skittish. A letter from her ex-husband who's also the prime suspect in a string of burglaries—"

Vin pinned Anthony's boss with a bland look. "Do I not look sensitive to you?"

Anth glanced up. "Vin."

His brother rolled his eyes. "I'll bring Jill. She's the hugging, cry-on-my-shoulder type if it comes to that."

"I don't doubt that Jill's good at delivering bad news, but you two are homicide detectives. You shouldn't even be involved."

"The letter was sent to *my* house," Vin said. "I'd say I'm pretty damn involved."

"*My* name is on the envelope," Anth shot back.

Ray held up a hand. "Boys."

Anthony gritted his teeth, irritated his boss had caught him in what was practically a sibling playground squabble over a girl.

"Detective Moretti, we appreciate you bringing this to our immediate attention. I trust you'll deliver any other letters as promptly," Ray said, the sharpening of his tone indicating that he was clearly pulling his rank.

Vincent, being no dummy, caught the edge in the man's voice and nodded reluctantly.

Ray turned to Anth. "Captain, you take the letter to Ms. Walker. If your name's on there, this shithead may have a message for us. And I doubt we're going to like it."

The deputy chief moved toward the door, giving Vincent no choice but to back out as well.

Anthony stopped his boss before he could exit. "I've changed my mind about police protection. I'd like to put a couple officers outside Mag— Ms. Walker's house. See if we can't catch Eddie trying to pay her a visit."

Ray Mandela shrugged. "You're in charge. Whatever you think."

Anthony nodded, ignoring the knowing smirk Vincent shot him before disappearing.

Anth knew his brother was thinking that the officers outside Maggie's house had more to do with Anthony's peace of mind than it did the off chance that Eddie Hansen would be dumb enough to show up.

His brother was absolutely right.

CHAPTER TWELVE

One thing a girl didn't expect to see through her peephole just minutes after getting home from a particularly crappy day at work: a six-foot-four police captain wearing a suit and a scowl.

"*Down*," she muttered to Duchess as she unlocked the chain. Although she honestly wasn't entirely sure if the command was to her overexcited dog or the butterflies in her stomach.

It was the first time she'd seen him after their flirtatious text exchange, and she expected him to look different somehow.

He didn't. Same frown. Same serious brown eyes.

Except he was *here*.

At her home.

"Hi," she said quietly. What she really wanted to ask, quite desperately, was, *Are you here as Anthony or as Captain Moretti?*

"Hi," he said back. Just for a second, his eyes seemed to warm as they held hers, a silent communication passing between them.

"You're wearing a suit," she said.

He glanced down. "We do that, occasionally."

"Oh." *You look ridiculously good. Please don't torture me like this.*

He cleared his throat. "May I come in?"

"Sure," Maggie said, stepping aside. "I hope you don't mind dogs."

He stared down at the dog who was now panting frantically, having rolled onto her back and giving him an awkward side-eye, which Maggie knew was doggie-code for *I'll die if you don't pet my belly.*

Moretti glanced back up at her, and for a horrible moment she thought he was going to either tell her to move the dog or simply step over Duchess.

Then he knelt down, slowly crouching until he could lay a big hand against the dog's stomach. Duchess's little tail went crazy, and so did Maggie's heart.

"Aren't you a pretty girl?" he said in a soft voice she'd never heard from him before.

"How did you know she was a girl?"

He glanced up at her with a knowing, crooked smile, and Maggie flushed. "Right," she muttered. "Her lady parts are rather on display, aren't they?"

He moved his big hand up over Duchess to her chest, scratching the sides of her face slightly before standing back up. Duchess got the hint and sprang to her feet, clearing the way for Moretti to enter her home.

"Guess you figured out the magic passcode," she said as he moved into her apartment.

He glanced down at her. "Does that work for you too? The belly rub?"

She froze in the process of closing the door, her eyes flying to his, watching as they crinkled slightly at the corners. "Relax, Ms. Walker. I'm kidding."

"Too bad," she deadpanned. "We modern girls so enjoy a good belly rub."

The hint of a smile dropped from his face, and this time she definitely didn't imagine the warmth in his eyes, or the way they moved over her. "Is that so?"

Maggie licked her lips and closed the door. "So, um..."

"What am I doing here?" he asked.

"Yes, that," she said with a little laugh.

His expression turned serious once more, and he glanced around her apartment. Maggie did the same, seeing it through his eyes. It was crowded even when it was just her and Duchess. But with Anthony Moretti's broad shoulders and commanding presence, her studio felt positively tiny.

His eyes locked on her tiny kitchen table. "Can we sit?"

"Oh boy," she said. "I'm pretty sure no good news has ever come following those words. But sure. Let's sit."

He moved toward the table.

"Can I get you something to drink?" she asked. "Water, tea, coffee, beer...I probably have some wine somewhere..."

"I'm fine."

"What about something to eat?" she asked, opening the fridge. "I don't have much but I could make some—"

"Maggie." The word was a quiet command.

She swallowed and joined him at the table, noticing the way he dwarfed her chairs with his long legs. Duchess, having no manners and even less shame, hopped up onto his lap uninvited.

Maggie immediately reached to remove her dog, but he held up a hand to stop her before laying the hand on the dog's head. "It's okay. I like dogs, truly."

"But your suit..."

He smiled. "You do an awful lot of worrying about my clothes. I told you that night in the rain, it's not like it's Armani."

"I never think of police officers as wearing suits," she mused. "I always figured it was a lot of polyester..."

"It is, early on," he said. "But past a certain rank, it's more or less a desk job, and the suit occasionally makes an appearance."

"And you like it?" she asked curiously. "You don't miss... walking the beat, or whatever?"

He raised his eyebrows at her use of the lingo, and she shrugged. "Luc and Lopez come in a lot after their shift."

"Ah. And yes, I do miss it," he said, his hand stroking over Duchess's rough fur. "Sometimes. But there are rewards on both sides."

"Such as?"

It was none of her business, but she found herself wanting to know him. To understand what made him tick.

He looked surprised, as though nobody ever asked him about his job. Then he shrugged. "There's something heroic about wearing the uniform. I mean, actually *wearing* the uniform. Your contribution is so tangible."

"And it's not while you're wearing the suit?"

He rubbed Duchess's ears and the dog looked ready to pass out from pleasure. Lucky dog.

"It's what I've always wanted," he said quietly.

"Being captain?"

He looked up. "And beyond."

Maggie put her elbows on the table and leaned forward. "Like *all* the way beyond?"

"All the way," he said.

She whistled. "So like father like son, huh? Police Commissioner Moretti the Second?"

He gave a small smile. "That's the plan."

Maggie opened her mouth, then shut it just as quickly, biting her lip to keep from asking even more things that weren't her business.

"Don't get shy on me now," he said, his voice teasing.

She took a breath and asked, "Is that what *you* want? Or what your dad wants?"

They were bold questions. Prying, even. But he didn't even flinch.

"Both," he said without hesitation. "I know the movie version of this story is the father pushing his own goals onto the son, and the son realizes too late that it's not what he wants, but…"

"But you *do* want it," Maggie said, searching his face.

He nodded. "More than anything."

More than anything*?*

Maggie couldn't imagine wanting a promotion more than *anything*.

She wanted to get her book published, rather desperately. Wanted to never have to fill another ketchup bottle for the rest of her days. She wanted to wake up and have her biggest problem be whether or not her characters did what her outline said they were supposed to do.

But she didn't want to publish a book more than *anything*.

Not as a stand-in for relationships. Not as a replacement for love.

Says the girl who can count her friends on one hand, who shares her pillow every night with a dog, and who can't even manage to flirt over text much less in person.

She was so not in the place to ask Captain Moretti where his personal life fit into those lofty career goals. She was pretty sure the answer would depress her.

"Ms. Walker—"

She sensed the mood shift abruptly, knowing that she was about to find out the reason he was here. And it wasn't to talk about his dreams and pet her dog.

As though reading her mind, he set Duchess gently on the floor.

"There's something you need to see," he said, reaching into his inside suit pocket and pulling out an envelope wrapped in a plastic bag.

She immediately tensed. She'd seen the TV shows. Whenever stuff was put in plastic, it was evidence, which generally translated to *bad news*.

He slid it across the table, and if the plastic baggie hadn't already alarmed her, the unexpected gentleness on his face did. If Captain Moretti was being gentle, she definitely wasn't going to like this piece of paper.

She started to reach for it, then hesitated, her hand hovering. "Can I touch it?"

He nodded. "We've already checked it for prints. Nothing usable."

She pulled it all the way toward her.

Somehow, she wasn't surprised to see her name written there. Why else would he be here?

But it had *his* name too. Which made no sense. And the mailing address was in Queens. She knew Anthony lived on the Upper West Side with his grandmother and Luc, so how had an envelope addressed to her, care of *him*, ended up in Astoria?

He was watching her carefully. "Do you recognize the handwriting?"

Maggie picked up the envelope to look more closely. She knew what he was really asking. *Is this Eddie's?*

She licked her lip. "It...could be."

He sighed.

"I'm sorry," she said automatically. "Eddie didn't...I took care of things like the bills and grocery lists, Christmas cards. I've seen his handwriting, obviously, but not often, and it's been a long time..."

"Nothing you may have kept? No photos with writings on the back, no love letters?"

She gave him a look and he shrugged.

"No, nothing," she said. "I could maybe recognize his signature, but this looks nothing like it. This is careful printing, whereas his signature was more or less a squiggle."

"Don't worry about it. We'll have the handwriting compared with the notes Smiley left on the scene, and that will tell us plenty."

She glanced up. "So you still think Eddie and Smiley are one and the same?"

His expression was grim. "Turn it over."

She did and saw a garish, unmistakable yellow face smiling back at her.

"So odd," she said, touching a finger to the plastic-covered sticker. "It seems far too eccentric for Eddie. But then, he also considers himself wildly clever. The mocking nature of this suits him."

Moretti nodded. "You ready to open it?"

She sucked in a breath. "I wish I didn't have to. I intentionally put this part of my life behind me, you know? I mean I *moved*. I cut ties with all our mutual friends. I changed my phone number..."

She closed her eyes and rubbed her forehead, not at all prepared for the firm warmth of his fingers when they touched the back of her hand.

"I can open it for you."

She looked at where his big fingers rested lightly on the back of her much smaller hand. She wanted to flip her hand over so they were palm to palm. Wanted to twine her fingers with his...

"Maggie," he said. "Shall I open it?"

She glanced up. "I'll do it."

Maggie felt slightly ill at the prospect, but she wasn't going to sit here and let him think she was so spineless she couldn't even open a freaking envelope.

She pulled the envelope out of the bag, surprised at how much revulsion she felt at touching something that Eddie had handled. *Especially* if Eddie was doing what they said he was— breaking into people's homes, taking what wasn't his, and then having the depraved cockiness to leave a note bragging about it.

"Careful," he muttered as her hands went to the flap.

Maggie glared. "Oh, so I shouldn't just tear it open with my teeth and use it as a coaster? Give me a break, Moretti. I may not be a cop, but I'm not an idiot."

He reached into his pocket and pulled out a letter opener. "Open it along the top. Preserve the Smiley sticker. Please." Then he half smiled. "Has anyone ever told you that you go from docile and abiding to sassy and difficult in the span of a couple seconds?"

"No," she muttered grumpily. "Because that's not typical. Only around you."

"Is that so?" he said mildly.

She narrowed her eyes. "Are you flirting? Trying to distract me from the letter?"

"Is it working?"

"You fluster me," she said, making quick work of the letter opener.

"Is that why you didn't respond to my last text?"

Maggie froze. "You *really* want to talk about that now?"

His eyes dropped to the letter in her hands, and then he gave his head a little shake. "No. That's not why I'm here."

Of course not, she thought. *Because you want to move up in your career "more than anything."*

She tugged the letter out of the envelope, and abruptly her mind shifted from the man sitting across the table to the man who'd written the letter.

She may not know Eddie's handwriting as well as she should, but she knew him. And she could all but hear his voice as she read his brief note.

Margaret.

I'm so glad I've found you again. I know why you left, but I'm fixing things so they're better for us. Tell HIM I say hello. It's been a pleasure watching him chase me.

> *All my love,*
> *E*

Maggie huffed out a sigh of disgust as she dropped the note on the table.

Moretti was watching her. "May I?"

She waved a hand, giving him permission.

His expression didn't change from its stony impassiveness as he read the note.

"Well?" she asked.

Moretti's eyes were still on the brief words. "He's cocky."

"He always was."

Moretti glanced up. "That's good. His self-confidence is justified thus far—he's eluded us—but it will work in our favor if he gets too smug. He'll get careless."

"So what's the plan?" she asked, putting her elbows on the table and leaning forward so her head was in her hands. "What's our next move?"

"*Our* next move?"

She gave him a tired look. "My name's on that envelope. I can't just sit and do nothing."

Her voice broke a little at the end, and Duchess, who'd been writhing her little body against Captain Moretti's calf for the past ten minutes, immediately remembered her loyalties and came to curl up on Maggie's foot.

Anthony searched her face. "This isn't your problem, Maggie. You know that, right? Not your problem to solve."

"Then why are you here?" she asked, feeling unusually snappy.

His smile indicated he was enjoying her waspishness. Strange man. "We couldn't open the envelope without a warrant. Which we could have gotten given the circumstances, but making the drive out to Brooklyn was a hell of a lot easier."

"No subway for you, huh?"

"Perk of the job," he said, slowly pushing back and unfolding his long body.

Her feet were cramped and her legs were exhausted from a long day at work, but she stood as well, just so he didn't tower above her.

Then she realized that even at her full height, she was barely eye level with his chest. He'd tower over her no matter what.

He'd also be just the right height to lean into. His arms would be big and warm and strong if they wrapped around her.

Moretti cleared his throat, and Maggie jumped, wondering if she'd leaned.

Duchess butted her nose once against Maggie's leg, as though to say, *be over there if you need me*, before scampering across the room and making a flying leap onto the bed, then diving onto her stuffed penguin and thrashing the thing ruthlessly.

Moretti moved toward the door, getting there in about two steps with his long stride.

Then he surprised her by looking around, as though seeing her apartment for the first time. "I like your place."

She laughed. "There's not much to like."

"It's..."

"If you say cozy, I'll punch you," she muttered.

He threw back his head and laughed, surprising her. "I was definitely going to say cozy."

She found herself smiling despite the reappearance of her ex-husband in her life, and the weird longing she had for this complex man who she couldn't get a read on.

"Yeah, cozy's a pretty classic synonym for tiny," she said. "I know Brooklyn's cheaper than Manhattan, but this is about all I could afford. After the divorce..." She shrugged.

"You don't have to explain anything to me, Ms. Walker," he said, his voice surprisingly gentle.

"Well, I wasn't explaining it to *Captain Moretti*," she said in exasperation.

He looked at her. "We keep doing that, don't we? Crossing wires."

She stared at his chest. "I just…I don't get you. You switch back and forth between Ms. Walker-ing me and then you touch my hand and call me Maggie, and—"

He took a step closer. "And what?"

"You confuse me."

"Do I?" His voice was soft. Thoughtful.

She frowned. "You seem far too pleased by that."

"I admit, it gives me a certain measure of relief. To know that I'm not the only one who's feeling a little off balance."

She snorted. "Yeah, you seem *really* disoriented here, Captain."

"You're hardly an open book, Maggie."

She glanced up in surprise at that. "Yes I am."

That was one thing she was very sure of. Her entire life, people had been telling her that she wore her heart on her sleeve, that her facial expressions hid nothing, that she was transparent. She was the definition of *open book*.

"Well, you're a book *I* don't know how to read," he said gruffly.

"Do you want to? Read it? Read me?"

"More than I should."

Was it her imagination, or had he moved closer? Or had she? Somehow they seemed to be standing closer than they were before. And they were certainly standing closer than necessary.

"You weren't at the diner on Sunday," he said gruffly. "My family won't leave me alone about it."

"They're blaming you? Why?"

His eyes roamed her face. "They got it in their head I had something to do with it."

Maggie licked her lips. "They wouldn't be wrong."

He flinched. "You were avoiding me?"

"No! Well, kind of..."

She put her hands over her face. "It's embarrassing."

"Try me."

Maggie dropped her hands and gnawed on her bottom lip. Decided to go for it. "I was hungover."

His eyebrows crept up and he made a *tsk*ing noise that contradicted his increasing smile. "Why, Maggie Walker."

"Shut up," she said, shoving a little at his shoulder. "It's your fault."

He moved closer. "How's that."

"Your text on Saturday night. The one about you being... *you know*."

His eyes darkened. "The one where I said I was jealous. Of the thought of you and Vincent together."

Maggie's stomach flipped over. She didn't know why, but this man's no-nonsense way of talking did funny things to her lady parts. There was no game playing with him. At least never intentionally.

"Yeah. That one," she said.

This time when he moved closer, she knew she wasn't imagining it. She started to take a step back, instinctively, but stopped herself. She was tired of being afraid. Tired of being skittish.

"That text freaked you out?"

"Let's just say I rather stupidly thought that liquid

courage might help me figure out an appropriately witty response."

"You never did respond," he murmured.

"Yeah, well, I'm not much of a drinker," she said. "A couple glasses of wine, and I wasn't any closer to coming up with a response. At least not an appropriate one."

"The *inappropriate* texts are the best kind. Keeps things interesting."

"Is that why you said what you said?" she asked, tilting her head up to look into his face. "To keep things interesting?"

"I said what I said because I meant every word."

"Oh."

The silence stretched between them, interrupted only by the occasional squeak from Duchess's toy.

"Maggie."

"Yeah?" It was more of a whisper, so she cleared her throat and tried again. "Yeah?"

His gaze was hot when it clashed with hers. "I'd like to hear that response now."

"You want me to text you back?" she squeaked.

He shook his head. "Tell me. No liquid courage, no cell phones. What were you thinking when I told you that I was jealous?"

She closed her eyes and shook her head.

His hand reached for her tentatively, his fingers hot through the fabric of her top, then firmer as his palm pressed against her waist.

"Tell me." It was a command. "Did you *like* that I was jealous? Did you want me to claim you as mine?"

The words sent a shiver down her spine. "I don't know," she whispered.

The silence stretched out, and she felt a pang as his fingers started to slide away. Her palm found the back of his hand, holding him still as she opened her eyes, trying to tell him with her gaze what she didn't know how to put into words.

"I'm bad at this," she whispered.

His jaw moved slightly, as though he was gritting his teeth.

Moretti took a half step forward, until they were toe to toe. If either of them leaned, just a little, they could be belly to belly, chest to chest...

"There's something I need to tell you." His voice was gruff.

Suddenly she became very aware what the heroines in her historical romance novels meant when they *waited with bated breath*. "Yeah?"

"There's a squad car outside your apartment building. And two officers."

Ice water. That's what his statement was. Ice water doused all over them.

"*What?*"

"We have every reason to believe that Eddie Hansen knows where you live. He knows where you work. If he should try to contact you."

Maggie took a step backward and gave a harsh laugh. "You're just telling me all of this now? What...what was with all of the flirting and the looks?"

Anthony's eyes flashed in anger. "You said you're bad at this. I'm bad at this too. I may not be handling this attraction between us well, but at least I'm trying!"

Maggie's eyes widened in surprise, both at the words and the blurted nature of them. Captain Moretti struck her as the type of man who was always in control, but he didn't look in control now.

"Fuck," he muttered. "I should go."

He backed away abruptly, turning to jerk open her front door.

"Wait!"

He paused and she went to him. Took a deep breath. "I wanted to text you that I could never date Vincent. I could never even *consider* it."

He didn't respond, but he did shut the door. Slammed it actually.

"And about the...attraction," she continued before she could lose her nerve. "I don't know what to do about it either. But I feel it. Like I've never felt anything before."

He closed his eyes. "You shouldn't have said that."

"Why not?" she asked, lifting her chin in annoyance that he'd all but begged her to tell him what she was thinking and was now scolding her for it.

He made a low growling noise. "Because now I won't be able to stop myself from doing *this*."

His hand pressed against her stomach, spanning the entire surface as he pushed her backward into the wall. His eyes were wild as they looked down on her, and the last thought Maggie had before his mouth slammed against hers was that Anthony Moretti completely out of control was the sexiest thing she'd ever seen.

His kiss was fierce. Carnal. Unapologetic. There was no soft coaxing to get her lips to open, he merely used his firm mouth to maneuver hers open and then he *took*.

The hand on her stomach held her pinned against the wall as his other hand came up to the back of her neck, keeping her mouth tilted up for his wonderful invasion.

Maggie hadn't had much experience with kissing. A couple awkward pecks in high school, a casual boyfriend in her two years at community college. And then she'd met Eddie, and if there had been any decent kisses early on in the relationship, the memories had been overwritten by the sloppy, drunken kisses near the end.

Anthony's kiss was possessive and giving. Like the man, the kiss was *deliberate*.

The way his tongue cleverly found all the most sensitive parts of her mouth, her lips, his teeth occasionally raking against her bottom lip, his—

He pulled back, just slightly. "Maggie."

Her eyes opened, eyelids heavy. "Hmm?"

His smile was surprisingly tender as he looked down at her. "You're thinking too much."

She blinked. "What?"

His thumb rubbed over her bottom lip, his eyes watching the gesture. "You're letting me kiss you, but *we're* not kissing. If you don't want this—"

Maggie went up on her toes, fusing her mouth to his to shut him up. Her teeth pulled none too gently at his top lip and she felt his rough growl of appreciation all the way down to her toes.

The tip of her tongue brushed against his, and there was a moment of stillness before everything changed.

No longer was it him kissing her, or her kissing him.

They were kissing each other.

Her arms wound around his neck, her fingers running through his short hair as both of his palms bracketed her waist.

The kiss was both endless and over too quickly.

His withdrawal was slow, his lips coming back to hers again and again, lingering until he finally pulled away.

Their eyes met, and somehow the eye contact was almost as sexy as the kiss itself. And even more important.

His hand moved up to touch a strand of hair that had come loose from her ponytail. "Here's the part where I tell you that we definitely should not have done that...that I've violated at least a half dozen of my own personal ethics, to say nothing of the department's."

Her heart started to sink, until he continued speaking with a rueful smile.

"It's also the part where I tell you that I wish I could do it all over again."

Her lips tilted up. "No regrets then?"

His eyes clouded over, and he didn't answer. "Maggie—"

She laid her fingers against his lips. "Can we just...not do that part tonight? Can I just have this moment? That kiss to think about?"

His smile was quick and sexy. "You're not going to hit the bottle again, are you?"

She smiled back. "Nope, learned my lesson. I'm a light-weight."

His lips pressed briefly against her forehead. "Good. I want you to remember every moment. Like I will."

Her eyes closed in pleasure, even as she wondered what the hell they were doing.

"I should go," he said, taking a step back. "The guys in the patrol car will no doubt be wondering what the hell I've been doing in here so long."

Maggie's smile dropped as she remembered the reality of the situation—remembered why he was here.

Eddie. *Smiley*.

"Hey," he said, touching a fingertip to her face. "Don't do that. Those cops outside are there for your protection."

"They're there to catch Eddie as much as they are to protect me," she pointed out.

"Yeah," he said, looking troubled as his hand found the doorknob of her front door. "The problem is, I care a hell of a lot more about the second one than I should."

Maggie opened her mouth, wanting to say...something.

But he was already gone.

CHAPTER THIRTEEN

Anthony was experiencing déjà vu. And not the pleasant kind that involved reliving a fantastic moment.

A moment, say...like kissing Maggie Walker.

No, today's déjà vu came in the form of a frowning paternal figure, a tart-mouthed grandma, a sweet but interfering mother, plus a whole slew of noisy, outspoken siblings.

"So you never said where you were with the Smiley case," Tony said, reaching across the table for Anthony's bacon.

Yup. Definitely déjà vu.

"No, I didn't, did I?" Anthony muttered, sipping his coffee.

His father chewed the bacon and frowned. "Why do you have so much more bacon on your plate today? You usually only get a couple strips."

Anth picked up a piece of bacon and bit into it, letting

the salty pork roll over his tongue. "Maybe someone noticed that my pieces always get pilfered."

"God, it's easy to be a man," Elena said, propping her chin up on her hand. "All it takes is throwing a couple extra slices of pork fat on the plate, and bam! He's in love."

Anth glared at his sister. "I'm not in love."

"Weird. *I* didn't get any extra bacon," Luc mused. "Did you, Vin?"

Vincent lifted a corner of omelet with his fork and pretended to look under it. "Nope, nothing here. Do you think...is it possible...could our Mags prefer the captain to us?"

Anth fixed his brothers with a look, refusing to be riled. "First of all, *bambino*, *you* didn't get any bacon because you insist on ordering a side of fruit. And Vin, you didn't get any extra bacon because—"

"—because he isn't come-hithering our waitress," Nonna chimed in.

Anth turned his glare to his grandmother. "I'm not come-hithering anyone."

"You are a little bit, dear," his mother said, patting his hand softly. "You keep looking at our Maggie."

Our Maggie.

Why did everyone think she belonged to the group? Anth resisted the urge to correct his mother—to claim her as *his* Maggie. Because she wasn't. Would never be.

But damned if she hadn't felt that way when he'd had her pressed against the wall with his hands all over her...

"You're off base," Anthony said, pointing his fork around the table. "Every last one of you. I'll have you know—"

"You still haven't said anything about Smiley," Tony broke in.

"Oh, for God's sake, Dad, that's enough!"

At first, Anthony thought that he might have snapped—that what he'd been thinking for the past three weeks had exploded out of his mouth instead of staying buried in his subconscious where it belonged.

But it wasn't Anth who had spoken. It was Luc.

Anth was torn with conflicting urges. He both wanted to scold his brother and utter a heartfelt *thank-you*.

But before he could speak, Elena beat him to it.

"Luc's right, Dad," Elena said. "You've got to leave Anth alone on this. He's handling it."

She leaned over to kiss their father's cheek to soften the blow, a move that was rendered pointless when Vincent too decided to join the fray.

"Seriously, Pops. I know you like to follow up on your kids, but spread the love, huh? Anth's been getting all the attention for weeks now. Anyone else getting bored of it?"

Nonna's hand shot up before she too reached over to grab a bite of Anth's pile of bacon. "*I'm* bored of it. This Smiley's a boring criminal. He's barely a criminal. I mean, he leaves thank-you notes..."

"That's not the point," Tony grumbled.

"What is the point, my love?" Maria Moretti murmured softly, stirring cream into her coffee.

"That every case matters," Tony said. "If he wants to move up—"

"Dad." Anth kept his voice gentle.

"Translation," Nonna stage-whispered. "Shut it, son."

Anthony felt a little stab of gratitude that his family so firmly had his back on this, although damned if he knew how to express it. *Thank you* wasn't very often in his vocabulary.

"I do it because I care," Tony Moretti muttered, looking both annoyed and properly chastened at his family's gentle scolding.

Anth waited until his father glanced at him, and held his gaze. "I know, Dad." Then he nudged his plate in his father's direction and saw from his dad's slight nod that Tony Moretti knew what it was. A peace offering in the form of bacon.

"Men," Elena muttered. "Communicating in food."

"So?" Vincent said. "You women communicate in shoes and chocolate—"

"And wine," came a soft female voice from the edge of the table. "Don't forget wine."

Maggie.

He knew his brothers would never let him forget it if he said it aloud. He very nearly did, though, just to hear her name on his lips. But somehow he knew this woman, not by her voice, or her look, or even her smell, but just by her presence.

He *felt* her. Felt when she was near. Felt when she was afraid. And felt when her eyes were on him.

Like now.

"You're a wine-o, Mags?" Luc said, forcing her to shift her gaze from Anth to his brother, and causing Anth to want to relieve Luca of all his teeth.

Maggie gave a small smile. "Let's just say that sometimes a glass of wine is just exactly the thing."

"Or a bottle," Ava chimed in. "Sometimes a bottle is just the thing."

Maggie grinned down at Luc's girlfriend. "Or a bottle," she agreed. "Although the hangover is rarely worth it."

She flicked a gaze at Anthony, and he gave her the

smallest of winks, reassuring her that he did in fact remember that her last hangover involved him and a series of texts...

Too late, he realized that his siblings would be watching him like a hawk, and no way were the Morettis the type to let one of their own off the hook.

"Did you just wink?" Elena asked.

Anth gave her his best scowl, but his sister merely shrugged. "Glare all you want. I know what I saw."

"Then why did you ask?"

"What Sister Dearest meant to ask," Luc chimed in, "was not did you wink, because obviously you did, but *why* did you wink, Anth?"

"I didn't wink."

"You totally winked," Ava chimed in. He transferred his glare to Luc's girlfriend, who merely beamed and stole a piece of his never-ending supply of bacon.

"You did wink," Maggie said, a smile lighting up her face as she looked at him.

And though Anthony knew it was insane...knew that his family would see right through him, he couldn't stop himself from smiling back.

Vincent cleared his throat. "Hey, Mags...I think there was maybe some mistake, but um, Anthony seemed to get *all* the bacon in the restaurant."

"Seriously, there are like, twenty pieces," Elena chimed in.

Anth leaned back in his chair and watched as Maggie's pretty features formed the picture of confusion. "I'm not sure what you mean."

Nonna pointed a long spindly finger at Anthony's plate. "Sure you do. You made sure he got half of a hog all because you two had *relations*."

Maggie gave one of those slow, secret smiles that only women seemed familiar with and leaned down so her lips were close to his grandmother's ear. "Mrs. Moretti, with all due respect…if I were to have *relations* with a man, he'd have all the reward he needs. You get me?"

Maggie stood up slowly, grinning a little when Nonna let out a delighted whoop and smacked her palm against Maggie's backside as Ava and Elena gave Maggie high fives. Even his mother looked strangely approving.

Anthony, meanwhile, was torn between grinning with the rest of his family and wanting to drag Maggie out the back door of the diner, press her up against the brick wall, and show her that when it came to *relations*, he was no slouch either.

Unfortunately, there was a time to woo a woman and a time to mind your manners. Sitting across the table from one's parents in a brightly lit diner after an extra long church service fell into the latter category.

Instead he settled for watching her as she joked with Elena, appreciating the way the youthful ponytail contrasted with the laugh lines around her eyes and mouth.

"You're staring," Vincent said under his breath.

Anthony immediately jerked his gaze away from her, locking it instead on the ivory porcelain of his coffee mug.

For years, he'd been ensuring not only that women didn't get the wrong idea about his intentions, but also that his family and friends didn't get the wrong impression either.

He'd told himself never again.

Not after Vannah had killed herself, citing him as the cause. He'd never forgive himself for being so wrapped up in his job that he didn't see how attached Vannah had become.

He'd been ignorant, and that was unforgivable.

He wouldn't be ignorant around Maggie.

He didn't want to let her imagine something that couldn't be.

His eyes fell on his father, watched as the often too-serious Tony Moretti smiled warmly at Maggie, let her rest a hand on his shoulder as she chatted with Anth's mother.

Maggie had always been comfortable with his family, and he'd never thought much about it, but things had gotten even more familiar as of late. The knot in his stomach tightened as he watched his father put his hand over Maggie's and pat it in a downright fatherly manner.

He should put a stop to this. Now.

But then she glanced over at him, and the guileless happiness in her eyes loosened the knot.

No doubt about it: he was in serious trouble.

"Anything else I can get you guys?" Maggie asked. "More coffee. Bacon?"

"I'd love a cup of tea, darling," Maria said. "If you have it."

Maggie laughed. "Mrs. Moretti, the day we stop having tea is the day you should find another diner."

"Never," Elena said, popping the last bite of her pancake in her mouth. "This place is our second home."

"But you should really consider selling booze, dear," Nonna said. "I could go for a nip right about now."

"It's eleven in the morning," Anthony's mother said mildly.

Nonna nodded emphatically and pointed at her daughter-in-law. "Exactly. Bourbon time."

Maria opened her mouth, but Maggie spotted the argument a mile away and broke in. "Mrs. Moretti—"

"Nonna."

"Nonna. I promise to let you know if the manager ever decides to pursue a liquor license, but in the meantime, how about a piece of pie, on me?"

"We will absolutely have pie," Anthony broke in, "but not on you. I'm buying."

"*I'm* buying," Tony broke in. "Bring us a piece of every flavor you've got, Mags."

She smiled. "Tea and pie, coming right up."

"And bourbon!" Nonna called after her.

Maggie didn't turn around to this last part, and Nonna grumbled under her breath before reaching under her shirt and pulling a silver flask out of—No. Anthony didn't even want to ponder where the hell she'd stashed the thing.

"Not to worry," his grandmother said proudly. "I came prepared."

"Wonderful, I know I'll rest easy knowing my mother-in-law keeps a flask in her bra," Maria said. "Son, hand me a piece of that bacon."

"Oh, this from Miss 'I'll just have a nice bite of oatmeal and some fruit'?" Nonna asked.

Maria pointed her piece of bacon at her mother-in-law. "Keep it up and I'll be stealing your flask."

That shut Nonna up.

Anthony enjoyed about two seconds of glorious, non-meddling silence from his family and then...

"Okay, so back to Smiley—" Tony said.

He was met with a chorus of groans, and his wife shoved a piece of bacon in his mouth.

Anth hid a smile as his dad sent him a victorious wink.

The wily old bastard had been after the slice of bacon the whole time.

Then Vincent had to go and ruin his burst of happiness with a rare moment of brotherly bonding.

"Maggie's not like her, you know."

Vin's voice was low enough not to be overheard by anyone other than Anthony, but Anth stiffened all the same. He took a sip of coffee and tried to block out his brother and the memories that came with his brother's words.

"Vannah was an emotional wreck," Vincent said, after glancing around and ensuring that the rest of the family was involved in a semi-good-natured argument about some new TV series about firefighters.

"Maggie's different. Fragile, maybe, but she has strength. Vannah was a selfish—"

"Don't," Anthony interrupted.

"I'll say whatever I damned well please," Vincent shot back. "I know we're not supposed to speak ill of the dead, but Vannah was a selfish bitch who refused to be happy and wanted desperately to take you down with her."

"She's dead, Vin," Anth said flatly. "She killed herself because I didn't pay enough attention to her. Because she begged me over and over again to see her, and I chose the damn job every time."

"Bullshit," Luc said.

Anth glanced around and saw that the family had taken notice of his and Vincent's discussion, and from the looks of things, they were all gearing up to take Vincent's side.

"Vannah begged you to pay attention to her, but it wasn't her *right* to do that. She didn't own you. And it wasn't your fault that she based her entire self-worth on whether or not her boyfriend texted her back within a certain amount of time."

"And she wasn't even your girlfriend when she died," Elena added gently. "You guys had been broken up for months."

Anthony's jaw clenched.

Two months. He'd officially ended things with Vannah two months before she'd swallowed a bottle full of sleeping pills.

Those two months were crucial, but not in the way his family seemed to think.

The way Anthony saw it, that time when they'd stopped seeing each other—his choice—were two months more that he might have helped her. Two months where he might have had the chance to see the warning signs. Two months he could have been there for her.

Technically, Vannah had been an ex-girlfriend when she died.

But that technicality meant bull-fucking-*shit* when you were named in the suicide note.

As the cause.

It was reasons like this that he couldn't pursue things with women like Maggie Walker. Women who would need him, and women who he couldn't be there for. Women who—

The clattering of plates disrupted his dark thoughts, and he and the rest of the Morettis shifted in their seats to see the cause of the commotion.

Anth's first impression was that that was a lot of wasted pie. A tray full of pie in every color littered the ground.

Seconds later, pie became the last of Anthony's worry, because then he caught sight of her face.

Maggie's face.

He was shoving at Vincent to move his brother out of the

booth seat, but his brother was already on the move. All of
his family was.

Ava had been sitting at the end of the table and made it
to Maggie first, her arm wrapping around the other woman's
waist and holding her up with surprising strength.

Maggie said nothing, her fingers reaching behind her to
pull at her apron. One of her fellow waitresses gently pushed
her hands away and did it for her.

"Maggie?" Luc asked.

She looked at Luc, eyes filled with panic. "It's my dad.
There's been an accident . . . I don't—they don't—my brother
says he's in surgery."

Her eyes moved around the circle of Morettis almost
frantically until they landed on his, and his hand reached out
for hers, wanting to somehow tug away the pain and fear he
saw there.

"Where do you need to go?" Ava asked. "Is your family
local?"

"New Jersey," she said faintly.

"We'll take you," Vincent said.

The rest of his family nodded in confirmation, and Anth
knew he was overstepping all sorts of boundaries, including
his own, but nothing—*nothing*—could have stopped him
just then.

He moved forward, oblivious to the fact that he all but
mowed over his brothers, until he was standing directly in
front of her. Elena and Ava stayed by her side, but he barely
noticed them.

"I've got you," he said quietly.

Damn it. What he meant to say was, "I'll drive you."

But when her eyes warmed in relief—and maybe
something even more important—Anthony realized that

maybe *I've got you* was exactly what he'd meant to say after all.

He wanted to hold her. To have her. To do anything and everything she wanted, to be everything she needed.

Because the woman in front of him felt like his.

CHAPTER FOURTEEN

Her dad had wrapped his Toyota around a light pole.

No other parties involved, just him, an inanimate steel object, and a bottle of vodka.

Actually, she wasn't sure about the vodka.

Knowing her father, it could have been whiskey. Or rum. Or a couple dozen beers...

"You know how crappy that road is, Bug, especially in the rain," her brother said from where he was slouched across from her in the hospital waiting room. "There are all those curves, and the city hasn't done shit to fix the potholes."

Maggie could only stare at him.

It was always like this with Cory.

Nothing was ever his fault. Nothing was ever their father's fault.

Cory had happily blinded himself to the fact that a pothole and a little bit of rain wouldn't have caused a car to go careening off the road with enough speed to practically split the car in two.

She studied him, waiting for the moment when this would click with him, even as she knew that the moment would never come.

Her brother looked exactly the same as she remembered.

Cory was good looking. Ridiculously so. He had the same brown hair and hazel eyes as Maggie, but whereas this translated to merely average on her, he had the added benefit of thick lashes, an excellent jawline, and white, perfect teeth.

It was as though fate had noticed the shortcomings of his character and decided to make amends by making him outright gorgeous.

"How long has he been out of rehab?" she asked quietly.

Cory snorted, not looking up from his phone. "He doesn't need to be in rehab. So he likes beer. What's the big fucking deal?"

"Your father is currently lying on an operating table in a trauma center. I'd say it's a big fucking deal," Anthony Moretti said from the spot where he stood in the corner of the waiting room.

Maggie tensed. It was the first thing Moretti had said since they'd gotten to the hospital. Mostly he'd done a lot of frowning.

He'd frowned when the nurse at the front desk had told them that her dad was still in surgery.

Frowned when her brother had greeted him with a *'sup*.

Frowned when Maggie had refused his offer of coffee.

Cory's expression turned from indifferent to sulky as he flicked his gaze to the pissed-off-looking man in the corner. "Sorry, who the fuck are you?"

Maggie dug her nails into her palms. "I told you, Cor, he's…"

"Yeah, I get that he's a big shot cop, Buggsie, but that's not what I'm asking. I want to know what he's *doing* here."

Cory had finally flicked off his phone screen and transferred his attention to her, but not in the way she wanted. She heard her brother's question loud and clear: *What is a cop doing here with* you*?*

"He gave me a ride," she said quietly.

Cory's eyes narrowed. "You just happened to run into an off-duty police captain who just happened to drive you out to fucking New Jersey?"

"I—"

Moretti cut her off. "Answer your sister's question. When did your father get out of rehab?"

The two men glared at each other for about twenty seconds before Cory looked away with an insolent shrug. "He was only there about a day or two. Didn't like it."

"He didn't *like it*?" Maggie said. "He's not supposed to *like* it, Cory. He's sick. He told me he wanted to get better and I—"

She broke off before verbalizing the extent of her foolishness, but knew from the curl of her brother's lip that he saw right through her. And she didn't have to look at Moretti to know what she'd see on *his* face. Disgust. Or worse, pity.

Maggie resisted the urge to dip her head all the way forward to bury her face in her hands. Instead she forced herself to sit up straighter. "What about the money?"

Cory's brow wrinkled. "What money?"

"Never mind," she said quickly, realizing her mistake.

Cory sat up straighter, looking alert for the first time

since she'd walked into the hospital. "No, seriously. What money?"

Crap. Crap, crap, crap.

Cory might have inherited the startling good looks of their mother, but he was thoroughly his father's son. Especially when it came to sniffing out money.

"Bug?" Cory prompted.

She felt Moretti's gaze on her. "I'm guessing your sister bankrolled your father's rehab stint," he answered for her.

Cory's expression turned thoughtful. "Huh. I wonder how much of that is refundable. Be a shame to let them keep it when he doesn't even need..."

Anthony very slowly pushed away from the wall he'd been leaning against, extending his long body to its full, impressive height.

Maggie's eyes widened a little at the look on Anthony's face, but her brother was too busy calculating how to get his hands on additional funds to recognize the danger until Anthony was standing in front of him, towering over Cory.

"I believe, Mr. Walker, that the *shame* here is that your sister is wasting her money on a man who doesn't have enough respect for himself or his family to get sober."

Maggie frowned and pushed out of her chair. "Now wait a second, *Captain.*"

He turned icy eyes to her, and she wanted to cower beneath the disdain there. Wanted to, but didn't.

"This isn't your business," she said firmly.

His eyes held hers. "Did you pay for your father's rehab?"

"Yes." She refused to be ashamed.

"Rehab he didn't finish. Rehab he barely even started," Moretti clarified.

"He wants to get better," she shot back. "If it was *your* father asking for assistance, you're telling me you wouldn't move heaven and earth to get him help?"

Moretti's face didn't soften. "How many times?"

She blinked. "What?"

"How many times has he gone to rehab?"

Maggie licked her lips. "It doesn't always work the first time. Alcoholism is a complicated disease—"

"Don't say another word, Bug," Cory said, standing up beside her so they were shoulder to shoulder, facing off against Anthony. "We don't even know this guy."

"She knows me," Anthony said, his eyes never leaving hers.

Her brother gave her a scathing look. "Don't tell me you're seeing this guy. A cop? Bug, *seriously*? You—"

Maggie was saved from having to respond by a tired-looking doctor who approached them. "Are any of you here for Charles Walker?"

"Yes," she and Cory answered in unison. Her hand instinctively wrapped around her brother's, looking for comfort.

He didn't squeeze it in reassurance like she wished he would, but at least he didn't shake her off.

"I'm his daughter," Maggie said, her voice surprisingly steady. "This is my brother."

"I'm Dr. Kim," the woman said, giving them both a perfunctory handshake. "Your father's out of surgery and in recovery. There was major internal bleeding and he's dislocated his shoulder. We were able to stop the bleeding and the shoulder will heal. He's got a nasty bump on his head, so a concussion is probable, but we're not seeing any brain swelling."

"So he'll live?" Cory asked bluntly.

"He's stable. His condition is still serious, but yes...I believe your father can make a full recovery."

Maggie's knees buckled, and a strong arm wrapped around her waist, steadying her.

Not her brother's arm.

Anthony was there, lending her all his strength, despite the fact that she'd just bit his head off. This, after he'd driven her forty-five minutes and waited with her for over two hours...

She should free him from this. Release him from the toxic grip of the Walker family. But for now, just for a moment, she let herself lean.

For someone who was used to everyone needing her— *using* her—it was nice to need someone else. Nice for someone else to *let* her need them.

"When can we see him?" she asked.

"I can let you in there for a few minutes now, but he won't be awake for a while yet, and when he does come around, he'll likely be groggy. One of the nurses will show you back," Dr. Kim said with a nod at one of the nurses who'd been hovering at the front desk.

Cory headed in the direction the doctor indicated, and Maggie started to follow, easing away from the wonderful warmth of Anthony reluctantly.

Dr. Kim touched her arm. "Ms. Walker."

Maggie turned. "Yeah?"

The doctor gave a questioning glance at Anthony, who started to back away, but Maggie instinctively reached out and grabbed his hand. "He's with me."

He stayed.

Dr. Kim's voice was quiet. "I didn't want to say anything

in front of your brother, who seems...upset. But your father's blood alcohol level..."

Maggie squeezed her eyes shut. "I know."

The doctor's face softened for the first time since she'd entered the waiting room. "In situations like this, the police will be involved. You should be prepared for questions, and when he wakes up..."

"We'll deal with that when he wakes up," Anthony interrupted.

The doctor gave him a sharp look, but relented at whatever she saw on his face. Anthony wasn't in uniform, so Dr. Kim couldn't know he was a cop, but it wasn't hard to read the authority on his face.

"Yo. Bug. You comin'?" Cory asked impatiently from where he hovered in the doorway with the nurse.

"Yeah," she said before glancing at Anthony, realizing she still held his hand.

"It's probably family only," she said quietly.

He nodded once and let his fingers slide from hers.

She looked up at his unsmiling face and, for the first time, realized that his features weren't harsh so much as strong. And oh how she wanted that strength now.

And it was precisely because of that longing that she needed to let him go. She wouldn't let a man like Captain Anthony Moretti get tangled up in the mess that was the Walkers.

She was willing to bet that he'd never been even close to the other side of the law, and that's exactly what he would be if he had to stand by her when she was questioned by the New Jersey police.

"Thanks for the ride," she said, dimly aware of Dr. Kim stepping away. "I...you can't know how much I appreciate it. Not just because of the convenience, but because..."

Maggie licked her lips, wondering how much to say. "It meant a lot that you waited."

He nodded, still saying nothing.

"I can take a cab home," she said quietly. "Or Cory can give me a ride to the train station."

His head tipped back slightly at the dismissal, and though his eyes didn't betray emotion—*any* emotion—she had to think he was relieved.

"Do you need anything?" he asked.

You. I need you.

"No, I'm okay. Not much to do until he wakes up, I guess."

Anthony crossed his arms. "And you'll let me know when he wakes up? Keep me updated?"

"Yeah. Sure. Of course."

"Bug!"

She glanced over her shoulder at her brother. "Coming."

She turned and headed toward her impatient brother and then followed Cory and the nurse into the harsh white lighting and cold floors of whatever lay beyond the sliding glass doors.

Maggie couldn't stop herself from glancing over her shoulder.

But Anthony was already gone.

CHAPTER FIFTEEN

Anthony was no stranger to hospitals. No police officer was. There were times you needed to question victims. And suspects.

But he hadn't been in a hospital for personal reasons since before his brother Marco had gotten stabbed in the shoulder after a convenience store robbery on the Lower East Side.

It had been a flesh wound and Marc had been out of the hospital within twenty-four hours, but Anthony had never forgotten what it felt like to be trapped in a hospital waiting room, desperate for information.

The waiting had been agony.

But today he'd experienced a different kind of agony.

Helplessness.

He'd never realized that watching someone else's pain could be worse than experiencing one's own, but watching Maggie try to physically hold herself together had nearly ripped him apart.

And that wasn't even the worst part; the worst part was that he was damned sure her father didn't deserve her. Didn't deserve her love, or her devotion, and he definitely didn't deserve her money.

Money she didn't have.

He'd seen Maggie's apartment. It was tiny. Old.

And he remembered the genuine dismay on her face when he'd accidentally caused her to knock her leftovers from the diner onto the ground.

Christ.

The woman could barely afford to feed herself, and she was tossing away God knew how much money on an alcoholic who hadn't made it past two days of rehab.

Sure, the fact that her father had even taken a step toward rehab was important. Vital even.

But Anthony hadn't made it to *Captain* without some damn good instincts, and his instincts were telling him that Charles Walker had known that the word "rehab" was the only way he'd get a penny out of his daughter.

And he was also betting the man had known *exactly* the refund plan when he'd entered rehab.

If he'd even gone in for treatment at all.

Anthony's hand fisted around his empty coffee cup, crushing the cheap paper before chucking it with more force than necessary into the garbage can.

He'd never met the man. Never even seen him. But if Charlie Walker were taking his daughter's hard-earned money to spend it on booze, only to wrap his car around a light pole, Anthony would find a way to make his life miserable.

He'd said as much to the New Jersey state trooper who'd come in to get a statement from the doctor. He hoped they threw the book at the bastard. And maybe her useless brother too.

Anthony slumped into the uncomfortable chair, eyes locking with a little girl who'd been playing some noisy game on her dad's phone while he paced around the room anxiously.

She grinned at Anth, probably too young to understand that a hospital waiting room generally meant bad news.

He smiled back, although the gesture felt awkward. Strained.

God, was he out of practice at smiling?

He was. He'd forgotten how to smile.

The little girl went back to her game, her purple-sneakered feet kicking happily back and forth.

He rubbed a hand over his face. He could leave. He probably *should* leave. Maggie had all but begged him to when she'd followed her brother back an hour ago.

But no way was he going to let her take a cab back to the city, and he sure as fuck wasn't going to let her get into a car with her brother. Cory Walker was a chip off the old block in the worst way. The man had reeked of booze.

Anth wondered if Maggie had noticed, or if she was just used to it. And where the hell was her mother? How long had it been just Maggie and two alcoholic moochers?

It bothered him that he didn't know these details about her, but at the same time, he knew he shouldn't ask. He already cared too much. It was hard enough to stay away from her when she'd just been the irresistible girl at the diner.

Now that he knew she had a criminal ex-husband and two degenerate family members? It made him want to fold her into his arms. Into his family. Into his life...

...where she'd be even worse off than she was now. Shackled to a cop who'd put his career first, every time.

She deserved more.

"What the hell am I doing?" he muttered, pushing to his feet.

Even if she were happy to see him when she came out, it would give her the wrong idea.

He—

He was too late.

"Anthony?"

Shit.

He turned around, prepared to tell her that he was just leaving...that he'd only come back for his cell phone or some lame excuse.

And then he saw her face and realized there was no way in hell he'd leave her.

He was in front of her in two big steps, his hands reaching for her, hesitating only briefly before finding her upper arms, tugging her forward gently.

And then he hugged her. Without agenda, without thought. Just because it was the right thing to do. He absorbed her shuddering breath, felt her hands find his shoulders, as though to push him away.

And then she sank into him, her forehead tilted forward until it rested on his shoulder, her hands slowly dropping downward until they slipped around him, settling just above his waist.

"You stayed." It was the tiniest of statements. Barely more than a whisper, but he heard it. Heard the surprise in it.

Of course I stayed.

"Where's your brother?" he asked instead.

She shook her head. "He took off a while ago. Said to call him when Dad woke up."

Asshole.

"Did he?" Anth asked. "Wake up?"

"No. They said it might be a while. That I should go home and they'd call me, but—"

His hands stopped their stroking motion on her back. "No buts, Maggie. I'm taking you home. And whenever you want to come back, I'll take you."

She blinked up at him. "But what if you're at work?"

She couldn't have known what a stab to the heart that was, but he felt it anyway. It was said without Vannah's snotty, passive-aggressive tone, but the message was the same.

What if you can't be there for me?

He forced a smile. "I promise, the Morettis will find a way to get you there. If not me, then Luc or Vincent. Plus, Elena loves making use of her company car. And if none of them, I'll pay for the cab."

The confusion on her face ripped at his heart. She looked utterly baffled that anyone would help her out.

"Anthony, I—"

He gave her a stern look. "You're not about to get weepy on me, are you?"

She smiled. "I admit, I was considering it. Between your kindness and the fact that my brother didn't even say good-bye, and then there's the fact that my dad is lying uncon-scious in a hospital bed..."

"He'll be okay."

She inhaled a long, steady breath. "You sound so sure of that."

"I've talked to plenty of doctors in my day, either updates on victims or the bad guys. If his condition was iffy, she would have said something to prepare you."

She nodded, and he saw her swallow bravely.

"Let's get you home," he said gently, holding out his hand.

She set her palm against his. Trusting him.

And damn, her trust felt good.

The ride home was silent, but not awkwardly so. He sensed she needed quiet to process everything, and he was more than happy to give it to her. Happy just to be near her.

"It's been a long time since I've ridden in a car," she said when they were nearing Brooklyn.

He glanced at her. "That's true of most New Yorkers. Beyond a cab of course."

She drummed her fingers against her knee. "I can't remember the last time I was in a cab either. They're sort of a luxury on a waitress salary, you know?"

It was on the tip of his tongue that perhaps she'd have a bit more money for the occasional taxi ride if she wasn't writing blank checks to her father, but he didn't. That discussion hadn't gone over well in the hospital waiting room and it wouldn't go over well now.

"Do I need to give my family a talking-to about their tips?" he said jokingly.

"Your family is more than generous." She glanced at him across the darkened car. "So are you."

He shrugged, and she twisted to face him. "No, I'm serious. Whenever you've come in alone, your tips are outrageous. Even before..."

Anthony glanced at her. "Even before you stopped spilling food and drink all over me?"

"I was going to say even before you *kissed me*."

Her words were like a bomb in the small space and he jerked his eyes back to the road. "I—"

"You shouldn't have done it," she said on a weary sigh. "I know."

Did you want me to do it? Do you want me to do it again?

They were silent for several minutes, the car barely moving thanks to road construction.

"Do you ever look at your life and wonder how you got there?" she asked.

He tapped his fingers on the steering wheel and considered. "No."

Maggie let out a little laugh. "I guess I already knew the answer to that. You've always wanted to be a cop, and that's exactly what you are."

He shrugged.

Maggie sighed and looked out the passenger window. "You're lucky."

"I take that to mean you *haven't* always wanted to be a waitress."

This time when she turned to face him, her expression was withering. "Does anyone? I mean, don't get me wrong, it's a decent job. And it has some of the hardest-working people you'll ever meet, hauling around heavy trays for mostly ungrateful customers."

"But it's not the dream," he completed for her.

"Definitely not."

"Then what is?"

She pursed her lips. "You'll think I'm silly."

"Doesn't matter," he said. "It's your dream. Doesn't matter what anyone else thinks."

She plucked at the skirt of her diner uniform. "I want to be an author."

"Nothing silly about that."

Her laugh was short. "It's a long shot. I read somewhere that like eighty percent of people want to write a book."

"Sure, but I'm guessing that most of them don't even try."

"Maybe," she murmured.

"Have you?" he asked, turning onto her street.

"Have I what?"

"Tried. To write."

"I've tried. I *am* trying."

"Yeah? What do you write?"

"Kids' books. Well, teens, specifically. I know it sounds weird, but I like the awkwardness of the age. The longing, you know?"

He pulled up to the curb in front of her apartment building. "I don't think teens have an exclusive on *longing*, Maggie."

Anthony hadn't meant the statement to be as loaded as it came out, but there it was. He didn't look at her as he turned off the car. Couldn't. Knew that he wouldn't be able to resist hauling her onto his lap and kissing away all the pain and stress of her day.

He could show her longing. He *lived* it.

"No," she whispered. "I guess that doesn't stop after our teen years, does it?"

They both stared straight ahead as he contemplated his options. He could either wrap a hand around the back of her neck. Tug her to him and kiss her like they both wanted.

Or he could...

"Looks like my babysitters are right where I left them," she said, leaning forward slightly and peering across the street.

Babysitters? Realization washed over Anthony like a brutally cold shower.

The cops outside her apartment. He'd totally forgotten.

He pulled a hand over his face. This woman messed with his head.

Anthony reached for the door handle and shoved it open before he could do something idiotic, like make out with Maggie with two of his officers watching.

Anth went around her side of the car, but she was already climbing out, not looking at him. All of the warm, sexual tension of the past moments completely evaporated.

"You don't have to walk me in," she said.

He ignored her, his hand finding the small of her back as he led her up the walkway to her apartment building, lifting the other hand in greeting to the officers who were watching them curiously.

Let them be curious. He wasn't about to explain why their captain was escorting Maggie Walker home at ten o'clock on a Sunday evening. Wasn't sure how he *could* explain.

And the hand on her back was professional—sort of. It was an old-school gesture that wasn't completely out of place for a captain and an informant.

But the heat of the contact, even through the fabric of her polyester diner uniform, didn't *feel* professional.

He could only hope the officers in the squad car wouldn't read it for what it really was.

Want.

And the subtle claiming of this woman as his. Not in the caveman sense, but in the sense that she was his to take care of when she was fragile.

Maggie's apartment building was a sad, decaying walk-up. No doorman, and the front door looked like it could blow open with a strong gust of wind.

Anthony knew from the one other time he'd come by that

it wasn't always closed tightly, its residents either too careless or too stupid to see that they were literally leaving a door wide open for criminals.

The ease with which Eddie Hansen could get at Maggie gave him chills.

Still, Eddie was likely the last thing on her mind at the moment, so he didn't lecture her. Maggie had enough to worry about with her father without adding her burglarizing ex-husband to the mix.

But *damn* the woman had a lot of bad men in her life.

When they reached her door, she dug her keys out of her bag and turned to face him. "Thanks for seeing me in."

Anthony searched her face. Her words were a dismissal. Plain and clear. But her eyes...

Gently he reached forward, his fingers wrapping around her wrist while his other hand coaxed the keys from her palm.

Wordlessly he reached around her and unlocked her door. Pushed it open.

A small cannonball exploded against his kneecaps.

"Oh, Duchess, my poor baby," she said, hunching down to embrace the dog. Or tried to embrace. The little mutt was wriggling too much for her to get more than a few pets in.

"I need to take her out. She's been alone all day," Maggie said, setting her purse inside the door before reaching for the dog leash on a hook.

"I'll do it," he said. "It's late."

She gave him a look. "It's not *that* late. Duchess and I are used to walking at all hours."

"Was that before or after your ex-husband started breaking and entering and then stalking you at work and sending you mysterious notes?"

Maggie rolled her eyes. "He's not stalking me. I'm still not even sure that was him at the diner, and even if it was, your watchdogs are right outside."

Anthony didn't budge. Held out his hand.

"Fine," she huffed and slapped the leash in his hand.

He glanced down. It was pink with little purple flowers. He glanced down at Duchess whose tail was wagging with enough motor power to lift the little dog right off the ground.

Maggie shoved something else at his chest. "Here are her poo bags. If you figure out how to get her to not go in the middle of the sidewalk, let me know."

He glanced down at the small plastic bags. "They're pink."

She patted his cheek. "It'll ease your rough edges. Show your officers out there your softer side."

Anthony made a growling noise before leaning down and clipping the leash to an ecstatic Duchess's collar.

He'd never had a dog. His mom was allergic. But when he was in eighth grade, he'd started a summer dog-walking business to earn extra spending money to buy a charm bracelet for Brenda Morris.

He didn't remember poop bags being pink back then. And he certainly didn't remember leashes being a fashion statement.

Once outside of Maggie's apartment, Anthony turned left, away from the squad car. The officers wouldn't miss the fact that he was walking Maggie's dog, but they'd hopefully miss the fact that the leash would have been at home in Elena's old Barbie Dreamhouse.

True to Maggie's warning, Duchess decided that her business would best be done in the middle of the street, and it took Anthony an ungodly amount of time to figure out how to open the fluffy pink plastic bag so he could do his pick-up duty.

Duchess, for her part, waited patiently, sitting calmly as Anthony picked up her poo before wagging her tail in a thank-you and trotting forward.

Anthony was itching to get back to Maggie, but he remembered that the poor little dog had been cooped up inside the apartment all day and let himself be led around the block to inspect every stop sign post, every shrub, every crack in the pavement before finally leading Anth back to Maggie's place.

He nodded at the officers staring at him. It was too dark to see their expressions, and Anth was glad for it. He imagined they were somewhere between shock and amusement.

Duchess raced back up the stairs so quickly that he had to take them two at a time to keep up.

He rapped a knuckle against the door, giving her a moment before his hand went for the doorknob. It turned easily in his hand, and he scowled, ready to scold her for leaving it unlocked.

But all cross words fled his mind at the sight of Maggie standing in the middle of the room. She was still in her orange diner uniform, and from the frozen look on her face, he'd guess she hadn't moved the entire time he'd been gone.

Even the hyper Duchess seemed to sense something amiss, approaching her mistress quietly and lowering herself on top of Maggie's feet protectively.

Up until that moment, Anthony had every intention of wishing her good night and escaping before the cops outside really started to wonder what the hell he was doing here, but at the sight of her lost expression, his plans went out the door.

He shrugged out of his trench coat, draped it over the

back of one of her kitchen chairs, and approached her slowly so as not to startle her.

"My dad never went to rehab," she said, blinking up at him. "He lied to me. Or at least he didn't *stay* in rehab. He took my money."

Anth swallowed his anger and gently set his hand against her waist, nudging her toward the bed. "Why don't you change into something comfortable? I'll find us something to eat."

She tugged at her ponytail. "Don't do that."

"Don't do what?" He moved toward the fridge.

"Don't be nice."

"Maybe I'm just an inherently nice guy."

She snorted and he smiled.

"I don't have much to eat," she said, her tone embarrassed.

She was right, he realized, as he looked through her fridge and pantry. She *didn't* have much.

But after a bit of rummaging, he found a box of pasta. "Can I use this?"

She shrugged. "Have at it. I hardly ever make pasta."

He blinked at her. "What?"

Maggie grinned and sat on the edge of her bed. "Easy, Mr. Italian. I know it's supposed to be a simple staple, but I can never make it taste as yummy as a restaurant's."

"Do you salt the water?" he asked, digging among her meager kitchen supplies until he found a pot big enough to fit the penne.

"Um, sometimes? If I think of it."

"Well, there's your problem," he said, flicking on the tap. "No food tastes good if it's under-seasoned. Pasta included. The water should taste like the ocean. Use a handful of salt."

"Well, even properly salted pasta is going to be a little un-derwhelming without a sauce," she muttered.

"Oh ye of little faith," he said, watching out of the corner of his eye as she stood and went to her dresser. Her shoulders had relaxed slightly, and at least she was finally going to get out of that horrible uniform.

"If you can find something to put on that pasta, I'm going to be very impressed," she said, pulling a couple clothing items out of the dresser and heading toward the bathroom.

It was on the tip of his tongue to say that she didn't have to change in the bathroom. But of course she did. She lived in a studio. No walls, no privacy. Even if he kept his back turned, he'd be able to hear her undressing and—

Jesus. Was he getting a boner from thinking of hearing her undress?

Yes. Yes he was.

Well now he had to for *sure* keep his back turned.

"You're ridiculous," he muttered.

"Sorry?" she asked from the doorway.

"Nothing. Change your clothes. I'll cook."

Maggie's voice was husky. "Captain Moretti, you have no idea how sexy those words are."

He spun around, but she'd already shut the door with a quiet click, leaving him with a raging hard-on and a mon-tage of images of what was happening on the other side of that door. Her creamy skin, her full curves, the way her soft hair would fall down her back as he—

"Get a grip." He yanked open the fridge again, staring at its meager contents. A bag of carrots. A block of some sort of cheese. Packaged hummus. Two eggs. Milk.

The pantry selection wasn't much better.

But by the time Maggie came out of the bathroom,

dressed in a gray T-shirt and red flannel pajama pants, he had a clove of a slightly dried-out head of garlic gently bubbling in olive oil as he grated what he was pretty sure was parmesan cheese.

She came up beside him. "How does something so simple smell so good?"

He glanced down at her head. Her skin was pink and dewy, like she'd just washed her face, and she'd pulled her hair into a messy braid. She smelled like vanilla.

"It's Italian food," he muttered. "It all smells good."

"Huh," she said, looking bewildered. "Who knew?"

"This would be better with red pepper flakes," he said, nudging the temperature down so the garlic wouldn't burn. "But your spice rack is nonexistent."

Maggie held up a finger and pulled open a drawer to her left, rustling around until she came up with a couple small white packets. "Will this work? My pizza delivery guy always gives me a big handful of these even though I only need one. I'm assuming it's the same thing you need…"

"It's the same," he said, pulling a couple packets out of her palm. "We've got a few minutes until the pasta will be ready. And since I'm doing the cooking, I was thinking you could provide the entertainment."

She glanced up at him. "Absolutely. Striptease?"

Anthony's hand slipped and he narrowly missed scraping his knuckle on the cheese grater. He glanced down at her impish smile and frowned. "You're evil."

"Oh, so not what you had in mind?" she asked, twisting so that she was leaning back against the counter. "I mean, I'm totally dressed the part."

She plucked at her oversize T-shirt and batted her eyelashes.

He needlessly stirred the pasta water to stop himself from telling her that he didn't give a fuck about her clothes. He cared about what was *underneath*. And his fingers were itching to duck under that ugly T-shirt and find out if her skin was as soft as he suspected.

"I was thinking you could read to me," he said gruffly.

Maggie's nose scrunched. "Read to you? Like a bedtime story? I don't really have much around here other than teen romance novels…"

"I mean your stuff," he said, setting the spoon aside and crossing his arms.

Her lips parted. "It's not finished, and it's probably terrible, and I—"

Before he could stop himself, his hand slid around the back of her neck, his thumb rubbing gently against her silky skin before he dipped his head and claimed her mouth.

It was a quick kiss. Just a brief melding of mouths, an exchange of startled breath. The quickest stroking of his tongue against hers before he pulled back.

"Read it to me, Maggie."

Her eyes were cloudy with desire, and the knowledge of how passionately she responded to even the simplest of kisses was a damn powerful aphrodisiac. And the thought of how she might respond if he pulled her across the room, pushed her onto the bed…

"Read," he commanded again.

"I've never let anyone read it. Only my best friend knows that I write. Or try to write. Well, and now you," she amended, her fingers going to her lips thoughtfully.

He pushed aside the surge of pleasure that she'd shared such a private part of herself with him. Only with him.

"You don't have to read it if you don't want," he conceded. "Although if you want any pasta..."

She groaned. "Now who's evil?"

She pushed back from the counter, moving toward the small table, and retrieved her laptop, hugging it to her chest. "It's all on my laptop. I don't have anything printed, and it's all rough draft."

He met her eyes and smiled. "I can't wait to hear it. In any form."

Maggie took a deep breath before shuffling over to the bed, pushing Duchess out of the way before pulling her legs up beneath her and opening the computer. "You can't say a word, okay? And you can *think* it sucks, but you can't *tell* me it sucks."

"Damn, because that was definitely my plan," he said, searching for a colander to drain the pasta. "To get you to share something incredibly private and then criticize it. Then I was going to move on to the list I keep of your flaws."

She narrowed her eyes at him. "You have a list of my flaws?"

"Absolutely," he said, giving up on the colander and instead just draining the steaming water into the sink while trying to lose as few pieces of pasta as possible.

"Name one," she said.

He glanced at her over his shoulder.

"Well, for starters. You haven't let me see you naked yet."

CHAPTER SIXTEEN

You haven't let me see you naked yet.

Yet. He'd said *yet.*

Later, much later, Maggie would think up the perfect comeback to Anthony's husky statement.

She would have let her voice go all low and sexy, and said, *You haven't asked.*

But yeah, that's totally not how it *actually* went down.

Because while Maggie considered herself relatively quick with a comeback when she had all of her senses, apparently, when faced with the prospect of being naked in front of one gorgeous, glowering Captain Anthony Moretti, wit was nowhere to be found.

"Relax, Maggie," he said, approaching the bed with two bowls in hand. "I'm not going to make a move on a woman who's had the kind of day you had."

Damn. "But—But..."

Yeah. Not the comeback she'd hoped for.

He shoved a bowl of pasta into her hands. "Eat. Then read. Or do both at the same time."

She shoveled a bite of pasta into her mouth. "Damn, you go from sexy to bossy so fast I get whiplash."

He looked at her. "Rumor has it some women find bossy sexy."

"And I'm one of those women," she said, licking a fleck of deliciously flavored oil from her lip. "But it will be a hell of a lot *more* sexy once you get me naked. I wouldn't mind you bossing me around then. At all."

Not so bad on the comebacks after all, Mags, she thought, mentally patting herself on the back.

He paused with his fork halfway to his mouth, his eyes dark with lust. At least she hoped it was lust, because she was about four seconds away from combusting with want for this man.

"Maggie…"

Crap. She knew that tone. His eyes had gone from hot to wary, and no way was she in the mood to get rejected. Not by him. Not today.

So she deflected.

"Your turn to relax, Captain. I'm letting you keep your virtue for the evening. Also"—she pointed with her fork to her bowl—"this pasta is *really* good. Especially for having, what, five ingredients?"

"Sometimes the simple pleasures are the best kind," he said, handing a bit of pasta to Duchess, who looked delighted to have confirmation that her begging techniques were at the top of their game.

She narrowed her eyes at him. "Either you just went all weird and Zen on me, or there's some sort of sexual innuendo wrapped up in there."

He smiled and jerked his chin toward the laptop she'd set aside. "Read."

She groaned. "I can't."

He shrugged, a gesture he did an awful lot of. Right up there with glowering. But his shrugs and glares were different tonight. Easier, somehow.

Part of the change was the lack of uniform. He was wearing jeans and a cream-colored sweater that could have easily been downright blah on another man, but on his oversize frame looked exactly right.

She nibbled another bite of pasta and, after realizing he'd already cleaned his bowl, offered hers to him.

He shook his head. "You eat it. You've had a long day."

Just like that, the memory of just how long—and awful— her day had been rushed over her. Her appetite disappeared. She dropped her fork and started to set it on the nightstand, when he reached out a hand to take it from her.

He stood and started to head toward the kitchen, but Maggie grabbed the sleeve of his sweater.

"Anth."

His eyebrow lifted at the nickname, and she looked away. "Sorry, your brothers call you that sometimes, and—"

"I don't mind."

Her hand dropped. "Will you stay?"

His gaze dropped to the bowls. "I shouldn't. The officers waiting outside will wonder."

"Right," she broke in. "Right, of course. I forgot all about them."

He made her forget *everything*. Eddie. Her brother. Her father. It was a wonder she remembered her own name.

Anthony looked like he wanted to say something else, but instead he swore softly and stomped toward the kitchen, where he washed the dishes with the amount of noise and force she would have expected from six police captains.

Maggie knew she should offer to help—the old, *you cook, I clean* cliché—but her limbs all of a sudden were tired. Hell, her *soul* was tired.

Tired, and a little lost.

So instead of cleaning, she let herself curl into the fetal position, where Duchess promptly curled up against her belly, snout resting on Maggie's bent arm.

"Tomorrow," she whispered against the dog's head. "Tomorrow I'll be strong and brave. But—"

A warm hand rested against her head. *His* hand. His fingers skimmed her temple.

Maggie's eyes fluttered shut.

"You are strong," Anth said, his voice gruff. "And you're brave too."

She gave a derisive laugh. "I'm not. You want to know something terrible?"

The mattress sagged as he sank down beside her, his hip warm against her back. "Tell me."

She smoothed a hand over the dog's head, wondering if it was as soothing for Duchess as Anthony's hand on her head was.

"The truth is," Maggie started. "The truth is, sometimes I look at my life. I *really* look at it... and I wish that all of the bad stuff would just go away and I could start over. Go back to when I was eighteen, back before my family got in the habit of relying on me for money. Back before I let Eddie trick me into thinking he was a good guy. Back before I gave up on the idea of college and started waiting tables because my dad had finally decided to get clean and needed money for rehab, stint one..."

He didn't interrupt her. Just kept up the soothing motion of his palm against her scalp and let her continue.

So she did.

She kept talking.

"Every time something happens with Cory or with my dad...*every* time, I tell myself that it's the last time. But it never is. I just keep making these same mistakes over and over again, and then I have to wonder...am I even capable of making different choices? What if I'm just...pathetic?"

They were silent for several seconds, until finally Maggie let out a little laugh. "So, Captain, this is the point where you tell me I'm not pathetic."

He cleared his throat. "Well, here's what I know. I know that I'm pretty fucking great. And since I'm, basically, the greatest guy around, I can tell you for an absolute fact that I wouldn't be here if you were pathetic."

She shifted slightly to look up at his face. "What if it's the other way around? What if you're only here *because* I'm pathetic? Because you feel bad for me?"

He stared down at her. "That's not why I'm here. Trust me."

"Then why are you?"

His eyes drifted over her face, but instead of responding, he reached over to her nightstand and picked up her laptop.

Then he opened it.

"Hey, what are you—"

"Either you read me your story, or I read it myself. Your choice."

She glared at him. Knew that if she told him to, he'd close the computer without question. And a part of her wanted to. A *big* part of her wanted to slam the laptop shut and toss it out the window where her book would never see the light of day. Never be exposed to criticism.

But maybe...

Maybe the shift from meek to brave wasn't one big, explosive transition.

What if it was born of teeny, tiny moments like this one, where you opened yourself up, just a little, to a complicated man who absolutely shouldn't be here, but was anyway?

"Okay," she said quietly.

"Okay what?"

"You can read it," she said. "To yourself, though. Not out loud."

Her bravery had limits.

He nodded, shifting on the bed so that his back was to the headboard, his legs stretched out in front of him.

He turned the laptop toward her, and wordlessly she pulled up her manuscript. Scrolled to chapter one.

He smiled reassuringly, and then, as if she wasn't already melting enough from the fact that he'd driven her to freaking New Jersey, waited in a horrible hospital waiting room, driven her home, walked her dog, cooked her dinner, and then cleaned up, he had to go and bump it up a notch. He opened his arm to her. "Come."

So she did.

She curled against him, her cheek against his chest, her arm draped across his waist as his wrapped around her back.

"What about the car outside?" she whispered. "They'll wonder what the heck you're doing up here."

"They will." He turned his head slightly so his lips were against her hair. "But I find I don't care as much as I should."

The admission was a small one. Hardly romantic-comedy worthy. But for a man who'd made it perfectly clear that his career was of the utmost importance in his life, it was a big statement.

And for a girl who was used to people choosing anyone
and everything over her, it was a heart melter.

"You going to read along with me?" he asked.

"Nah. I know what it says."

She'd read it a dozen times. Hell, she could probably re-
cite chapter one from memory.

"You're just going to lay here and let me read silently?"
he asked. "You'll be bored."

Maggie tilted her head up and met his eyes. "It's been
years since someone's held me. Trust me, I won't be bored."

His gaze softened before turning to the computer screen,
where he began to read.

Maggie waited for the rush of panic to set in. The rush of
fear she got every time she thought about her book being exposed to the world.

But there was no panic. No fear. There was only the
steady heartbeat of an uptight police captain who, against all
odds, was the first person in a very, very long time to *care*.

CHAPTER SEVENTEEN

Son of a fucking bitch," Anthony said, throwing the report back on his desk with so much force his pen cup slid off the back. "Damn it."

The report was from Greenwich, Connecticut.

There'd been a break-in in some rich, uppity, gated community. As far as crimes went, it was a snoozer. Parents out of town, a teen that forgot to set the house alarm before sneaking out for a midnight rendezvous with her boyfriend. A picked lock, a couple stolen TVs, and a missing necklace.

All boring as shit crimes, with one very crucial detail.

There'd been a note.

With one Goddamn yellow smiley-face sticker on it.

"Yeah," Anth barked at the knock on the door.

It was his boss.

Mandela's eyes took in Anthony's livid expression. "You've read it."

"It's not him," Anthony said, standing and locking his

hands behind his head as he paced in circles. "It's not Smiley."

"You read the file all the way through, right? Because the first responders found a note—"

"*It's not our guy.*"

Ray Mandela kept his face blank and his voice easy as he dropped into one of Anthony's guest chairs.

"You're thinking copycat?"

"Yes."

Ray lifted his hands. "Why the hell would anyone want to copy Smiley? The guy's a second-rate criminal at best. Not usually the ones to inspire fans."

"I disagree. For premeditated crimes, what's generally the perp's number one objective?"

Mandela shrugged. "Depends on the crime. To rob the bank, to kill the guy who stole your wife, to hot-wire the car—"

"Wrong," Anth interrupted. "Your number one objective is *not to get caught*. That's what the copycat is copying. He doesn't care about the crime, he cares about the thrill of getting away with it."

Mandela leaned back in the chair and considered.

Anthony charged on. "Eddie might be in the kiddie pool of criminals, but he's not in the news because of that stupid yellow sticker. He's in the news because there've been *lots* of those damn stickers. The guy's dodged us for weeks, and the Cretans of the tri-state area are going to notice. They're going to want in on the fun."

Ray scratched his head and looked skeptical. "It's possible, I suppose, that there could be another player, but without any proof, we've got every reason to assume we're dealing with the same guy. The MO's the same—"

"It's not," Anthony interrupted, knowing he was out of line and not caring. "Eddie Hansen has hit ten homes, all on the Upper West Side. All within five tiny blocks of each other. And now he's in fucking Connecticut? I don't buy it. As far as we know, Eddie Hansen doesn't even have a car. Also, this house has an alarm system. Eddie never touches the ones with alarm systems, regardless of whether the alarm systems are actually *set*."

"He's a criminal, Moretti. A thief. He can damn well get a car if he wants one."

"But why would he?" Anth said more to himself than to his boss. "The guy's been doing just fine with his current MO. Why would he change it up?"

"Maybe he's bored. Or hell, maybe he's smart. Doesn't want to push his luck, especially now that this sketch is all over the place. Speaking of which, are you telling me we haven't had one damn person come forward and say that they've spotted this guy?"

Anth grunted. "It's worse than no one coming forward. *Hundreds* have come forward. I've got my people looking into it, but you know how it goes. We're not exactly in Small-town, USA, asking the local baker to keep an eye on Main Street. According to the reports, Eddie Hansen's managed to be on every possible subway platform from here to Jamaica all within the same hour."

"So you're saying we've got nothing."

Anth sank back into his chair. "That's exactly what I'm saying."

"Wrong," the deputy chief said, leaning forward to tap his finger against the latest file from Connecticut. "We have a brand-new case. The potential for prints..."

"It's not him."

Mandela breathed out long and steady, as though searching for patience. "You want to tell me what the hell is going on here? Why you're being so bullheaded?"

Anthony lifted a shoulder. "My gut says it's not him."

"And I know that in our world, a hunch says a hell of a lot. But Moretti...you're a captain now. You can't afford to rule out a related case because of a hunch. In the past you could pass on your report to your superior and they'd make a note of it, but they sure as hell explored every option."

Anthony opened his mouth, but his boss cut him off. "You see this through. That's an order."

Anth clenched his jaw in anger, although it was at himself as much as Ray. His boss was right. Beyond right. Anth would bet his entire pension plan that this wasn't Smiley, but normally it wouldn't do any harm to treat this latest Connecticut break-in like it was until proven otherwise.

But this wasn't a normal case. This was a high-profile, unsolved string of crimes...

That had now just gone and crossed state lines.

This was bad. Really bad.

Because it meant...

Mandela leaned back in his chair and gave Anthony a steady gaze. "The FBI wants in."

"Fuck," Anthony said, shoving the case file across the table. "I knew it. *Fuck.*"

It was exactly what he'd been afraid of, although no less than he'd expected. Any case that happened in Anthony's precinct was *his.* Even if Smiley had hit another part of the city, it would still be his, if perhaps in partnership with another captain.

But when a string of crimes crossed state lines, you could kiss your case good-bye.

Because that gave the FBI jurisdiction. And when it was a case as high profile as Smiley's had been in the local news lately, you could bet your ass they'd be all over it first chance that they got.

"Ray, you've got to tell them—"

His boss held up his hand. "I told them you had it handled, but Moretti...do you?"

Anth spun around to glare. "What the hell is that supposed to mean?"

"It means that we have a name and a picture of the guy, plus the name and location of his ex-wife, and we still can't catch the fucker. And then I'm hearing reports of you seeing Ms. Walker in your spare time..."

Anthony groaned. The NYPD was worse than a high school hallway after lunch period when it came to gossip. Of course his and Maggie's... *relationship* would get back to his boss.

Because he was a fucking idiot.

Anth pinched his nose, remembering the way he'd stupidly insisted on staying at her house last night.

Remembered the way he promised himself reading just one more page of her story, just one more minute in her presence. Just one more minute of listening to her quiet breathing while she slept cuddled against him as though he were her everything.

He hadn't left until two a.m.

He hadn't glanced at the officers parked outside when he left. He'd merely sent up a silent prayer that whoever was on duty would keep his or her fucking mouth shut.

God, apparently, had been focusing on things other than Anthony Moretti's irrational obsession with Maggie Walker.

"What's going on, Moretti?"

What *was* going on?

Anthony wasn't entirely sure that he knew. For years now—his entire life—he'd had an unshakable focus. It was this clarity of mind that had gotten him to where he was today.

The same ambition that had him wanting to eventually follow in the footsteps of the man in front of him, and beyond.

An ambition he hadn't thought about in days.

Not since he kissed her.

Anthony took a deep breath to steady himself, extending his hands in front of him and resting them lightly on the desk. Focused himself to refocus on the goal, and work was the goal.

Smiley was running circles around the NYPD. No, running circles around Anthony. And so far, he'd let him.

No more.

This was what his father had been trying to tell him. That this case, while seemingly harmless, was a crossroads of his career. If he handled the case flawlessly, it would likely soon be forgotten; it wasn't big enough to register in anyone's memory.

But if he failed; if he fucked it up, they would remember that. A captain who couldn't handle even the simplest of cases was exactly that. A captain. Always. There would be no promotion if he lost this case to the Goddamn FBI. He'd be starting from scratch.

Anth met his boss's eyes. "Ray. I need time."

Mandela shook his head. "You've had time. We need fresh eyes. It happens, Moretti. Nothing to be ashamed of."

"So you've had the FBI take over your cases?"

"No," Mandela said, causing a sinking feeling in Anthony's stomach. "No, but I've had them *try* to take them away from me once or twice."

"How'd you keep the case?"

His boss shrugged and stood. "I offered to partner with them. Let them consult, even though I ran the ship."

Anth nodded even though the thought of partnering with anyone chafed mightily.

"This Connecticut case," Anthony said before his boss could leave. "If it's *not* Smiley, they'll have no jurisdiction, right?"

"Sure," his boss said slowly. "But, Moretti... treat it like it is Smiley. I don't know what's going on with you, but get your head out of your ass."

Anthony drummed his fingers against the desk.

"And in the meantime," Mandela said, leaning back and motioning someone out in the hallway. "This is Agent Garny."

A short blond man in glasses appeared in Anthony's doorway, and Anth would have known who he was dealing with even without his boss's use of the word "agent."

The FBI wasn't just closing in on him. They were *here*.

"Captain," the man said, stepping forward and extending a hand.

Anth stood, shaking the man's hand even though he wanted to order him out of the office. Agent Garny's handshake was firm and efficient, his gaze shrewd and alert.

His expression was friendly without being condescending.

Damn it. Nothing to dislike about the man. So far.

"Captain Moretti, I appreciate you working with us on this one. I hope we can proceed without the stereotypical animosity between the FBI and the local law enforcement."

"'Local law enforcement' makes it sound like I'm a sheriff in a one-horse town in the Wild West," Anth muttered, gesturing for Garny to take a seat. "We're the NYPD."

Translation: We have nearly as many resources as you do. And probably more television shows based on us too.

"All the same, now that Eddie Hansen has moved beyond the city—"

"Allegedly."

Agent Garny's gaze sharpened. "You don't think it's him?"

Anthony glanced at the doorway where Ray Mandela mouthed *partner!* before disappearing.

"No, sir, I don't," Anthony said, shifting his attention back to the agent.

Garny leaned back in his chair. "You're new, right?"

Shit. Not this.

"New to the title of captain, yes. New to the NYPD, no."

"Related to retired Police Commissioner Moretti?"

"His son," Anth said.

Garny nodded. "Never met the man myself, but he's a legend. Didn't like us coming in on his cases any more than you do."

"No, Agent."

"Drop the Agent. Garny's fine. Or Craig."

Anthony sat forward, folding his hands. "Well, Garny, respectfully, let me lay this out. I'm well aware of the fact that from the media's standpoint—and probably the FBI's— Eddie Hansen is running circles around us. But we're close. I swear to you, we're close."

To Anth's surprise, Garny didn't argue or even look surprised. He merely nodded. "The wife, right?"

"Ex-wife." Honestly, why did nobody remember to add that crucial first bit?

"Margaret Walker. Waitress, Brooklyn resident. And still very much the obsession of Smiley."

"Ms. Walker is our only link to Eddie," Anthony agreed. "And we're fairly sure he knows where she works. Probably knows where she lives."

"Good."

Again, Garny surprised him.

"Sorry?" Anth said.

"I've read the reports that you've got her under surveillance. That's good. But I think we bump it up a notch."

"Increase her protection?" Anthony asked, surprised at the suggestion. Not that he would argue with it, but resources in cases like this were iffy considering it was a nonviolent criminal they were dealing with.

"We won't let anything happen to Ms. Walker."

Anthony's eyes narrowed, sensing that he was missing something.

Garny cracked his knuckles. "It's time to tighten our noose, Captain."

"Spell it out for me," Anth said warily.

The agent leaned forward, his eyes gleaming behind the thick glasses. "It's time we put Smiley's affection for Ms. Walker to use. We'll use her to set a trap."

Anthony's stomach twisted at the thought. "You want to use her as bait."

Agent Garny's brow wrinkled. "That's a rather emotional way of putting it, Captain. You've never used an asset to catch a perp before?"

He had. Dozens of times. And he hadn't thought twice about it. If done right—and he always did it right—there was virtually no risk to the person used to entice the bad guys.

But this wasn't just *any* person.

This was Maggie, who snored when she slept, who wrote amusing love stories about teenagers and was damn *good* at it.

Maggie, who'd already been used mightily by every man in her life.

Anthony saw the resolve on Garny's face.

Even worse, he knew Garny was right. This *was* the best shot at getting Smiley. A long shot, but it was something. More than he had now.

He closed his eyes briefly.

God help him. Once again, he was going to choose the job over the woman.

CHAPTER EIGHTEEN

You look like shit."

"I'm going to let that slide, only because you brought whiskey," Anth said, accepting the glass Vincent dangled in front of his face.

His brother sat in a chair across from where Anthony sat slouching on their parents' couch. Sunday dinners had become a "come if you can" affair over the past few years (unlike brunch, which was mandatory), and since Luc had picked up an extra shift and Elena was on a date, it was just him and Vin tonight.

"Where is everyone?" Anthony asked.

"Dad's on the phone with Uncle Mike, and Nonna and Mom are arguing about the brand of pasta Mom switched to."

"So everything's normal then," Anth muttered distractedly.

He felt his brother studying him and narrowed his eyes. "What?"

"Nothing."

Anth snorted. "Since when have you picked up passive-aggressive skills? I know that look. It's not *nothing*. Say it."

Vincent swirled his glass, watching the ice clink against the sides of their mother's crystal tumblers.

Whiskey might not be an Italian thing, but it was definitely a cop thing, at least in this house. There was always a decent supply of bourbon, Scotch, and Johnnie Walker on hand for the shitty weeks.

And this was definitely a shitty week. A shitty *month*.

"Pops told me about the sting opp," Vincent said. "To catch Smiley."

"It's not an opp yet," Anthony muttered. "Just an idea."

A crappy idea, he'd decided. The very thought of putting Maggie in the middle of Bryant Park with an open invitation to Eddie Hansen to come to her made him want to hurl the crystal tumbler against his mother's wallpaper.

"What's the holdup?" Vincent asked.

Anthony took a long swallow of his drink. "Maggie's not on board."

Vin frowned. "You mean she doesn't want to participate?"

"Meaning...I haven't asked her yet."

Vincent stared at him. "Dude."

"Don't *dude* me. You've been talking to Marco too much. Picking up California surfer talk."

"You sound like a grumpy old man," Vincent grumbled.

"This from Mr. Sunshine?" Anth shot back. "Last time I checked you weren't exactly riding a white unicorn around the city, passing out candy to children."

"Yeah, because I'm not a child molester, you sick fu—"

"Problem?"

Both brothers turned to see their father standing in the doorway.

"Yes, there's a problem," Vincent said, standing and going to the sideboard where he refilled his glass. "Your eldest son has his head up his ass. Drink?"

"Yeah," Tony said gruffly, ambling over to the second chair where he sat across from Anthony. Vincent handed his father a glass, then took the chair next to Tony's.

Anth rolled his eyes. "Great. Facing the firing squad."

"I only *wish* I had my gun," Vin said.

Tony took a sip of his drink before setting it on the table. Started to lean back, then shifted again, reaching for a coaster and replacing his beverage.

Anth nearly smiled at the gesture. His father may be the patriarch of the house, but his mom definitely was in charge.

"This about the girl?" Tony asked Vincent, never taking his eyes off Anthony.

"Obviously," Vin said.

"He likes her," Tony said.

"Definitely," Vincent confirmed.

Their father nodded thoughtfully. "You haven't told her about the sting opp?"

Anth pointed a finger at his own chest. "Oh, I'm sorry. Are you talking to me directly now? I thought the two of you would just proceed like I wasn't here."

"Wouldn't *that* be nice?" Vincent said into his glass.

Tony leaned forward, linked his fingers together, and studied his oldest son. Anth resisted the urge to squirm. He was thirty-six. Well past the age where he should have to explain his career or his love life to his father.

But of course, they were Morettis, and the distinction between career and family was nonexistent.

"You know, Anth, the sooner you catch Smiley, the sooner you can date Maggie, clear and free."

Anthony blinked in surprise. Not what he'd expected his father to say, and since he didn't do well with the unexpected, he blurted out something he wasn't at all sure was true. "I have no intention of dating Maggie."

"Bullshit," Vincent said around an ice cube. "Your head's so far—"

"Oh, fuck off." Anthony's temper ignited as it often did when confronted with the most irritable of his three brothers. Vincent pushed his buttons on the best of days, but then there were times when his younger brother just plain went too far.

Vin held up his hands. "Hey, don't take it out on me just because you—"

"Oh, enough," Tony said, directing the order at Vincent for once. "You, of all people, don't get to badger your brother about being an idiot when it comes to women."

Vincent had had one foot crossed over his knee, but he dropped both feet to the ground and sat up at his father's statement.

"What do you mean, 'me of all people'?"

"You know exactly what I mean." Tony took a sip of his drink.

"Obviously not," Vincent snapped.

Anth watched the entire interaction with interest. He knew, of course, what his father was talking about. *Who* his father was talking about.

Jill Henley was Vincent's other half. His cuter, nicer, more smiley half, obviously. But if there was ever a male/female duo destined for romance, it was those two.

Only his brother was too damn blind to see what was right in front of him.

Anthony studied Vincent, saw the torment there, and silently amended his previous thought. Or maybe Vincent knew exactly what was right in front of him. Maybe there were reasons he held himself back from Jill.

Reasons Anth had never bothered to ask.

"This isn't about me," Vincent finally grumbled. "I'm not the one who's got a boner for an informant."

Anth mentally crossed his fingers that his father would linger on Vincent's love life a bit longer, but no such luck. Tony's attention swung back to him.

"Son, do you know how many sting operations I did in my day?"

"A billion?" Anth said, knowing his father was going to name some astronomical number to prove his point, and wanting to get it all over with.

"Close," his father said with a decisive nod. "And you know how many went south?"

Anthony didn't bother to respond, just continued to sip the now watered-down whiskey until his father got down to it.

"One. One case."

"Oh, BS," Vincent said. "You're telling me all but one were successful? No way."

"Well, no, I didn't say they were all successful. But collateral damage? Only one case. One case out of hundreds."

"I thought you said it was a billion?" Anth asked.

His father jabbed a finger in his direction. "You're deflecting. Deflecting because you're scared something will happen to the girl and it'll be on you. But, son, this isn't that girl. Maggie isn't that Vannah character. And her life isn't on you."

"It sure as fuck is if I put her in the middle of a criminal investigation!" he lashed out, angry that his father would dare to mention Vannah.

"We're not talking about luring a serial killer to a lone woman in a deserted warehouse. We're talking about a B-player criminal coming to a public park in the middle of Manhattan."

Anthony stared stubbornly into his drink.

"Pops is right," Vincent said, surprising Anth with his gentler than usual tone. "Maggie won't be in any danger. You'll be there. The FBI will be there. Luc and I will be there, plus Jill—"

"And I'll *for sure* be there."

All three men turned to see Anthony's grandmother standing in the doorway.

"Mother, no way in hell will you be anywhere near this," Tony said wearily.

Nonna folded her arms across her flat chest, her eyes getting that narrowed, stubborn look that Anthony knew all too well. It was a trademark Moretti move.

"I'll bring my sharpshooter."

"Question." Anthony lifted a finger. "Do you know what a sharpshooter is?"

"Absolutely. And I'll bring one."

"Wrong," Anth said, making a buzzing noise. "A sharpshooter is a person."

Nonna scowled. "Well, fine. If you're going to be particular about it, then I won't *bring* a sharpshooter, I'll *be* a sharpshooter."

"Oh my God," Vincent muttered.

"Maggie would want me there," she persisted.

"Not with a firearm, she wouldn't," Anth's mother said, coming into the doorway.

Nonna bristled. "I know how to shoot."

"When was the last time you actually held a gun?" Maria said, folding her own arms to match her mother-in-law's posture.

"1964," Nonna said proudly. "Back when people weren't so—"

"Okay," Tony said, standing. "Enough. Mother, no guns. No anything. Just . . . stay out of police business."

"Well, who will take care of my Maggie?" Nonna said.

"Anthony will," Maria said. Her tone was matter-of-fact.

Anth rolled to his feet, starting to put his glass on the table and then tugging a coaster toward him when he caught his mom's look. "Ma, it's not that simple. Even if I did feel good about putting her into the middle of a trap for Smiley, there's the not-so-minor problem that she hasn't agreed to do it yet."

"She refused to help?" Maria asked.

Anth tugged his earlobe. "Not exactly. More like—"

"He hasn't asked her yet," Vincent said for him.

"Right. More like that," Anthony said sheepishly.

"Well, don't worry," Tony said with a wave of his hand, heading out of the room toward the kitchen as though it was all decided. "That woman is strong. If she can handle the Darby Diner on a Sunday morning shift, she can handle sitting pretty in a park with a dozen policemen swarming around her."

"We're asking a bit more than that," Anth said quietly. "The woman crossed state borders and changed her phone number to get away from Eddie Hansen. We're asking her to face him again."

"True," Maria said thoughtfully. "But she has something now that she didn't before."

"A gun?" Nonna asked. "I could teach her to shoot."

His mother's eyes never left Anthony. "No. She has *you*."

His mom gave him a meaningful look before regally leaving the room. His father and grandmother followed, leaving him and Vincent alone.

Anthony gave his brother a bemused look. "You know what I can't wait for? When it's your turn to be under their microscope."

"Not gonna happen," Vin said, clamping him on the shoulder as he walked past.

"Why, because your cop record is so flawless?" Anthony asked irritably.

"Nah," Vin said into his whiskey glass. "Because I've never been stupid enough to fall in love."

His brother turned away and missed Anthony shooting him the bird.

Anth wasn't *in love*.

He didn't know what *in love* felt like.

But he did know that whatever the hell he and Maggie were mixed up in was complicated as hell.

CHAPTER NINETEEN

Maggie had long ago recognized that the best things in life were often the simple pleasures.

Taking your shoes off after a double shift.

Heck, taking your *bra* off after a double shift.

A glass of cold water on a horribly humid August afternoon.

The happy grin of a baby on a subway.

And today, Maggie was discovering a new pleasure, long forgotten since Gabby had moved to Denver:

Girl time.

Actually, if Maggie were totally honest, she'd have to admit that she hadn't had this sort of unabashed girl time since even *before* her best friend moved across the country.

It wasn't that Gabby had dumped her after Maggie had gotten divorced. Far from it. But Gabby's relationship had been soaring just as Maggie and Eddie's had been exploding, and although her best friend had had her back—

fiercely—back then, their conversation had all been about Eddie, and Maggie's escape from him.

It had been years since she'd enjoyed the pleasure of chatting with women about absolutely nothing of substance.

"No, no, no," Elena was saying as she shifted half a dozen shopping bags from one hand to the other. "No *way* are we going lingerie shopping. We've already been to like a million different stores."

"Um, no," Jill said as she led the way down the crowded sidewalks of SoHo. "*You* went to a million different stores where the rest of us couldn't even afford a key chain, and watched you buy eighty pairs of shoes with your attorney salary."

"Hey!" Elena said, swinging one of her bags so it hit Jill in the butt. "Who insisted we go in all of those designer stores, and who insisted I need all the shoes?"

Jill sighed. "I can't help it. I'm a glutton for punishment."

"Well, *that's* obvious," Ava chimed in. "You're partnered with Vincent."

"Right?" Jill said, turning around to walk backward, incredibly managing not to walk into anyone. "Get this. Yesterday we went into Starbucks and when I ordered my usual mocha he asked if I was *sure* I wanted the whipped cream. Then he looked at my hips. And *then* he walked away, so I had to pay for his boring drip coffee."

"You could petition for a transfer," Elena said, slowing slightly to check out the window display of a store Maggie had never even heard of. "I mean, there's got to be a way not to be stuck with the same grump for your entire career."

Maggie watched Jill carefully at this suggestion and noted that the other woman's smile slipped slightly at the suggestion, before the smile widened again even brighter than before. "Totally! I should. Okay, but seriously, El, we're not going in that store. I want to find some sexy panties for my date on Friday."

"And I need a couple new bras," Ava added. "My favorite ones keep getting ripped when Luc—"

Elena held up a hand. "And *this* is why I don't want to go lingerie shopping with this crew. One of you is banging my baby brother and the other *wants* to bang my big brother."

"I do not want to bang Vin!" Jill exclaimed.

Ava and Elena both gave her a look, and her wide blue eyes blinked. "Oh. *Ohhhhhh.*"

All three of them turned and stared at Maggie, who'd been eyeing a gorgeous blue wool coat in the window that she could never, ever afford.

"What am I missing?" she asked.

Ava flicked her shoulder. "Don't tease us. Are you doing it with Anth or not?"

Elena dry-heaved, but then immediately resumed her curious stare. "So gross. But yes, are you?"

"No!"

The other three women exchanged a glance, and Maggie narrowed her eyes at them. "Is this why you let me into your little shopping circle today? To pump me for information?"

Jill giggled and linked arms with Maggie. "You said 'pump' in the middle of a conversation about sex. Well done, you! And no, silly. We asked you because we *like* you. And because you round us out."

"How's that?" Maggie asked warily, letting herself be dragged forward by the pint-size blonde who was surprisingly strong for being like five-foot-one.

"Well, I'm the bubbly one, and Ava and Elena are always

vying for the spot of sophisticated and sassy, but you are sweet and fierce."

Sweet and fierce?

The sweet, she got. Not because she thought she was, but because she'd been hearing it most of her life. It's what people called other people that they could push around. Maggie didn't exactly consider it a compliment, but she knew Jill didn't consider it an insult either.

But the fierce—

"I'm *so* not your girl for fierce," she said.

"Oh stop," Ava said, coming up on her other side. "If you try to take on the label of self-deprecating, we'll kick you out of the group. No room for that."

"Nope, none," Elena said. "And you are too fierce. I've seen you lift those trays at Darby's. And more important, I've seen you stand your ground to every one of my family members. My dad when he's trying to order the sausage he's not supposed to have, Nonna when she tries to talk about her favorite sex positions, the boys when they're, well, *boys*. You even manage to manipulate Mom into ordering the freaking pancakes instead of oatmeal once in a while, and that is no small feat."

"So, I'm thinking all of that translates more to manipulative than it does fierce," Maggie said.

"Yes!" Ava said, holding up her hand for a high five. "Even better! Manipulative we can work with, assuming, of course, you never manipulate *us*."

"Is that even possible?" Maggie asked dryly. "To manipulate you three?"

"That's a negative," Jill said. "Oh look, here's my store."

Elena threw herself in front of the door before Jill could enter. "Or, another idea…we skip the bra shopping for today so I don't have to imagine my brothers having sex with any of you, and in exchange, I buy us all wine?"

"Done," Jill said quickly.

"Well, that was easy," Elena muttered.

Jill caught Maggie's eye and winked. Maggie smiled back. Apparently she wasn't the only one that could be manipulative. Elena had definitely just walked right into Jill's mission for free wine.

"I know just the place," Ava said. "They have happy hour seven days a week and an awesome by-the-glass list."

She glanced at Maggie. "Do you like wine, Maggie?"

"Love it," Maggie said. "Although I don't really *know* it."

"Fear not," Elena said. "We've got you covered. I know my way around the menu. Although honestly, it's boozy grape juice, so you really can't go wrong."

The sidewalk narrowed again, so they had to walk two by two, Elena and Ava ahead, while Jill fell into step beside Maggie.

"Hey, if this is weird for you, you can say so," Jill said quietly, tugging nervously on her short blond ponytail.

Maggie glanced at the shorter woman. "What do you mean?"

Jill bit her lip, as though debating how much to say. "Vincent told me about your dad's accident. The cause of it. I didn't know if—"

"You want to know if I skip booze because my father's an alcoholic."

Jill winced. "Well…yeah. I mean, I'm just saying we don't want to pressure you to drink after what happened."

Maggie felt a strange lump in her throat at the other woman's caring. It was a tiny gesture. A small thing, really. But the kindness meant something.

"My dad's mistakes are his own," Maggie said quietly.

"How's he doing?" Jill asked.

Great question, Maggie thought. The day after the accident, she'd had every intention of heading back to the hospital first thing.

She'd called to see if he was awake.

He was.

And he hadn't wanted her to come.

It's a long trip, Bug. Don't worry about it. Cory's coming by later and we're going to watch the game.

She'd argued, but he'd been insistent in his easygoing way.

Maggie would like to say that her eyes hadn't watered when her dad had outright rejected her, but the truth was it had stung. A lot. Why wouldn't her dad want his only daughter there after a major car accident?

And then he'd laid it on her.

You really want to help, Bug, I'm going to need a hand with these damn medical bills. Do you have any idea how much they charge for a fucking catheter these days...

It wasn't that her dad didn't need her.

He did. He needed her *money.*

Money she didn't have.

She squeezed her eyes shut. "He's fine. Recovering."

Jill nodded. "I'm glad. And if you ever want to talk...I had an uncle with a drinking problem. It's hard, watching them destroy their lives, you know?"

Maggie knew. She *sooooo* knew.

"Hey, slowpokes," Elena said. "Hurry it up!"

"It's a good thing alcohol's not your vice," Jill said with a grin. "Because the Morettis are so not the people to hang out with if you do. They can drive a saint to drink."

"Yeah, figured that out pretty quickly," Maggie said. "The time I got a sexy text from Anthony, I sought liquid courage and had only a killer headache to show for it the next morning."

Jill skidded to a halt before letting out a whoop and grabbing Maggie's arm, dragging her forward to the door of the wine bar that Elena and Ava had just entered.

"Elena, honey, I thought you'd like to know that Maggie here has been sexting with your brother."

Elena shrieked in horror and Ava tilted her head thoughtfully. "Does one sext *with* someone? Or do you just sext them. Is sext the verb?"

"We didn't *sext*," Maggie said, shooting an apologetic smile at the couple who'd turned around to stare at her. "We just—he just—"

"Say no more," Ava said, holding up a hand. "Not until we get to a table; I want to hear every last juicy morsel."

"And *I* want to know if his incredibly tall stature translates to an impressive stature in other places," Jill chimed in as they crowded into a small four-top in the corner.

Elena swatted Jill across the back of the head. "Maggie, if you answer that question, I'm reneging on my offer to pay."

"I couldn't answer even if I wanted to," Maggie admitted. "We, um..."

"Haven't done it?"

"No," Maggie said, slowly warming up to the topic of talking about sex. It had been a long time since she'd talked about this stuff. Hadn't realized that she wanted to. "But the mixed signals are killing me."

"But he's kissed you, right? You've got to at least give me something; I'm going through a dry spell," Jill said.

Maggie's body tingled as she remembered the feel of

his hands on her back. In her hair. His tongue against hers as he'd pressed her into the wall, coaxing moans from her mouth.

Ava gave a knowing laugh. "I know that look. That's a yes."

Elena propped her chin on her hands and looked at Maggie. "Okay, I don't want to know details. Obviously. But can I just say how glad I am that he's found someone like you?"

Maggie glanced warily around the table. "Well, I don't know that he's really *found* me. I don't even know what's going on. And sometimes I think he only wants me because of my connection to his case."

"No, that's just it," Jill said. "He wants you *in spite* of his case. That's huge. Especially for a guy like Anthony. Especially after everything that he's been through."

"You mean because of that girl...the one you mentioned when you and your mom came into the diner?" Maggie asked Elena, fishing shamelessly.

Jill and Elena exchanged a glance. "It's really his story to tell."

Ava's fingers wrapped around Elena's wrist. "You have to tell her. Anthony never will."

Elena blew out a long breath. "Okay. Fine. It's not like it's any big dark secret or anything. But first...we wine."

Maggie waited impatiently while the other three women debated the wine list, caring not at all about red vs. white, but caring an awful damn lot about this mysterious woman in Anthony's past.

"Okay," Elena said, once they'd decided to start with a bottle of Pinot Grigio, and everyone had a full glass in front of them. "You're sure you want to go here? Because I think we all know, once you go prowling into a guy's past, it's a hell of a lot harder to get out of his future. You'll become entangled."

I want to be entangled.

"I'm sure," Maggie said, taking a sip of wine for courage.

Elena blew out a breath. "Okay, so I don't know all the details. To be honest, when Vannah came onto the scene, we all thought the relationship had the staying power of wet Scotch tape."

"That's...oddly specific," Ava muttered.

"She was a model, and looked it. Tall, thin, waif-ish..."

Pretty, Maggie silently added. Vannah would have been very, very pretty.

"I don't know what the hell she modeled," Jill muttered.

"You knew her?" Maggie asked.

Jill shrugged. "Our appearances at Moretti events over-lapped occasionally. I remember her being...vacant. One of those women who was always claiming to be busy, but never seemed to *be* busy. And despite the fact that she was like ninety pounds, she had this way of sucking the energy out of the room."

Elena nodded. "None of us ever figured out what Anth saw in her, and apparently he couldn't figure it out either, because he slowly stopped bringing her around. When he finally ended things altogether, nobody batted an eye."

Elena dipped her dark head down, staring into her wine, and Maggie watched as her usual confident, smiling face shadowed. And because Maggie already knew how this story ended, she had a pretty good guess what Elena was feeling.

Sadness. Maybe even guilt at her flippant dismissal of this Vannah.

"And then she died," Maggie said softly.

"Yeah." Elena ran a finger around the rim of her wineglass.

"But they were already broken up," Maggie said quietly. "I can see why Anth would be regretful at the loss of life. It's horribly tragic, but...did he still love her? Is that why it continues to haunt him?"

"No," Elena said quickly. "I don't think he ever loved her in that way. And yes, he was saddened by the death of someone so young. We all were. But for Anth, it was more than that."

"Vannah committed suicide," Jill blurted out.

Maggie's fingers covered her mouth.

"God," Ava breathed.

Maggie glanced at Luc's girlfriend. "You didn't know?"

The brunette shook her head. "Luc and I have only been dating a few months. And we've talked plenty about his brother, but he's never really mentioned Anthony's personal life."

"That's because Anth doesn't *have* a personal life," Elena said. "Not since Vannah."

"He blames himself," Maggie said. It wasn't a question. She knew Anthony Moretti. Knew the way he took responsibility for just about every single person and thing that crossed his path. Of course he'd blame himself.

"Yes," Elena said bitterly. "He does. He'd blame himself even if it hadn't been for Vannah's suicide note."

Maggie groaned, already fearing what Elena was about to say. "She blamed him?"

Elena lifted a shoulder. "Him. Her mother. Her psychiatrist. Her landlord. But yeah, Anthony had a whole paragraph dedicated to him."

"That's just… selfish," Maggie said. She knew she wasn't supposed to dislike a dead woman, but she did. She absolutely did.

"What did the note say?" Ava asked, sounding horrified.

"I don't know the specifics. I only know about it at all because Luc told me, and I suspect Luc only knows because he lives with Anth. Anthony barely talks about the good stuff in his life, much less the bad stuff. But I'm guessing it's got something to do with him never being there for her. She was *always* whining about that."

Maggie's heart twisted. That must have shattered Anthony. He made no secrets about his life's dream of being police commissioner, but if this Vannah was the needy, clingy type—and it sounded like she was—then they were doomed from the start.

No wonder he tried to push Maggie away at every possible turn. He had no idea how to reconcile being a cop with being a boyfriend, and after what had happened, was probably too scared to try.

Jill tapped her nails against her wineglass and pursed her lips. "Okay, so here's what we know. Anthony breaks up with his girlfriend, and she kills herself. He takes it to heart, and from what we can tell, hasn't had a serious relationship since. Right?"

"Pretty much," Elena said.

Jill blew out a breath as she reached for the wine bottle and topped off Maggie's not yet empty glass. "You're going to need this more than the rest of us, honey."

"How's that?" Maggie asked.

Jill's wide blue eyes looked at her sympathetically. "Well, based on his history with this Vannah girl, he was bound to keep his distance from you no matter what. And then when you throw in the fact that you're also connected to his most high-profile case…"

Maggie waved this away. "Not anymore. I haven't heard from Eddie since that weird note, which I'm pretty sure was more about messing with the cops than it was about me."

"Perhaps," Jill said. "But things are more complicated now. He already has it in his head that he can't be a good cop *and* a good boyfriend, and now, when he might actually want to *try* to be both, his superiors make him go and choose."

Maggie scrunched her nose. "Hold up, not following. His superiors said he's not allowed to date me?"

"No," Jill said. "I don't even think they know about your guys'…um…thing. But Vin said this sting opp with Smiley is *killing* Anth. Normally Anthony wouldn't think twice about it, but since it's you, he's hesitating and he hates that."

Maggie was about to take a sip of her wine but set the glass back down. "Sting opp?"

"Yeah, the—" Jill's eyes traveled around the table before widening in horror. "He talked to you about this, right? It's common knowledge?"

"I'm thinking maybe the good captain hasn't mentioned it," Ava said quietly.

Maggie's mind was reeling. "Sting opp. That's like… they want to set Smiley up, right?"

Jill covered her face with her hands. "Don't ask me. I can say no more."

"Yes, that's what it means," Elena said quietly. "They basically lure the suspect into a situation they think he'll be likely to enter willingly."

Everything clicked into place at once. "And they think he'll come to meet me."

Ava touched the back of Maggie's hand. "We shouldn't

have said anything, sweetie. I'm sure that the department was figuring out a plan, wanting to get all the details sorted out before mentioning it to you."

"Or," Maggie said, her voice sharp with anger, "*maybe* a certain captain didn't have the guts to tell me about it."

"I'm sure he was planning on it," Ava said. "Eventually."

Maggie pushed back from the table, leaning down to grab her purse. "Ladies, if you'll excuse me . . . I believe *eventually* just got upgraded to *right now*."

CHAPTER TWENTY

It had been a long time since Anthony answered his door to an angry woman. And in the past couple years, at least, the ones who had come by were all out for Luca's blood.

Anth tended to be long gone before women even had the chance to get angry at him.

But Maggie Walker was definitely standing outside of his door. And she was *definitely* angry.

Which was a shame, because she also looked beautiful. He was used to seeing her in her uniform or casual clothes, but today she was wearing form-fitting black pants, some sort of high wedge-shaped shoe, and a tight green sweater that made her eyes sparkle.

Sparkling with rage, but still pretty.

Wordlessly he stepped aside so she could enter.

"Captain," she said icily as she stepped into the apartment he shared with Nonna and Luc.

And speaking of his grandmother...

"Oh, Maggie!" she said, appearing at his shoulder. "I didn't know you were coming over! Had I known, I wouldn't have made plans with my latest beau."

Anthony refrained from rolling his eyes. He was unfortunately all too accustomed to his grandmother having a "latest beau." She was on a one-a-month schedule, although where she met them, she refused to say.

"Hi, Mrs. Moretti," Maggie said, her expression softening slightly when she looked at his grandmother. "I didn't know I was coming over either."

Nonna clapped her hands together. "A surprise booty call. I love it!"

Anthony pinched the bridge of his nose. "Where did you hear the words 'booty call'?"

"*The Bachelor*," she replied matter-of-factly. "Which, I've been thinking, I wonder if there isn't room for that type of show for the older generation. Maybe set in a retirement home and instead of handing out roses, they could hand out walkers—"

"I'm not here for a booty call," Maggie said.

Nonna frowned, finally noticing the edge in Maggie's tone, the tension around her mouth. "Uh-oh. You're mad at him? Why?"

Anthony fully expected Maggie to demure, make some polite excuse until they were alone. She didn't.

"I am mad at him, yes. I just learned that he's been arranging a sting operation in which I am the bait and forgot to mention it."

"Oh, he didn't forget," Nonna said, waving her hand. "He's been scared to tell you, because—"

Luc emerged from his bedroom, scooping their grandmother's purse off the kitchen table and coming up beside her to slide it over her shoulder in one smooth motion. "Nonna, let's get going, shall we?"

"Where are you going?" Anthony asked his brother. "Thought we were going to watch the game."

Luc held up his cell phone. "Ava texted. Told me to clear out."

Maggie nodded at that. "She was there when I found out. She's also the one who gave me your address. Helpful girl that Ava."

Anthony grunted. "I'll be sure to thank her."

Luc blew Anth a mocking kiss before leaning down to peck Maggie's cheek, all the while ushering their grandmother out the front door.

"I can be your sharpshooter!" Nonna hollered just before Luc closed the door.

Normally, Anthony relished the silence when he got a moment to himself. Solitude was a rarity with two roommates who also happened to be family.

Now, however, the silence felt different. Dangerous.

Maggie took a step forward, and he barely remembered to hold his ground despite the fact that he had several inches on her.

Yep, he was definitely in danger all right.

He cleared his throat. "Ava told you?"

"Jill, actually. Although it could have just as easily been Elena or Ava, because of the four of us on the girls' shopping expedition, I was the only one left in the dark."

Shit. On one hand, he was glad that the females of his family had decided to include her. Maggie needed them. Needed friends. Needed decent people in her life.

But on the other hand...

Shit.

He had not seen this coming. He'd thought he'd have time to figure out how to phrase things.

"Can I get you a drink?" he asked, taking the coward's way out and moving toward the kitchen.

"I'd rather have answers."

He pulled out two beers anyway, popping the cap off both before handing one to her. She took it but didn't drink. Just stood there watching him with quiet, simmering eyes.

"I was planning to tell you."

"Were you now?" she asked.

"I just... we needed to get all the kinks worked out. I wanted to have all the information in place, the plan in place, so that you knew you wouldn't have to worry."

"Uh-huh. So keeping me in the dark was for my own benefit."

"Yes," he said, a little relieved that she understood.

"I'm calling BS," she said, taking a sip of her beer and sauntering farther into the apartment as though she belonged there.

"Sorry?" he asked, distracted by the way the black pants hugged her ass, and the way her high heels made her hips sway when she walked.

She turned back around and leveled him with a steady gaze. "I think you didn't mention it because you were scared. I just don't know if it's because you were scared of my reaction, or scared of something else."

Of course I was scared of the something else. Scared that something will happen to you, and it'll be on me.

But since admitting *that* wasn't an option, he opted for sarcasm.

"Gosh, I can't imagine why I'd be scared of your reaction. You're not overreacting at all."

Her eyes turned lethal, and he amended his previous assumption. Sarcasm was *not* safer. With a furious woman, it was gas on a flame.

She moved toward him slowly, setting her beer bottle on the counter and then continuing until they were nearly chest to chest.

"Do you have any idea," she said softly, "what it's like to be the last to know? To have other people making decisions about your life as though you're not worthy of having a say?"

Panic made his chest tighten and he set his own beer aside, reaching for her arms. "No. No, that is not what this is."

Her eyes clouded. "Then what? You want to use me as bait, and you can't even tell me?"

Anth tightened his fingers a little on her arms. "You make it sound like I wanted to trick you into it. That's not—I just wanted to make it really easy for you to say yes. I wanted to show you that there was no danger, and that—"

"You didn't have to convince me," she said quietly.

His brain derailed. "What?"

"You wouldn't have had to convince me. If you'd just told me you thought that it was your best shot of catching Eddie, I would have said yes."

"I don't think you understand. We want to use you as bait. Put you out in the open, by yourself, and use you to lure Eddie Hansen in."

"I understand all that." She set her hand on his chest, the touch tentative. Then she looked up at him. "But I trust you."

He gritted his teeth. "You shouldn't. You don't even know me."

She smiled then, the first smile since she'd come storming in looking for a fight. "I know you're a good cop. The best cop."

Anth ran a hand over his face, feeling tired. "That's just the thing, Maggie. I am a good cop. A damn good one. But only when that's *all* I am. With you…things are muddied. Complicated. You may trust me, but I don't trust myself."

She flattened her palm more firmly against his chest, over his heart.

"What is it you're afraid of?"

I don't know.

He couldn't put a name to the stark fear inside him. Could barely even acknowledge it to himself, much less to her.

All he knew was that he was used to being in control. *Had* to be in control. And with her…

He wasn't.

Not even close.

She nodded her head slowly when he didn't answer, and he had the strangest feeling that this woman understood his silence. Understood the words he couldn't say.

"I don't know how to do this," he said quietly.

She smiled up at him. "What makes you think I'm asking you to do anything?"

Her tone was playful, but he'd never been good at playing games, so he spoke straight.

"You're here. You're touching me. You want something."

Her eyes went smoky, and too late Anthony realized he was wrong: Maggie Walker's next words proved that she wasn't playing games after all.

"You're right. I do want something, Captain Moretti. I want *you*."

Her hand slid up behind his neck, pulling his face down to hers.

And she kissed him.

CHAPTER TWENTY-ONE

For a heartbreakingly awful moment, Maggie was terrified he'd push her away. Or not respond at all, just enduring the kiss, which would be infinitely worse because it meant he felt *bad* for her.

Then that horrible moment turned into two... and then to five...

And then Maggie had to face the fact that his lips weren't moving against hers. His hands weren't touching her.

It was just her on her tippy toes, kissing a man who didn't want to be kissed. At least not by her.

Oh my God.

Maggie pulled her mouth away from his the same time she sank back to the balls of her feet, although it took her a few seconds to realize that her hand was still hooked—yes, *hooked*—around the back of his neck like a desperate cat trying to climb an immobile object.

She jerked her hand away from him, using it to cover her mouth, then her entire face.

"Oh my God," she muttered, out loud this time.

"Maggie." His voice was gruff.

She could only shake her head. "Don't. I'm sorry I did that. It was...oh my God," she muttered yet again.

"Stop." His fingers wrapped around her wrist, yanking it away from her face. "Don't do this. Don't be embarrassed."

She stared at him, aghast. "Oh, I'm well past embarrassment. Not an hour ago I was sitting across from three women who I sincerely hoped might become friends, only to find out they knew more about my life than I did. *That* was embarrassment. Fast-forward fifty minutes or so, and it gets worse, because I go and throw myself at a guy that doesn't want me back—"

"I want you back."

His blunt admission stopped the rest of her rant.

"You do?"

"Yes."

"Then why—"

"Because I don't do this."

"Sex?"

His eyes flared, all but searing her with the sudden heat flashing between their gazes. Between their bodies.

"I don't do relationships," he said through gritted teeth.

"I don't remember asking for a relationship," she shot back. "I remember putting my lips against yours and feeling nothing. It was like kissing a fish."

This time when his eyes flared, there was anger, and his grip on her arm tightened. "I'm not going to have casual sex with you, Maggie."

She lifted her chin. "Why not?"

"Because I like you!"

He looked as startled by the outburst as she felt.

It was hardly romantic, especially when blurted out reluctantly. But from a man like Anthony Moretti who, from what she could tell, kept his thoughts close and his emotions closer, it was enough to make a girl swoon.

"I like you too," she said softly.

He swallowed and took a step back. "So, you get it."

She blinked. "No, I don't get it. Pretty sure we're not even talking the same language."

He reached for his beer, although he didn't take a sip, which told her it was more a self-protection mechanism than anything else. "You're *good*, Maggie. You deserve the kind of guy that will make you dinner every night. Take you out on weekends. Bring you coffee in bed, and stop by and see you at work on his lunch break. I'm not that guy. I'm at work more than I'm at home, I barely remember to call my mother, I bring my work home with me more often than not..."

She stared at him for several seconds, trying to read the flurry of emotions on his face —frustration, want, anger— and wasn't surprised in the least when he settled on stubbornness.

Something shifted then. The balance of power. And this time it was in Maggie's favor.

For as long as she'd known Anthony Moretti, she'd been trying to measure up. Trying not to embarrass herself, trying not to spill on him, embarrassed by her small apartment, embarrassed by her family, even her dog...

But something was shifting.

This time, Maggie understood that maybe his life wasn't any easier than hers. That he had his own demons to fight.

Only ... he wasn't fighting. He was giving up.

She felt an unfamiliar spark of anger.

She could sympathize about what had happened with his ex-girlfriend certainly, but did that really excuse the fact that he was letting external circumstances dictate his life?

The fact was, he was being a coward. By shutting himself off from risk, he was also shutting out the chance for something *more*.

"I can't do complicated," he said when the silence stretched on.

Maggie nodded. Pursed her lips. Maybe it was time to take a risk.

Time to call this complicated man's bluff.

She picked up her beer and took one last sip before setting it back on the counter. "Okay then," she said simply.

Maggie started to move past him toward the front door. She paused when their shoulders were even, although she didn't glance up at him. "That's too bad. Because this is one time when 'complicated' would have been *really good*."

She didn't even make it to the door before he reached for her, pulling her around so hard she slammed up against his chest.

Anthony's fingers were rough as they plunged into her hair, but she welcomed the slight pull. Welcomed even more the possessive pull of his lips on hers when he claimed her mouth, sinking his tongue into the depths of her mouth without preamble or apology.

Maggie's fingers were equally greedy as she held on to his hair, her mouth moving restlessly against his. Anthony tilted his head to take the kiss even deeper and Maggie moaned.

This is what kissing was supposed to be like.

He pulled back, just slightly, his breath hot and heavy against her face. "Say you want this."

Her own breath was ragged. "I already told you that."

His lips found the underside of her jaw. "Say it again."

Maggie closed her eyes. "I want this."

I want you.

Anthony lifted her then, as though it were nothing. Just wrapped his arms around her and swooped her up, Southern-belle-style.

"A girl could swoon with moves like this," she said, lifting her face up so her lips could nuzzle his neck.

Anthony kicked open his bedroom door, and she had the vague sense of a Spartan room—a perfectly made bed, a small dresser, not the tiniest bit of clutter—before he set her on the bed.

Maggie started to scoot back to make room for him, but his hand found her knee, stopping her. "I'm in charge."

Mouth. Dry. Other parts . . . not.

She swallowed, acutely aware that this man could do more with three words and a hot gaze than most men could do with an entire night of lovemaking.

Not that she'd had much experience, but . . .

His eyes drifted over her body before the hand on her knee slid down, over her calf, his thumb sliding under the hem of her pants just below her ankle. Definitely not an erogenous zone that she had known before then, but the brush of his finger against that thin skin did things to all of her nerve endings.

He removed one shoe, then the other, setting them carefully next to the bed instead of tossing them aside, and she wondered what it would take to get him to lose his iron-fist control.

Anthony sat on the edge of the bed then, but instead of climbing over her, tugged her up so she was over him, her knees on either side of his hips.

A hand slid to the nape of her neck and he pulled her mouth down to his, halting her when her lips were mere inches from his.

"Kiss me," he ordered.

She did. Oh, she *so* did.

She kissed him long and hard, and soft and sweet, but all of them—the fast and the slow—were *hungry*.

He kissed her back, his mouth as urgent as hers, although he let her lead the kiss. Let her flick her tongue at the corner of her mouth, let her rake her teeth over his bottom lip, let her nibble his upper lip just a little bit hard, and oh, he liked that one.

His hands were under her shirt now, stroking up her sides, over her back. They toyed with the edge of her bra, and briefly she wondered which one she was wearing, hoping it wasn't too ugly. It didn't matter, however, because his fingers found the plump upper curves of her breasts, tracking back and forth in teasing, toying motions.

She whimpered and his fingers slid downward, under the fabric of her bra so the rough backs of his fingers scraped against her nipples.

Yes. She gasped and pulled away from his mouth, and the way he watched her face as he played with her was almost as erotic as the touching itself.

Only when she was squirming against him, silently begging him for more, did he stop.

"Shirt. Off."

His voice was still commanding, but huskier now.

She tried for one of those sexy shirt-removal things that

girls in the movies always did, but it got stuck on her earring and he gently helped free her.

Her face was flaming when he finally set the shirt aside, both from her awkwardness and realization that she was *not* wearing one of her cuter bras, but in fact, an ugly, light pink cotton affair that had seen better days. Come to think of it, it might have seen better *decades*.

Bras were expensive. One didn't replace them often when nobody else would see them.

But someone was seeing them now.

And from the reverent look on his face, he didn't seem to care that it wasn't fancy lingerie.

His hands bracketed her waist, tilting her forward slightly so that his mouth could reach her breasts. He kissed her softly there, just above the cup, then licked, his tongue diving just under the fabric and she hissed, her hands moving behind her back to remove her bra.

He grabbed her hands before she could undo the clasp, fisting her wrists with one hand. "I'm in charge. Remember?"

She looked down at his glowing brown eyes and slowly nodded, watching as his mouth moved forward again, repeating the sensual touches that were enough to make her pant, but also not nearly satisfying enough.

"Please," she whispered finally, when she could take no more of the almost-touches. "*Please*."

He released her hands then, sliding his own up her back, fingers trailing her spine until all of a sudden the bra was gone, tossed aside with a bit more roughness now, she noticed.

Then his hands slid forward, covering her, and she didn't notice anything at all. There was only the feel of his fingers on her nipples, his rough palms on her soft skin.

And then his mouth—oh, his mouth, and a scrape of

teeth, as he tormented the tip of her breast, then the other, until Maggie thought she'd explode.

"Easy," he breathed against skin moist from his mouth. "Easy, Maggie."

Then he moved her gently off of him before using his body to push her back to the bed, covering her completely as he claimed her mouth.

He was lying between her open thighs now, his hands on the back of her legs, rocking against her, torturing them both with the slide of fabric against fabric.

Impatient, she reared up, sinking her teeth into his shoulder as her nails dug into his back.

He swore softly and pulled back long enough to pull off his shirt. His fingers went for the button of her pants, but she stopped him, sitting up on her elbows so she could look at the magnificence of Anthony Moretti without a shirt.

The man was a masterpiece, all sculpted muscles and firm skin. He had just the right amount of hair on his chest, exactly the way she liked it, and her mouth watered.

"Really?" she asked. "Aren't you supposed to be all about the donuts?"

He gave her one of his rare grins and started to lean down for a kiss, but she slapped a playful hand against his bare chest. "I'm serious, how am I supposed to compete with a six-pack? I haven't seen a gym since high school, things that were never that perky in the first place are starting to sag, and—"

His mouth closed around her nipple, and her words fled.

It was an effective way to shut a woman up. Very.

"I like the way you look," he said when he finally lifted his head.

"Okay," she said dumbly. It was all she could manage, because then her pants were off and then *his* pants were off, and if he'd looked really good with no shirt, he looked even better wearing only boxers.

Her panties didn't match her bra—of course they didn't—but he didn't seem to care when he slid his hand under them, his fingers delving into her wetness without hesitation or apology.

Maggie's back arched and he slid an arm under her head, pulling her face into his neck as his skilled fingers explored her.

Later she would be embarrassed at how quickly she fell apart, shattering against his hand, but in the moment there were only fireworks and gasping breaths.

When she finally opened her eyes, he was watching her with an unreadable expression.

She smiled shyly, and he smiled back, his expression almost tender.

He leaned back, sat up, and rummaged around in his nightstand before unabashedly pulling off his underwear and sliding a condom on in a smooth, practiced motion.

He turned back to her, fingers hooking into the elastic of her panties and pulling down.

She expected him to touch her then, but he merely flicked his eyes back to hers. "Open."

God, why did she find this bossy thing so damn hot?

She spread her legs then, and he was over her.

Her eyes fluttered closed.

"Look at me." His voice was harsher now, as though his self-control was wearing thin, and the second she obeyed, meeting his eyes, he plunged forward, entering her in one glorious, smooth stroke.

He made a sound of guttural pleasure as he sank all the way into her. Then his mouth brushed hers softly, surprising her with the gentleness before his hands found hers and wrapped them around his neck. "Hold on."

He took her roughly, and she relished every moment, loved the agony when he pulled out, loved even more the ecstasy when he pushed back in.

His pace quickened, his fingers greedy where they dug into her thighs. "Maggie, I can't—I—it's . . ."

She scraped her nails down his back then, and when he came with a quiet roar, Maggie wrapped her arms around his back, holding his large body to her own soft one.

When his breathing finally slowed, he lifted off her, turning away before heading toward the small bathroom connected to his room.

He didn't glance back at her.

Maggie's pleasure slowly gave way to discomfort.

What now?

Gingerly she sat up, glancing around until she spotted her shirt and reached for it. Another scan of the darkened room showed her panties and bra scattered across the floor.

She bit her lip, scooting toward the edge of the bed, realizing she was going to have to wander around his bedroom, picking up her various clothing items like a . . . like a . . . she didn't even know what, but it didn't feel good.

Maggie swallowed. This was what she got for thinking she could do casual.

Anthony Moretti had known her better than she'd known herself. She didn't like this at all. She wanted cuddles and postcoital affection, or at least conversation, and he'd all but told her that he wasn't the man for that—

"What the hell are you doing?"

She glanced up to see him standing unabashedly naked in the doorway.

Maggie held up her ratty bra in explanation.

He was across the room in two steps, tossing the ugly garment aside. His arm around her waist was firm as he pushed her back toward the bed, using his other hand to yank back the covers. "I'm in charge, remember?"

She licked her lips, thoroughly confused. "I thought that was only in bed."

"Which is exactly where we're going," he said.

He slid beneath the covers, scooting to the middle of the bed before looking up at her expectantly.

She stared at him. "You want me to . . . stay?"

He lifted an eyebrow.

Her heart swelled. Yes, actually swelled, and she didn't care that that wasn't an actual medical *thing*.

"Okay, but can I borrow a T-shirt, or—"

He gripped her wrist, tugging her forward into the bed.

Okay then. They were sleeping naked, apparently.

"Bossy," she muttered as she rolled to her side and felt him curl up behind her, the best Big Spoon *ever*.

"You once said you liked me bossy," he whispered.

"So I did," she murmured, all but purring at the warmth of his big arm around her.

"Maggie," he whispered, just as her eyes started to close.

"Hmm?"

He was silent for a long moment. Then, "Nothing. Go to sleep."

So she did. But in her dreams, he finished that sentence with something else entirely.

CHAPTER TWENTY-TWO

Are we sure this will work?"

Anthony shot an annoyed look at the speaker, a cocky-looking FBI agent whose name he'd already forgotten, but Ray Mandela beat Anthony to the setdown.

"Nothing is ever *sure* when we're dealing with known criminals," Ray snapped.

Anthony's hands were on his hips as he made what had to have been his hundredth pace across the floor of the office building they'd taken over for what the other guys had started referring to as "Sting Smiley."

The neon lights and deserted cubicles were depressing as hell, and the whole place carried the faint smell of tuna, but the floor was vacant, which was ideal.

Even more important, it had an unobstructed view of Bryant Park, where Eddie Hansen would hopefully be coming to meet Maggie in—Anthony glanced at his watch—twenty minutes.

Vincent appeared by his side. As a homicide investigator in another precinct, he absolutely shouldn't be here, but Mandela had become resigned to the fact that Morettis traveled in packs, and said nothing. And everyone else was likely too wary of Vin's ever-present glower to even suggest he should be elsewhere.

"She'll be fine," Vin said gruffly. "Jill's down there. So is Luc."

So were a dozen of Anth's best men and women, but he felt better knowing that his family was surrounding Maggie, and could be at her side in seconds.

He only wished *he* could be. Being up here, watching it all go down...he felt helpless.

"You think he'll show?" Vincent asked, for Anth's ears only.

Anthony's shoulder lifted. "Hard to say. Maggie doesn't have his phone number or current address, but she's pretty confident that one of the people she reached out to will know how to contact him."

That had been one of the worst parts of all this. Forcing her to delve back into a life she'd obviously tried to put behind her.

No, that wasn't the worst part. The worst part was the nagging suspicion that she was doing it for *him*.

It didn't feel good.

But the sex...oh God. The sex had felt *great*—more than great.

Everything that happened after though...

The morning after their night together, he'd come out of the shower to a sleeping Maggie. And had wanted nothing more than to crawl back into bed with her, when what he'd *needed* to do was head into the office and tell that the opp was a go.

And then it had gotten worse, because she opened her eyes. Smiled at him.

His heart had felt both too big and too small in that moment. Maggie Walker's smile had always gotten under his skin. Maggie Walker's smile while naked in his bed...

Anthony growled at the memory. He was in serious trouble.

"Quit with whatever you're thinking," Vin said, snapping him back to the present. "She agreed to this. Free will."

"Yeah, but why," Anth said, hands resuming their previous stance on his hips. "*Why* the hell would she help us out? She gets nothing out of it."

His brother's look was almost pitying. *You know why.*

And there it was. Confirmation of exactly what he was afraid of. That she was doing this for him.

The noise in Anth's earpiece had mostly been a bunch of chatter and setup until this point, but things had quieted down. It was nearly time.

He glanced again at his watch. 12:55. Maggie's message to their mutual friends had been for Eddie to meet her at one o'clock at one of the benches on the north side of the park. The side where Anthony and his team would be able to see her most clearly.

His eyes skirted around the area, seeking and immediately finding the plainclothes officers ready to move in the second they had eyes on Smiley.

To his right, he saw Luc and Jill, where they sat laughing on a park bench, looking to the rest of the world like a happy couple completely absorbed in each other's inside jokes. He knew better. Knew that both of their eyes had been moving constantly. Watching. Waiting.

Only then did he let his eyes go to Maggie.

They'd agreed it would be best if she wore her diner uniform. Eddie would likely watch her before approaching, and the hope was that he'd be less wary if it looked like she was just coming or going from a work shift.

Her long brown hair was back in a ponytail, her purse tucked by her side as she sat alone on the park bench.

He knew everyone else was seeing a pretty waitress taking in some fresh air in a public park, but Anth saw her differently.

Saw the way her fingers clenched too tightly in her lap. The unsmiling flat line of her mouth. The tension in her shoulders.

She was nervous.

He wished he could talk to her. He could, of course. She was wearing an earpiece so that they could tell her to get the hell out if it came to that.

All he had to do was un-mute and tell her...what, exactly?

Agent Garny's voice crackled over the line. "You're doing just fine, Ms. Walker. You're doing great. This will all be over in minutes."

As they'd instructed her, Maggie didn't respond. Didn't jump. But the thumb of her left hand ran idly over the inside of her right wrist. Their signal that she'd heard, that she was okay.

He focused his binoculars, zeroing in on her face, just for a second, willing her to look at him even though she shouldn't.

Her eyes never lifted.

Good girl. All it would take was one wrong glance on her part at one of the plainclothes cops or up here to their location and Eddie would hightail it out of there.

Of course, the damn man had to show up first.

"Where is he?" Vin muttered.

The thought was echoed shortly after by Agent Garny, who was giving Anthony a run for his money in terms of the award for pacing.

Anth didn't blame him. This whole fool plan had been the FBI's idea. Not that Anthony was opposed to the concept, it was just...his gut wasn't feeling good about this one. Smiley had been smart so far. And based on the note he'd sent Maggie, he knew she was connected to the NYPD. Connected to *him*.

But if there was even a chance that Eddie's obsession with Maggie was stronger than his sense of self-preservation, they had to take it.

His binoculars scanned the park, looking for anyone that resembled Eddie Hansen, focusing on the people wearing hats and sunglasses in an effort to disguise themselves.

"Red jacket, northeast corner." A low female voice crackled in his ear. Officer Teeks. One of his best.

Anth swung the binoculars in the direction she'd indicated and immediately spotted the man in question. Average height, light blond hair, and sunglasses despite the overcast, might-rain-any-minute weather.

Anthony tensed, then watched as the man strolled, hands in pockets, into the park.

Tensed further when he saw the man was indeed ambling toward Maggie.

He glanced at her, but if she recognized him as Eddie, she wasn't giving anything away.

The man grew closer and Anth swore his heart was in his throat. Saw the officers circle imperceptibly closer under the guise of doing something else...throwing away the trash, talking on the phone...

The man in the red jacket approached Maggie's bench. She glanced up. Glanced away again, nothing flickering on her features.

"It's not him," Anth muttered. "Damn it."

The man walked past, continuing his easy amble, as though he didn't have a care in the world. Completely unaware that had he so much as *looked* at Maggie Walker he'd have been surrounded by law enforcement.

"It's one fifteen," Mandela said. "How much time do we give him?"

"Till one thirty," Garny said. "Ms. Walker said Eddie always runs late."

"Yeah, but you don't *run late* when the ex-wife you're not over finally contacts you," Mandela argued.

"You do if you suspect there might be a greeting party," Vincent muttered low enough so that only Anth could hear.

"Heads up." It was Luc's voice. "Maggie's one o'clock."

Anth immediately looked in the position his brother indicated, seeing nothing out of the ordinary. Only a kid...

A kid who was approaching Maggie.

It could be nothing. The boy looked around twelve, and could just be practicing his flirting skills, or looking for directions...

Or he could be handing her a motherfucking note.

"What the hell?" Vincent said as the kid handed her a piece of paper.

"Grab him," Anthony and Agent Garny said at the same time.

The boy was flanked by two cops seconds later, but Anthony's eyes never left Maggie.

Watched her face as she glanced down at the note in

confusion. Watched as she opened it. Watched as confusion turned to dismay.

She glanced up at the window of the office building then, and though she'd have no way of knowing where he stood, her eyes seemed to find his immediately.

"Abort," Garny said.

Maggie was surrounded then, and everyone started talking at once.

"What does the Goddamn note say?" Mandela asked.

Maggie handed it over to Sergeant Corvalis, who read it aloud.

Margaret—

>*He'll never have you.*

>>*—E*

"The *fuck* does that mean?" Mandela asked. "Who'll never have her?"

Anthony couldn't answer. His mind was too busy reeling with the reality of what he'd done.

Deep down he'd always wondered if maybe his strict delineation between work and pleasure wasn't overkill. If maybe it wouldn't be the end of the world if those two worlds collided.

But now he knew.

Knew who the *he* Eddie referred to was.

Eddie had seen them together, and it had tipped him off.

And just like that, his feelings for Maggie might have just cost him this case.

CHAPTER TWENTY-THREE

It's not like she went throwing herself into his arms. She didn't go hump his leg like a needy little dog.

But in the forty-five minutes since the entire team had come out of that damn office building and into the park, Anthony hadn't looked at her. Not once.

She told herself it was because he wanted to talk to the kid that delivered the note first. That made sense.

Then he needed to talk to his people. That made sense too. He was a cop first, and she got that. Respected it.

But he was also a *man*. She knew that better than anyone here. The night they'd spent together was nearly a week ago, but she could still feel his mouth on hers. His hands on her body.

Yes, he was definitely a man.

A man who was one hundred percent avoiding her.

"Damn bureaucratic bullshit. It's always like this when

the FBI is involved." This from Luc, who hadn't left her side. Neither had Jill.

Even Vincent was hovering nearby. He'd rested a heavy hand on her shoulder when he'd first seen her.

"*Totally*," Jill agreed with a quick nod. "There's all sorts of crazy protocol to follow."

Maggie gave them both a knowing look. "And this protocol doesn't involve interacting with the bait, is that it?"

Luc and Jill exchanged a look, both opening their mouths to cover for Anth at the same time.

Maggie held up a hand to stop whatever ready excuses they had. She understood their loyalty.

She could even appreciate it.

But it didn't mean she was going to sit around and wait to listen to them spout off some bullshit as to why Anthony seemed to be talking to *anyone* but her.

Even the FBI agent had come over and told her that she'd done everything right, and they were doing everything in their power to make sure she'd be safe. He'd been perfectly nice.

Kind, even.

A man with salt-and-pepper hair made his way over to her. He was wearing a suit, so she figured FBI, but he introduced himself as Deputy Inspector Mandela.

"Anthony's boss," Luc muttered under his breath.

"Ms. Walker, I can't thank you enough for your participation today."

She gave a forced smile. "I only wish it could have turned out better."

He blew out a breath. "Yeah, well…at least we know you were able to reach him. Able to draw him out, even if not directly. You're a link to him we didn't have before."

Agent Garny came up beside the police inspector and they exchanged a look. Finally the agent cleared his throat.

"Ms. Walker, we hate to pry into your personal life, especially given what you've already done to help us out, but… any idea which man your ex referred to?"

Maggie's heart skipped a beat. Strange that she hadn't been prepared for this. She'd been so busy trying to figure out how Eddie had known about her and Anth. Too busy trying to figure out why Anthony wouldn't even look at her…

It hadn't occurred to her that there'd be questions.

Of course there'd be questions.

She just wasn't at all sure she wanted to give answers.

"I'm not really sure," she said, fiddling with her necklace. An ugly locket that was the one and only possession she had from her long departed mother. "The note was vague. It could have been anyone."

"Do you have a boyfriend he might be referring to?"

She shook her head. "No boyfriend."

That much at least was true, she thought, glancing at the broad back of Anthony as he stood talking to one of the female officers.

"Anyone you've been hanging out with, even casually?" Mandela asked. "Anything would help."

She licked her lips, fairly sure that guilt was shimmering off her in waves. She'd never been good at lying.

"Um—"

Luc's hand found her back. "Why don't you take a day to think about it, Mags? No need to add to your stress right this second."

Agent Garny looked ready to argue, but after a glance at Luc and Vincent, he seemed to change his mind.

"Sure." He pulled a card out of his wallet. "If you think of anything. Any names..."

"I'll be sure to tell someone," she agreed.

If he caught the vagueness in her use of the word "someone," he didn't show it.

Both men started to turn away, but Maggie reached out a hand to stop them. "What happens next?"

Mandela ran a hand through his hair, then seemed to remember that there was too much gel and dropped his arm. "We'll regroup."

"Do you think Eddie will steal again?"

"Hard to say. He knows we were onto him here, so he may lay low for a while. Or he may get cocky. The thrill of eluding us outright like this might give him a boost of confidence to act soon."

Agent Garny eyed her. "What do *you* think he'll do?"

Maggie bit her lip, considering. "I think he'll strike again. Soon. He thinks highly of himself. Knowing that he was onto your plan will feed his ego."

"Do you think he'll contact you?"

"I have no idea," she said. "Truly."

They looked disappointed but not surprised.

Maggie really was telling them the truth. She had *no* idea what her ex-husband's next move would be. None. What none of these people seemed to understand is that she didn't know Eddie anymore.

It had been two years since they'd been married, and a lot longer than that since she'd really understood him. If she ever had.

This Eddie who was breaking into other people's homes—she didn't know this version. Not because he'd been particularly upstanding or law-abiding when they'd been together, but because he'd lacked any kind of drive. Even the criminal kind.

She certainly hadn't expected him to hire a kid to deliver a note, although *that*, at least, was in keeping with the Eddie she knew. Lazy and not particularly inventive.

"Did the boy that delivered the note have any information?" Luc asked.

Anthony's boss shook his head. "No connection to Eddie that we can tell. Just a random kid skipping school because he forgot to study for his math test. Said a blond lady pointed out Maggie. Handed him a twenty-dollar bill and asked him to deliver the note."

"Did he say—"

Mandela shook his head. "Nope. He's twelve. Didn't think to ask who the lady was, or what the note was, or where she'd gotten it. Didn't care."

"So this whole thing was for nothing," Maggie said.

"Not entirely. We at least know that whomever you spoke to when you were trying to get ahold of Eddie is in contact with him."

"Which means that they lied when we questioned them about Eddie," Mandela grumbled.

Agent Garny looked unperturbed. "They usually do. People protect their own."

Maggie didn't care about any of that. She'd reached out to old neighbors, old friends, Eddie's sister...everyone she could think of. Only about half of them had bothered to get back to her, and the ones that had bothered had been oozing nosy curiosity.

She hadn't told them crap, not a single detail about her new life, but in the end it hadn't mattered.

Eddie still knew about her and Anthony.

And she had no doubt that the *he* in Eddie's creepy note was, in fact, the tall captain who was still standing with his back to her as though she didn't exist.

Agent Garny and Mandela moved away after thanking her for her help and reminding her to give them a call the second she thought of anything.

Maggie let Jill lead her to a nearby bench, Luc and Vincent following so close behind them Maggie almost smiled at how quickly her life had gone from serving these people their omelets on Sunday mornings to being one of them.

Almost.

Almost one of them.

The back of her neck tingled then, and her eyes immediately sought out Anth, only to see his head turn away before their eyes could meet.

"What's his deal?" Jill muttered to Luc and Vincent.

The two brothers remained silent, loyal to their brother, but Jill's allegiance apparently lay with Maggie because she grabbed her hand and squeezed. "He looks at you every time he thinks you're not paying attention."

"Well, gosh, that's practically better than flowers," Maggie said irritably.

Jill laughed. "I love when you get cranky. For the longest time I thought you were just this sugar puff who never had a cross thought."

Maggie snorted. "Trust me. My thoughts can get very cross."

Luc sat down on the other side of her. "Don't ruin the dream. I picture you as the type that wakes up before the sun, all smiley and full of song as small woodland creatures flock to you."

"Not so much," Maggie said with a wry smile. "I do seem to attract much less delightful creatures, though."

"Ah, of course. Like Smiley?" Luc asked.

"No, more like—" Maggie broke off when she saw Luc had been teasing her.

Maggie blew out a breath. "I guess I should get to work."

"I thought you took the day off?" Vincent asked. "The department was supposed to speak to your boss. Explain the situation."

"They did. I don't *have* to go in. But I might as well. It's not like I'm of any use here."

As she said the words, Maggie sat up very straight, realization clicking into place in the worst possible way.

"I'm not of any use here," she said again.

Jill gave her a puzzled look. "Well, not right this second, no, but—"

Maggie wasn't listening to whatever Jill said next, because she knew. Knew that was exactly why Anthony Moretti had turned his back on her.

You little fool.

She should have known better. Should have seen immediately what was going on.

Anthony no longer needed her.

And people only ever wanted her around so long as they *needed* something from her.

With her mom, it was to have a cute mini-me. When Maggie was little and cute, her mom had taken her everywhere, basking in the compliments over Maggie's darling clothes, adoring the way people occasionally asked if they were sisters.

And when Maggie had grown into awkward pre-teen years and stopped being declared *darling*, her mother had grown bored with the mom role. Maggie had been discarded.

With her dad, the need was money. Always money. And lots of it.

Cory was subtler than her dad; his requests came under the guise of "investments" or "a little help" or "calling in favors."

Even Gabby, as good a friend as she'd been over the years, had pulled back on their friendship once she'd started her family and no longer needed a wing woman to go out on the town at night, or someone to analyze her latest boyfriend's text messages.

And Eddie . . .

Eddie had been the worst. Eddie had *always* needed something. Dinner. His laundry folded. Money for a lottery ticket. Her to fetch him his beers. Her to find the remote. Her to get his sister a birthday present, and call his mom on Mother's Day, and make nachos when his friends came over for the game.

And when she'd finally stood up for herself—told him she wanted to feel *wanted*, not needed, he'd gotten nasty.

But Anthony . . . He was supposed to be different. She was supposed to be something more than a tool for him to use to get his way.

She'd known that he'd *wanted* her assistance on the Eddie case of course, but he'd been oh-so-convincing in his reluctance to involve her, and she'd fallen for it, all but *leaping* at the chance to help him out.

But his plan had been flawed; it had backfired. In his efforts to lure Maggie into luring Eddie, he'd in fact scared Eddie away.

He'd taken a gamble and it hadn't paid off. *She* hadn't paid off.

And now he was done with her.

"I'm such an idiot," she muttered under her breath.

"Hey," Vincent said sternly, kicking the tip of her toe softly with his shoe. "None of that."

"No, I am," she said, standing up. "I'm an idiot."

"You're leaving?" Jill asked.

"Yep. I can't think of anything else you guys need from me, can you?"

"Hey!" Jill said, looking stung. "That is *not* why we're here. You're our friend."

Maggie was instantly contrite. "I know. I'm sorry. It's just...I really don't know what else I can do to help. Eddie's not going to come to me as long as the cops are lurking around me, and the cops aren't going to bother lurking around me if Eddie won't come to me, so..."

"We'll figure out a way to get the guy without you," Luc said softly. "You've done enough."

"Apparently," she said with one last glance at Anthony, only to realize that he'd disappeared. Without a good-bye, much less a thank-you.

She gave Jill a hug and kissed Vincent's and Luc's cheeks, ignoring everyone's worried expression.

"You'll be in touch, right, hun?" Jill said.

"Sure," she said brightly.

Just so long as *Captain* Moretti keeps his distance.

CHAPTER TWENTY-FOUR

Have you called her yet?"

Anthony glared across the dimly lit bar to where his brothers sat across the table. "You mean since you asked me five seconds ago? No."

Luc frowned, and Vin took over. "It's been over a week since Smiley dropped that note off in the park. You haven't talked to her once?"

He slammed his beer down with more force than necessary. "What the hell would I talk to her about?"

Vincent's face flashed with anger. "Dude, I *get* the asshole vibe. I've got some of that going on myself. But you don't sleep with a woman, ask her to do you a rather major professional favor, and then not call her."

Anthony scowled right back at his brother. "You're telling me you call every woman you sleep with?"

"No. But I don't sleep with women like Maggie. I sleep

with women who know the score and are in it for the same thing I'm in it for."

Anth's eyes narrowed. "How do you know I slept with her?"

"Luc told me."

Anth's gaze shifted to his other brother. "How do *you* know I slept with her?"

"Dude, I *live* with you. I know your 'just got laid' vibe, and you were practically radiating it after that night when Maggie came over."

Fuck.

This is exactly why he'd never intended to get involved with her. Now the whole damn family was in on it, and they knew how to complicate everything, and this situation didn't need any complicating.

It was fucked up enough on its own.

Two days after the failed sting operation, there'd been three break-ins in a row. All Upper West Side.

All with mocking thank-you cards, sealed with a fucking smiley-face sticker.

The only good news in the entire thing was that Anthony had been proven right on the Connecticut case being a copy-cat. Turned out the kid living next door to the victims hadn't appreciated their habit of calling the cops when he played his music too loud.

And the kid, being spoiled, entitled, and too smart for his own good, had launched a rather elaborate revenge plan, complete with a scapegoat in the form of Smiley.

Only the fool kid wasn't *that* smart. He'd forgotten the public nature of social media and had bragged not so subtly about his stunt on Twitter.

A full confession followed, which Anth couldn't have

cared less about except that it meant the FBI had backed off.

They'd claimed it was because the Smiley case was back to being a local one, but Anthony was reasonably sure that a bit of pride was involved. Their sting operation had sucked balls, and nobody had any other ideas.

Anth had tripled the•patrol of the Upper West Side in recent days, but Manhattan was a busy town. There was always someone on the streets. Trying to keep an eye out for one man was a needle in a haystack.

Making matters worse, there'd been a reference to Smiley on a national late-night talk show. A small, passing reference, but still...Smiley's notoriety was rising, and with it, Anthony's prestige was slipping.

Hence, he'd agreed to drinks with his brothers, thinking it would be a stress reliever.

It was proving the opposite.

The three of them—four, when Marc was around—had always had one another's backs when it came to women. Respected one another's boundaries, understood one another's limitations.

At least he'd *thought* his brothers understood where he was coming from.

But apparently they had different standards when it came to Maggie. Higher standards.

"Ava thinks you've discarded Maggie now that Smiley's avoiding her. Said you dropped Mags like a hot potato when she quit helping you with the case."

Anthony's beer turned sour in his mouth. "That's bullshit. Where'd she get that idea?"

"Maggie told her. She came over for dinner last night. I stuck around for a while, then cleared out so they could have girl talk."

"*That* was the girl talk? That I'm not calling her because I don't need her anymore?"

Christ.

Vin shrugged. "Well it's either that or you don't *want* her anymore."

"I fucking want—you know what, can we not talk about this?"

"Sure," Luca said easily. Then he turned to Vincent. "Hey, Vin, now that Maggie's available, have you thought about asking her out—"

"Oh, come off it," Anth grumbled. "The family's already tried the 'make Anthony jealous by setting her up with Vincent' routine."

"Yeah, and it worked," Luc said.

"I love how that's the *only* possible reason anyone would set Maggie up with me," Vin grumbled. "As part of a ploy."

Anthony and Luc both ignored him.

"How is she?" Anthony heard himself ask Luc.

It wasn't what he'd meant to say. He'd meant to not care. To let her go for her own good. Because if he let her get even more tangled up in his career than she already was, it would hurt all the more when she realized that the job would always come first.

"She's fine," Luc said.

Anthony nodded, telling himself he was relieved that she was unscathed. Happy that she wasn't missing him.

"On the outside," Luc continued. "But she's different. Sadder."

Shit. *Shit.*

"What the hell happened, bro?" Luc asked.

Even Vincent looked interested. And worried. And when Vin looked worried, things were bad.

"That note that Eddie left," Anthony said, taking a sip of beer. "He mentioned me. I mean he didn't name me, but I *know*—"

"Yeah, we figured that was a reference to you," Luc said. "Dude's pretty familiar with Upper West, and the note happened just days after Maggie came by our place. *On the Upper West Side.*"

"The fucker was watching you. Watching her," Vincent said, looking pissed.

"Do the bosses know?" Luc asked. "That you're the guy in question?"

He shook his head. "No. I'd tell them if it would help with the case, but as it is, it'll only serve to get me yanked from the case."

"Would that be a bad thing?" Vincent asked.

Anth felt white-hot rage flow to his knuckles. "Are you fucking kidding me?"

Vin held up his hands. "Hear me out. This case has been dragging on forever. And while nobody can blame you for getting pulled in by Maggie's appeal, you can't deny you *have* been dragged in. Your perspective might not be what it usually is."

He hated his brother for saying it, but hated the truth of the statement even more.

"So what, I give up the case?" he asked.

"It might be best," Luc said. "Or at least step down. Let someone else lead it."

Great. Now both brothers were siding against him.

"If my first case on record is a fail, I'm going to have a hell of a time moving up," he said.

Luc met him steadily. "Are you sure that's what matters?"

"Of course I'm sure. It's *all* that matters."

His brother's eyes flickered in disappointment, and Luc looked away. Even Vincent seemed troubled.

"Oh, come on," Anth said a little desperately. "If anyone should have my back...if anyone should get it, it should be you two."

"What exactly is it that we're supposed to get?" Vincent asked skeptically. "And are we going to need more beers for this?"

"Look, let's just be straight about this," Anth said, ignoring Vin. "Cops don't make good boyfriends."

Luc opened his mouth, but Anthony cut him off by holding up a finger. "Yeah, yeah, you and Ava are solid, but it took you *months* to get there."

His brother closed his mouth.

"Didn't it?" Anth persisted. "Did you or did you not have serious doubts about whether it made sense to get into a relationship with her? After what you saw go down with Mike. After you saw Mike's widow..."

Luc slapped his palm on the table. Not hard, but from someone as generally easygoing as Luca, it was enough to take Anthony aback. His brother's eyes were angry as they bored into him.

"After I saw Mike's widow," he said, picking up where Anth left off, "I realized what an idiot I'd been."

Anthony frowned.

"Yeah. That's right. I was a *moron*. I thought I was being noble by pushing Ava away. Protecting her. But really I was protecting myself. I was a selfish ass."

And from the look on his younger brother's face, Luc clearly thought Anthony was being an ass as well.

"But—"

"What the fuck are you scared of, man?" Vincent asked, already looking bored with the heart-to-heart.

"I'm not scared." The words were automatic.

"Well, obviously you are if you can't even so much as look at the woman."

"I don't want her to get the wrong idea." He took a sip of his beer but it was warm, and he made a face.

"What idea is that?" Luca asked.

"That I can be a boyfriend. That I *want* to be a boyfriend."

"Huh. And that's what Maggie wants? A boyfriend?" Luc asked.

Anthony opened his mouth to say *yes, of course*, only to shut it just as quickly.

His brother gave him a smug, knowing look. "You've never asked her, have you?"

Anthony slumped back in his chair, feeling foolish. And also feeling like a bit of an ass.

He'd just been assuming, because Maggie was as nice and wholesome and good as they came, that she was only interested in a relationship with staying power.

But that wasn't fair to her. He was shying away from demands that *she'd never placed on him*. Hadn't even had the courtesy to have an adult conversation with her; he'd done a hell of a lot of rambling about his own limitations, but never once had he bothered to ask about her expectations.

"Luc's point is excellent," Vincent said, with a fist bump to his youngest brother. "I mean, here you are assuming that she *wants* to be a groupie of an irritable, egotistical captain, when really—"

"Yeah, yeah, I get it," Anth said irritably. "She may not want me at all."

Except she did want him. In the physical sense. She'd

said so. And he wanted her just as much. More. Their bodies had been perfectly suited, and the way she'd responded to him, arched for him...

"I can't wait to see this," Luc said gleefully.

"We're going to need popcorn," Vincent said. "And maybe a video camera so we can record the moment..."

"What are you two clowns muttering about?" Anth asked, managing to pull his sex-addled mind away from the memory of how she'd felt beneath him.

"We're talking, of course, about getting to watch you apologize," Luca said.

"Pretty sure that'll be a first, you apologizing," Vin said, draining the last of his beer and glancing around for their server. "I'm thinking you'll want to practice on us first, and I've got a long list of grievances with which you can start."

"Fat. Fucking. Chance." Anth stood, reaching into his back pocket and pulling out a few bills, which he threw on the table. More than enough to cover another round for his brothers and the tip.

"You're buying?" Luc asked in surprise. They generally had an unspoken agreement to split the tab equally. Leveled the playing field and allowed them to drink as brothers, not as cops with different ranks.

"Yeah," Anth said tersely. It was as close as he would get to a *thank-you* for their not-so-gentle wake-up call. "But I'm not staying."

He had serious amends to make.

Except not in the way his brothers thought. They wanted him to ask Maggie if she wanted a relationship, and perhaps he would—if he could figure out the words.

But they also assumed the answer Anthony was looking for was *no*. That she *didn't* want a relationship.

They assumed right. If Maggie told him she wanted nothing more than a casual fling, it would be...great. Convenient. *Perfect*, even.

So why did his stomach feel tied up in knots at the thought?

CHAPTER TWENTY-FIVE

In the week since the failed sting opp, and since Captain Moretti had discarded her like a pair of holey socks, Maggie had gotten more writing done than ever before.

Writing had always been a passion, but now it was like a fever. The words were flowing faster than she could get them onto the screen—she could literally see the story unfolding when she closed her eyes.

Her characters' emotions were her emotions—their heartache her own.

Not that Anthony Moretti had broken her heart. Nothing so maudlin as that. But neither had he exactly, um, *called her*.

Nobody from the NYPD had, although the squad car continued to park outside her apartment every evening without fail. Her most frequent babysitters were Officer Jonas and Officer Corrigan who she'd found were actually quite lovely.

She'd started bringing them a slice of leftover pie from the diner whenever she brought some home, and they never said no. Judging from their twin bulging bellies, she was guessing "no" wasn't something very often said when it came to baked goods.

They were kind, and friendly . . . and completely unnecessary.

Because Anthony wasn't the only one that had completely forsaken her. Eddie too had apparently decided that she was no longer worth the effort. She'd kept an eye out for him. On the subway. On her walk home. Through the windows at the diner.

She was really, truly, alone.

Forgotten by men.

Fine. That was just fine.

Maggie shoved a tortilla chip in her mouth, then offered one to Duchess. She still had her dog.

And Elena had invited her tomorrow night to binge-watch some reality show Maggie had never even heard of, so she was on her way to making girlfriends again.

"We don't need males, do we, baby?" She glanced down at the dog and offered her another chip. "Well, *you* certainly don't, being spayed. And *I* don't, because I'm strong, and independent and—"

There was a knock at the door.

She stuffed one last chip in her mouth, fully prepared for it to be the new neighbor next door. A cute twenty-something hipster who liked to stop by on a near nightly basis to see if she'd mind him playing the guitar.

It was considerate, and a little bit flattering considering she was pretty sure it was more a ploy to talk to her. She was far too old for him, and she suspected he knew it, but he was a little shy, and if he wanted to practice talking to women—hey—she could use the eye candy.

But it wasn't the boy next door.

It was a *man*. A very somber, pissed-off-looking man.

"You really should tell your neighbors to make sure the front door is closed behind them," he said irritably.

"So good to see you, Captain," she said as he pushed past her into her apartment.

She wasn't the least bit glad to see him, even if he did look yummy in his uniform.

Duchess, on the other hand, was making Maggie doubt her earlier assertion about the dog being spayed, because she was practically humping the man's leg.

"She's never been a great judge of character," Maggie said, slamming the door with more force than necessary.

He was hunched down, sitting on his heels to pet the dog, but he glanced up at her then, his brown eyes unreadable. "You're mad."

She made a little whatever shrug. "I shouldn't be, right? You told me it was just sex, I said the same. We had an agreement. Nobody got hurt."

"You did."

She went on high alert. "I didn't."

"Well, fine, you didn't," he snapped, standing so quickly and his tone so tense that Duchess gave him a baleful look and retreated to the bed, where more friendly company awaited in the form of her stuffed raccoon.

"Good, so we're sorted then," she said, moving toward the table where her manuscript sat on her computer, interrupted. "So glad you came over to chat about it."

He glanced at her laptop. "You were writing."

"Yes."

"How's it coming?"

She eyed him warily, wondering what his angle was. "Fine."

He looked disappointed at her curt response, and she found herself softening slightly. "It's actually coming along better than fine. I'm nearly done, and it feels...it feels really good," she said, feeling just a little foolish.

He smiled then. A small smile, but a real one. "I'm glad. Can I...what part are you at?"

She started to tell him—*wanted* to tell him all about how her muse was on freaking fire—and how she'd taken the plunge and started researching literary agents that very afternoon, but then...

Then she remembered all of his constant reminders that he couldn't do "this." Didn't want to.

Remembered the sting when he'd turned his back on her. *Literally*.

She shut her laptop with finality, seeing from the flicker of dismay on his face that he saw exactly what it was—a rejection.

"You don't get to have it both ways," she said quietly.

He shook his head, indicating he didn't understand. *Men*.

"I mean you don't get to tell me you're only in it for no-strings-attached sex and then come by whenever you feel like it, pretending like you care."

"I care."

"Yeah?" she asked. "I didn't really get the *caring* vibe when I sat on a cold park bench for a serial burglar to seek me out, and then didn't get a glance much less a thank-you."

He swallowed. "Yeah. About that."

She lifted an eyebrow.

Anthony looked anywhere but at her, then blew out a long

breath, before shrugging out of his jacket. "Got anything to drink?"

"No."

His shoulders rolled, and she sensed he didn't want the drink so much as a distraction. But then he surprised her by speaking plainly.

"The last serious girlfriend I had committed suicide."

"I know," she said quietly.

Surprise had his head jerking back. "I swear to God, my damn family—"

"Cares about you," she completed for him.

"Luc?" he asked.

"Elena," she said. "She didn't tell me in a gossipy way. I think she just wanted me to understand you."

"Do you? Do you understand me?"

She thought about this. "Having a loved one—even a past loved one—end their life would affect anyone, but I think it would haunt someone like you."

"Someone like me?"

"You take responsibility for everything. And everyone. Even if they're not yours to assume responsibility for."

"That's not true."

She smiled softly. "It's *so* true. Your brothers and sister, perhaps, I can understand. Older sibling syndrome. I suffer from it a bit with Cory, although I'm less...controlling. But you do with your parents too; trying to limit your dad's bacon intake, treating your mom like a delicate flower. And with your grandmother, making sure she doesn't get too out of hand. And at work...I imagine you've been labeled a micromanager at work once or twice?"

His wince told her she'd hit the nail on the head, but she continued anyway. "But, Anth, what happened with

Vannah... that wasn't your fault. I imagine she was troubled long before you entered the scene."

"She was my girlfriend," he said quietly. "I should have seen—"

"How long were you dating?"

"Four months. Maybe a little less." His answer was reluctant. Wary.

"And how serious were you? Living together?"

"No, but—"

"How many days a week did you see her? Seven?"

"No, once or twice during the week, and weekends, if I wasn't working, but—"

"And when was the last time you saw her before she died?"

His eyes were shuttered. "Two months. Almost three."

Maggie nodded. "Okay, so just so I'm clear... you dated this woman for less than four months, but it wasn't serious. You saw her for a couple hours each week, and you'd in fact broken up—"

"I get where you're going with this," he interrupted. "You think my family hasn't tried this exact same lecture a million times?"

She reached out, touched his arm softly, despite the fact that she was still a little angry. "Then maybe it's time you start listening to us. We can't all be wrong."

"With all due respect, it doesn't matter what you all think the situation was. Or should have been. She *did* blame me for her unhappiness, whether or not she was right to. She said as much in her note."

"I know, but—"

"No, you don't know," he said, raising his voice. "Do you have any idea what it's like to have someone you once cared about dead of their own choosing? To learn that the reason they did it was because you never made time for them? That you cared about your job more than you cared about her? To have her say *outright* that she wouldn't have done it if you hadn't broke up with her?"

Anth's tone had resumed its monotone drone, but his eyes were agonized, and Maggie swallowed a fierce burst of rage at Vannah's unspeakable selfishness. She'd been miserable, and Maggie was sorry about that, but she'd wanted to ensure that Anthony was miserable too, and for *that*, Maggie was pissed.

"She was sick," Maggie said. It was the kindest thing she could think of.

He ran a hand over his hair. "She was right though. I chose the job over her time and time again. I canceled dinner, canceled dates. Even when I was there, I wasn't. My mind was always on a case."

"So you weren't that great a boyfriend," Maggie said with a shrug.

He let out a little laugh.

"It's not a crime," she said, keeping her voice matter-of-fact. "I've dated a handful of crappy ones. Heck, I married one. I promise that no matter how bad you were, Eddie was worse."

"Yeah, but—"

"No but." She kept her voice gentle. "We all get to choose how we respond to the people around us, and she chose *wrong*. It's tragic and awful, but it wasn't your fault. And I think you know that."

He was staring at a spot over her head, lost in thought. "Can I take Duchess out?"

Um, what?

Duchess had been frantically thrashing her raccoon on the bed, but she knew her name, knew the word "out," and knew that the two words combined meant good things. The dog all but threw herself off the bed, beelining for the front door, her nose pointing toward the leash where it hung on its hook.

"I guess that's a yes," Maggie said, bemused. It was an odd request, and even odder timing, but she suspected he needed a moment, and Duchess was due for a pee, so ... why not?

"We've got to get you a better leash," he muttered as he clipped the bright pink leash onto the dog's collar. "There's no dignity in this one."

"Clearly you know nothing about girls," Maggie called after him.

He shut the door without a backward glance and she shook her head.

She tried to get back to her story while he was gone, but her concentration was completely shot, and she ended up deleting more words than she added by the time he finally returned.

He said nothing as he took Duchess's leash off, and they both watched as the dog did frantic, happy laps around the tiny apartment before rediscovering an ancient bone on the small rug by Maggie's bed and settling down for a quiet gnawing session.

She opened her mouth to break the awkward silence, but he beat her to it.

"I'm never going to be the long-term kind of guy."

"Um, okay?"

"I don't want to get married. Ever."

A little dagger twisted in Maggie's chest at the finality of his statement, but she nodded again, respecting, even if she didn't like it. "Okay..."

"And I'm not good at balancing things. I've always been sort of an all-or-nothing kind of guy, and more often than not, my job requires *all*."

"With all due respect," she said quietly. "You've more or less said all of this before."

He put his hands on his hips, looking annoyed, although not at her so much as the situation. "I want to know what you want."

She closed her laptop again, buying time. "You want to know if I want long-term. If I want to get married again."

He nodded.

"Yes."

He winced, but she held up a hand. "I'm not done. I want those things, *eventually*, but that doesn't mean I'm looking for them right this second. It doesn't mean I'm looking for them with you."

His eyes flickered with something, but became impassive seconds later.

Maggie stood. "But I *do* want someone that won't drop me the second I stop being useful."

Anth's hands fell from his hips and he looked defeated just seconds before he looked angry. "You can't seriously think—"

She moved toward him, her rage from this entire week rising again to the surface as she remembered just what an ass this man could be in the name of his job.

"I do think. I think there's a very good chance that you slept with me so I'd help you with a case. You couldn't so much as look at me the second you realized you'd misjudged my pull on Eddie."

"That's not—"

"—You used me, Captain, and some of that's my bad because I let you, but my eyes are wide open now, and so please—*please*—just respect me enough to tell me why you're here. What you *need*. You want me to send him an e-mail, or call him, or send him a freaking telegram? Just be straight with me."

His eyes burned into hers. "You want me to be straight with you."

She nodded.

"About why I'm here," he continued.

"Yes." She kept her voice patient, because he seemed to be speaking very slowly.

He nodded.

Then he moved.

He was in front of her in two steps, his hands finding her waist, sliding around her back to lift her up to him. His mouth found hers, his tongue sweeping deep before he pulled back and sipped at her lips in tugging, teasing motions that kept him in complete control over the kiss.

When he pulled back, his eyes were tormented. "I'm here because I can't stay away. I shouldn't be here, for all the reasons I've already said. If I were even a *little* bit decent, I'd walk out the door right now, leave you to find a nice banker or an electrician or someone who—"

She hooked her hand around the back of his head, yanking it down to hers for a brief, shut-up kind of kiss.

"You know," she said quietly when she finally released his lips. "For the strong silent type, you talk way too much."

He smiled slowly. "My mouth does other things too."

"Yeah?" She smiled back. "Show me."

CHAPTER TWENTY-SIX

Maggie's dog had never had a male visitor that stayed around for sexy times, but Duchess apparently sensed that she did *not* want to be on the bed at this particular moment. She hightailed it to the bathroom, where she promptly resumed chewing her bone on Maggie's bathmat.

"Smart dog," he growled as he placed a hand high on Maggie's chest and marched her steadily backward until the backs of her knees hit the bed.

She sat, watching as he removed his belt and set it carefully aside.

Their eyes met for several seconds. Held. And then they reached for each other, falling back on the bed in a graceless heap as hands turned greedy and frantic.

Maggie untucked his uniform shirt, sliding her hands up under to the firm male skin of his back as his hands slipped under her sweater, fingers trailing over her rib cage until his palms found her breasts.

He groaned. "No bra."

Then his hands took advantage, his thumbs stroking her nipples into hard peaks so that she gasped his name, nails digging into his back.

He teased her for several seconds before lying back slightly, shoving her sweater up roughly under her chin, not bothering to take it off before his mouth fell on her, sucking a nipple hot and deep while his fingers rolled the other one.

He'd been a wonderfully rough lover before, but this was different. He was less in control this time, his touch more desperate, and Maggie relished every moment of pushing this man past his usually strict limits.

He alternated between wet licks and toying nips until she couldn't take any more, and she tangled her hands in his short hair, jerking his head up to hers where she took control of the kiss, using her body weight to maneuver over him.

He let her, complying when she straddled his hips and began unbuttoning his shirt, only to hiss in frustration at the white T-shirt he wore beneath.

His smile was both playful and strained. "That's not what you wanted? You were hoping for skin?"

In response, she narrowed her eyes, her hand sliding down over the hard line of his cock and his eyes rolled back. "Jesus."

Maggie trailed her fingers over his long erection, her turn to torture, before she went for his belt buckle. She made fast work of his button and zipper as well. Apparently faster than he'd been expecting, because his eyes went wide in surprise when she jerked his pants down over his hips, taking his boxers with them.

"Maggie, wait. Let me—"

She didn't wait.

She kissed the tip of his cock, tentatively at first. She'd done this before but had never really wanted to.

But with him—she wanted to—badly.

Anthony had started to lift his head off the bed, but he dropped it back with a quiet groan at the touch of her mouth, and she felt a rush of triumph along with a fierce stab of desire.

Her tongue came out to touch him, softly at first, then more confidently as his hands tangled into her hair with a muttered oath.

She loved him with her mouth, using his groans and gasps as her guide, tasting him thoroughly. His breathing grew quicker, his hands on her head gripped more firmly, his hips jerking off the bed before he made a ragged, snarling noise and pulled her mouth off him.

She whimpered in protest as she was flipped onto her back, only for all protest to scatter when his fingers slid down under the front of her pants, toying with the lace edge of her panties.

Maggie was reasonably sure her underwear wasn't any more attractive than last time, but she didn't care. Couldn't even think about it, because his thumbnail was teasingly skating around the edge of her panties, getting close to what she wanted but never actually touching her.

"Please," she said.

"Please what?" he asked, his voice all innocence.

"Touch me."

"I thought I was." His fingertip slipped under the fabric just barely and she gasped.

"Oh, like this?" he asked in mock befuddlement. "Is this what you wanted?"

Again with that wicked swipe of his thumb.

"Well, if you liked this, I'm wondering if you'll like this," he said, sliding his forefinger all the way under her panties, then sliding it in her, slick and wet.

"Oh my God." It was all she could manage.

He withdrew his hand, tugging her pants down and off before returning his fingers to her. His eyes flickered to her face only briefly before he returned his gaze to his fingers, watching as he slid a finger back inside her, followed by another one so that he stroked her with two fingers.

Then his thumb found her clit, and Maggie cried out, deciding there was nothing more erotic than watching this man watching his hand work her over.

He replaced his thumb with his tongue, and she realized she'd been wrong. *This* was the most erotic thing she'd ever experienced. His tongue wet and hot against her, his fingers pushing into her with the perfect rhythm.

As with the last time with him, she didn't see it coming. Not until she was in the throes of it, her cries echoing off the walls of her small apartment, her body arching to the ceiling in the ultimate ecstasy before dropping back down in helpless wonder.

His face bordered on tender as he moved back up her body, pushing her messy hair out of her face.

"You're . . ."

She looked at him through hazy eyes. "Hmm."

"Everything," he said quietly.

The admission took her breath away but she didn't have time to dwell on what it might mean, because his hands were under her sweater again, pushing it up as he stroked her, quickly bringing her back to a point of breathless want.

He rolled back only long enough to shed the rest of his

clothes, giving her only a second to admire his nakedness before he groaned in dismay. "Tell me you have protection."

She scooted toward the edge of the bed, rummaging around in her nightstand until she proudly presented a box.

He took it, holding it up with lifted eyebrows. "Unopened?"

Maggie blushed. "I bought it the day after we...slept together."

Before you decided to start ignoring me.

But she didn't let herself dwell on the negative thought, instead choosing to take what he was offering, even if it was only *right now.*

She tugged her ugly sweater over her head and pulled her pants all the way off over her ankles.

He'd made quick work of the condom and she started to scoot back on the bed to make room for him, when he set a hand on her waist to pause her. Then his other hand found the other side, and he was turning her, kissing her shoulder as he rolled her onto her stomach.

"I want to see you like this," he said hotly against her ear.

He paused, as though giving her time to protest.

Her only answer was to lift her hips, rubbing her butt against his cock and smiling when he swore and swatted her.

Then his hands were on her hips, lifting her as he nudged forward, pushing slowly at first, as though to test her readiness, before thrusting all the way.

They both groaned when he was seated fully inside her.

He reached around her, finding her hands, folding her fingers into the comforter.

And then he took her, fiercely, wonderfully, waiting until she was begging for release before reaching around and fingering her to completion at the same time he let himself come with a harsh string of profanity that oddly turned her on with its rawness.

He pulled out, resting his forehead to her back briefly before collapsing beside her on the bed.

Maggie lay on her stomach, turning her head to face him, unable to stop herself from gently laying a hand against his cheek.

He surprised her by turning his face and pressing a gentle kiss to her hand.

And sweet as the gesture was, it turned Maggie's thoughts in a dangerous direction.

What if this wasn't enough? What if he was right to be scared of her and her demands?

What if she did want... *more*?

CHAPTER TWENTY-SEVEN

For the first time since she could remember, Maggie woke up to someone else making her breakfast.

And not just anyone.

A tall, broad-shouldered cop was standing in her kitchen, making eggs and bacon, from the smell of it.

Then the sleepiness wore off and she sat up groggily. She didn't have any bacon. Or eggs.

"Did you go to the store?" Her voice sounded all croaky from sleep. And sex. Lots of sex.

He turned around, his eyes landing south of her face.

Whoops. Naked.

She dove for her sweater on the floor, belatedly aware that it was not what a savvy, confident woman would have done.

Anthony gestured with his spatula toward the laminated weekly calendar she kept on the back of her door. "Says you work the dinner shift tonight. Figured you had the day off."

She nodded, still trying to reconcile having a handsome man in her kitchen. "Kim asked me to switch with her. But don't deflect. Where'd the bacon and eggs come from?"

"You didn't have anything," he said, pouring coffee into her favorite *Real Women Read Books* mug, hesitating. "Black?" he asked.

"Sorry, I'm not that hardcore. There's flavored creamer stuff in the fridge."

He gave a rueful smile as he added some to the mug. "It feels wrong, all this time you pouring coffee for me at the diner, and I don't even know how you like yours."

"That's different," she said with a smile as he approached the bed, mug in hand. "You *pay* me to know how you like yours."

"I think I got payment last night," he said, leaning down to kiss her, settling for her cheek when she moved her mouth away. Morning breath.

"So that's why I get breakfast, huh?" she asked, taking a bracing sip of coffee. "I traded sexual favors for breakfast and didn't even know it."

She glanced at the clock and her eyes bugged out. "That's not the time. Is it? I have to take Duchess out, poor thing…"

"Already done," he said, returning to the stove and stirring the eggs.

Maggie glanced to her left, and sure enough, there was her dog, curled up for a late-morning nap.

She scratched her cheek as she quietly tried to take all of this in.

Captain Anthony Moretti had not only made love to her three times, but had stayed the night, then taken her dog for a walk, gone to the store, and made her breakfast.

All with the squad car presumably still parked outside.

"Who's on duty this morning?" she asked.

"What?"

She took another sip of coffee. "My watchdogs. Who's out there? Jonas and Corrigan?"

He took a sip of his own coffee and shrugged without turning around. "Yup."

"Did you talk to them?"

"Yup."

She resisted the urge to throw her mug at him. "Will it be a problem that you stayed the night?"

"As far as they know, I didn't. They assumed that I'd shown up early again this morning to discuss the case, and I didn't correct them."

"And they don't think it's weird that you're walking my dog?"

He glanced over his shoulder. "They probably do. But I told them I'm a dog person and can't have one of my own because of my long hours. I'm the boss. They're not going to argue."

"Huh," she said, not sure how she felt about this.

On one hand, she didn't want him to get in trouble—didn't want his career at stake because of her.

On the other hand, she didn't exactly like being some dirty little secret either. She supposed some women might get off on the clandestine, secretive part of sleeping with someone you probably shouldn't, but she wasn't one of them.

She was a nice girl who wanted a nice guy who walked her dog. And made her breakfast. Who was kind to his mother.

Oh crap.

She wanted *him*. All of him. Always.

There was a better than good chance that she was falling in love with him. Might already be there. Fallen. All the way.

Oh crap.

Oh crap. Oh crap. Oh crap.

Maggie squeezed her eyes shut in horror, relieved that he'd turned his back once again to check the bacon and couldn't see her face. Knew that he'd read it in an instant if she wasn't careful.

She opened her eyes again, willed herself to reevaluate.

The man had gone out of his way twice now to tell her all the ways he didn't want a serious relationship.

Had flat out told her that a career would always come first over a woman.

Anthony had all but spelled *I will never love you* in big, fat neon letters.

She couldn't be this stupid. Could she? It was just a brief moment of Crazy, brought on by the great sex, and dog walking, and the smell of bacon. It would pass.

"Hey, so," he said, flicking off the burners on the stove and piling eggs and bacon onto two plates. "I'm off today, and you don't have to be at work for several hours so I was thinking..."

He grabbed two forks and then walked toward her, handing her a plate before sitting on the edge of the bed.

Duchess immediately wiggled between them, planting her butt directly in the center where she'd have the best chance at reaching rogue bits of bacon.

"You were thinking...?" she said warily when he didn't finish.

He shoveled a bite of eggs in his mouth. Chewed it slowly, but methodically.

He swallowed. "I was thinking since we have some time,

I could read the rest of your book? I was left hanging last time."

She stared at him, eggs and bacon untouched.

He wanted to read her story.

This wasn't a phase. The man had gone and done it. He'd made her fall in love with him.

All the way.

He finally noticed her stricken expression, and he set his fork carefully on the side of his plate, shifting to face her more fully, giving her his full attention. "Everything okay? You like bacon and eggs, right? I mean I've only ever seen you serve them, not eat them, but—"

"No!" she said, her voice coming out all shrill. "No, I love them."

She took a bite. Huge bite. Too big a bite, as it turned out, because it took her several seconds and a huge swallow of coffee to wash the eggs down.

"Very good," she said.

Very good? You dork.

"You're sure you're okay?"

"Mmm," she said around a piece of bacon.

Even Duchess was looking at her strangely.

"If you don't want to let me read your book, you don't have to," he said quietly.

"No, I'd...I'd like that," she said finally.

And to her surprise, she found it was true.

She'd been terrified last time he'd read her work, but it had also been wonderfully freeing. Since then she'd even gotten the courage to sign up in an online writing community where she'd found a few critique partners to exchange work with.

But she'd always remember that he'd been the first. He'd

been the first to read the early chapters; he should be the first to read the last ones as well. "Maybe a little later?"

His smile was slow and wide, as though she'd granted him a great honor.

They ate the rest of their breakfast in companionable silence. He reached for her empty plate, but she batted his hand aside, instead reaching out her hand for his. "I'll clean."

Anth played tug-of-war with Duchess on the bed before piling all of her pillows against the headboard and propping his back up against it to read something on his phone.

She was almost done scrubbing the egg out of the pan when he spoke again. "How's your dad? On the mend?"

Maggie let out a little harsh laugh, although the question didn't bother her as much as it usually did. "Out of the hospital," she said. "He had no insurance, and as I'm sure you can imagine, the bills were…extravagant."

He said nothing as Maggie snapped the dishtowel off the back of its hook, drying the pan with more aggression than necessary. "Oh, and he needs a lawyer. He's made a list of attorneys with a strong track record of getting people off DUIs."

She scrubbed at the pan harder. "The man has barely made the effort to take out his own garbage can in decades, but he finds *plenty* of time to devise ways to dodge a criminal charge."

"He wants you to pay for the lawyer." It wasn't even a question, which bothered her all the more.

She put the pan in its proper spot before bracing her hands against the sink. Heard him come up behind her. Felt his palms, hot and strong on her shoulders as he turned her.

"You don't have to keep doing this, Maggie."

Her eyes watered. "I know."

"What about your brother? Surely he can help with something."

She laughed and wiped her nose. "He's in Fort Lauderdale with a new girlfriend. Hasn't answered his phone since Dad got home from the hospital."

His thumbs ran over her cheekbones. "How does a family of such utter pricks get someone so wonderful as you? Do you take after your mom?"

Maggie licked a tear from the corner of her mouth. "I hope not. The best thing she ever did was leave. I was twelve. Came home from school, excited to tell her that I got asked to the end-of-the-year sixth-grade dance by the boy I'd liked all year, only to find her loading up her fake Louis Vuitton suitcase into the trunk of her boyfriend's new car. I didn't even know she had a boyfriend."

"Jesus," he muttered.

"I get a Christmas card from her every year. She's currently living in Paris with husband number four and a Pekinese named Bubbles. Her Louis Vuitton luggage is the real deal now. She'd make sure of it."

His hands were on her arms now, rubbing up and down in kind, soothing gestures. "Promise me you won't give Charlie a penny."

She looked away.

"Maggie."

"I can't let him go to jail," she said desperately.

"That's exactly where he belongs. This latest DUI's the longest in a string of many. He shouldn't be on the road."

She shook him off. "Said the cop."

"Maggie, I get family loyalty. I understand it. But what

has that man ever done for you other than take your money? Do you even have any money left?"

"I'll make some," she said defensively. "I'll take extra shifts. I don't need much for myself, and I can live cheaply—"

"For God's sake, you didn't even have *eggs*. You eat pie for dinner more often than not, and do you really want to be a waitress at the Darby Diner for the rest of your life?"

She turned away.

"Do you?" he pressed.

"What I want doesn't matter," she said, whirling back around. "I want my father not to be an alcoholic, or to at least stick with treatment for more than forty-eight hours. I want my brother to act like a man instead of a pre-teen. I want my mom to not have ditched us, and my ex to not be a con, and I wish you—"

She broke off then, catching herself.

His eyes went wary. "You wish I'd what?"

"Nothing."

"No, there's no nothing. You don't get to start sentences like that and not finish them."

"Yes, I do!" she said, feeling peevish. "This is my apartment. Mine. And this is my life. You don't get to barge into it, demanding answers you don't even care about."

"I care!"

"Do you? Do you *really*?"

Do you care enough*?*

His jaw was tight and they glared at each other for several seconds before he took a step backward. "I should go."

"Probably."

He held her gaze. "I don't know when I'll see you again. If I come by too often, the guys outside will start to get suspicious. They know you're a family friend, so I've gotten away with it thus far—"

She held up a palm to stop him. "You don't have to spell it out for me. I'm fine, really. No expectations, remember?"

He nodded but looked worried by her easy acquiescence, and even as angry as she was at him, she softened, just slightly, because she understood. They'd gotten themselves into a terrible mess.

"I'm fine, Anth. I really am. I'm not going to crumble because you're gone. I'm not going to wait by the phone, I'm not going to watch the clock, I'm not even going to think about you when you're not around, I promise. I'm not putting any demands on you."

I'm not Vannah.

He watched her for another long second and took a deep breath before repeating, "I should go."

Her heart twisted. But after the rather fabulous speech she'd just made, she couldn't very well beg him not to go.

"Okay."

He reached for his coat on the back of the chair, glanced across the room at Duchess, almost as though he meant to say good-bye to the dog, then shook his head and reached for the door handle. Jerked it open.

The door slammed shut as quickly as it had opened, but he stayed inside the coziness of her apartment.

Hadn't moved.

"Do you like movies?"

"What?" she asked.

"Movies. Do you want to go to one?"

Her jaw dropped. He'd rendered her good and truly speechless.

"With me," he clarified. "Today. A matinee before you have to head to work."

"I'd like that," she managed finally.

"Good." He returned his jacket to its spot on the back of the chair.

"But first, I get to read your story."

CHAPTER TWENTY-EIGHT

Y ou ate all the popcorn. All of it."

Maggie sighed happily. "I know I did. But I have no regrets, Captain. None. Also, Milk Duds? I thought those were more urban legend than actual candy."

"Watch your mouth, Walker. Duds are classic."

Maggie heard herself give a girlish giggle that sounded nothing like her usual laugh—it was younger...freer. "*Duds*. Very cool of you, old man."

"Admittedly I am feeling old right about now," Anthony muttered, taking a surreptitious glance at the people around them.

Maggie spread her arms out to the side. "Welcome to Williamsburg."

It was trendy, hipster Brooklyn at its best, and the two of them didn't exactly fit in, but it had the best movie selection of anything even remotely near her apartment.

"Where the average age is like, what, twenty-two?" he asked grumpily.

She shrugged. "Pretty much. And it's Saturday afternoon, what do you expect?"

"Exactly, it's Saturday *afternoon*. I'm positive that group over there is inebriated already."

She rolled her eyes. "Easy, Grandpa. They're just laughing. And I'm sure your scowl will keep everybody in check."

"I'm not scowling."

She flicked his bicep. Hard. Yummy. "You're always scowling."

"It's just my face."

She smiled. "Well lucky for you, I happen to like it just the way it is."

He glanced at her, surprise registering before he resumed his usual passive, well, *scowl*.

"The response you're looking for is 'thank you,'" she said, exasperated. "Really, complimenting you is a bit like talking to a black hole. I have no idea what's going on inside."

She meant the words jokingly, but he was silent for several moments, his expression thoughtful as they walked out of the theater and toward a nearby restaurant where they'd agreed to grab a quick bite before the start of her shift.

"Thank you," he said finally.

His hand brushed hers then, so tentatively that she thought it was an accident. Then his pinky touched hers, lingering this time. Not an accident, but still he didn't reach for her hand. Didn't take hers in his and link their fingers.

It made her smile.

This man who was so in control of his life—in control of others' lives—this man who was controlling and demanding and possessive in bed, didn't know how to initiate the basic handhold.

Maggie's smile widened. Well, lucky for him she wrote young adult romance; she knew *all* about the importance of a handhold and how to initiate a proper one.

She brushed her pinky back, encouraging. Then she slid the rest of her fingers along his, giving him a chance to chicken out.

Once they were palm to palm, the world around them seemed to disappear, for one lovely moment.

And then his fingers entwined with hers, and the world snapped back into place, but it was a better place.

It was a place where Anthony Moretti held her hand.

"So what's next for your book?" he asked.

"Um, finish it?"

He squeezed her hand. "I mean after that."

Maggie blew out a breath. "Well…editing."

"You mean like spell-check?"

She smiled. "No, I mean like *editing*. Going back through and adding scenes and deleting scenes and just making it…better."

"Okay, so you make it better. And then you sell it?"

"You make it sound simple. But yes. Basically. I'd like to get a literary agent. Someone to shop it to the publishing houses," she explained before he could ask.

"If it does well, do you think you'll quit Darby—"

"I can't think like that," she interrupted before he could finish the sentence.

"Fair enough," he said easily. "But what about in your dreams? What do you dream about?"

Maggie glanced at him in surprise. It was a lovely, whimsical thing to say. Completely out of character.

Or perhaps not. Perhaps it was just another facet of his character. One he kept hidden.

"In my dreams?" she said, happy to play along. "In my dreams, I get to write all day. No bright orange Darby uniform. No uniform of any kind, other than what feels comfy at that particular moment. No carrying trays or pouring coffee, or—"

"Or dumping food/beverage in people's laps?"

"Well, only if they deserve it."

They exchanged a smile as he held open the restaurant door for her. It was crowded, so they found a spot at the bar, both opting for a beer and cheeseburger.

"What about you?" she asked, taking a sip of her beer and turning to face him. "What are your dreams?"

"Police commissioner," he said without hesitation.

"Well, I know that," she said teasingly. "But get specific. What does it *feel* like?"

He took a sip of his own beer, considering. "Nobody's ever asked me that before."

She shrugged. "You want it *so* badly. So I figure it must have the same sort of pull on you that being a published author does for me. I was just hoping to understand. As much as you *can* understand someone else's passion, that is."

He looked uncomfortable. "I don't know how to explain."

Maggie patted his hand. "That's because you're a guy. I'll help. What about it lights you on fire? Is it the prestige? The control? All the good you can do?"

Another sip of beer before he spoke slowly. Hesitantly. "It's a goal achieved. That satisfaction of wanting something, reaching for it...and getting it. And, yes, it's about the good I can do. It's a political position, sure, but you also have the ability to shape a massive law enforcement organization that is at the heart of this city."

"The heart of this city, huh? You sound kind of like Batman."

"Great. That's just what we cops like to hear. That we sound like vigilantes."

Their burgers arrived, looking every bit as juicy and decadent as Maggie had hoped for. She swirled her fry in their homemade ketchup. "Okay, so you're police commissioner in your future, dream life. What else?"

He paused in his chewing, brow furrowed. Swallowed, then washed down with a sip of beer. "What do you mean, what else?"

"Well..." She wiped burger juice off her chin. "Your dad was police commissioner but he must have had hobbies."

"Sure," Anth said hesitantly. "He liked to fish, on the rare times that he could get away. And he loved sports. Still does."

"And he was a father. And husband," she added, dunking three fries at once and biting them neatly with her front teeth.

Anthony had gone very still beside her, and as she swallowed the deliciously greasy potatoes, she realized what her statement must have sounded like.

She set her burger down. "Anth, I didn't mean...I wasn't hinting."

He was looking down at his plate, looking troubled. "I did want those things. Once."

"But then...Vannah?"

He set his burger aside, reached for his beer. "Yeah. That was the ultimate reminder of just how opposing my goals might be."

"But they weren't for your father," she said before she could stop herself.

"True. But my mother was also in the police business, so to speak. She was a dispatcher. It's how they met."

"That didn't mean she was hardwired to accept a husband who wasn't around, whose job was life-threatening every day," Maggie argued.

"No," he agreed. "But she went in eyes wide open. She'd spent years watching the realities of law enforcement before she agreed to marry my dad. It's something... you can't understand unless you've been there."

"Ah," she said. *Got it. Loud and clear. I'll never understand because I'm a waitress and an author.*

He touched her hand lightly. "Hey."

She glanced at him. Wary.

His eyes were intense. "I've had a really nice time today. And last night. And I just... I need you to know that even though I don't want more, if I did..."

She put her hand over his mouth then. "Do not finish that sentence, Captain."

He frowned and pulled her hand away. "Why not?"

She leaned forward, gave him a quick kiss on the mouth.

"Because you're already very, *very* close to breaking my heart."

CHAPTER TWENTY-NINE

Smiley had gone and done it this time.

His latest hit was a state senator's house.

As the *eleventh* time he'd eluded police, it would have made the news regardless, but the high-profile victim ensured that the story moved beyond New York.

Smiley had turned the NYPD into a national laughing-stock.

"Where the hell is this guy?"

This from Jozlin, Ray Mandela's boss, who'd called a meeting to discuss "the problem."

"We don't know, sir," Ray said quietly.

"Obviously," Jozlin snapped.

He was a tall man. Taller even than Anthony himself, which was rare, and rail thin, with dark hair and a matching goatee that didn't show even the faintest hint of gray despite the fact that Anthony knew him to be close to fifty.

He glanced around at the room, frustration coming off

him in waves. Anth didn't blame him. The guy reported directly to the police commissioner, and it was rare that they bothered themselves with crimes and issues as small as nonviolent home invasion.

But then, it wasn't every day that a frazzled state senator gave an impromptu, irritable assessment of the NYPD as a bunch of "incompetent figureheads."

Jozlin fixed his sharp blue gaze on Anthony. "Captain."

"Yes, sir."

"You've been working on this case the longest. You're seriously going to tell me that your people have no clue where to find this guy? He strikes the same neighborhood every damn time, for God's sake."

Anthony refused to flinch. "I've got all my resources on it, sir."

"I should hope so. What about family? This guy didn't come out of thin air. Someone's got to know where he is. A mother, a girlfriend…"

"No current girlfriend that we know of. We've had eyes on the ex-wife since day one."

Maggie.

It was hard to imagine that the woman whose soft voice and softer skin, which felt like heaven, had once been married to the man who was shaping up to be Anthony's very own private hell.

"Right. Ms. Walker," Jozlin said, looking down at his file. "But we've already tried that route, right? And she failed to bring him in."

It was on the tip of Anthony's tongue to say that *Maggie* hadn't failed at anything. Eddie *had* been following her.

But then he'd seen Anthony with her and run scared.

It was a hard truth that Anthony had come to swallow in

the past couple days. If he hadn't gotten involved with Maggie, Eddie wouldn't have known just how close she was to the NYPD.

And the man would likely be behind bars by now.

Maggie was Eddie's Achilles' heel, but Anthony's inability to keep his dick in his pants had also made Maggie Eddie's weapon.

The guy let them know with every one of those damn smiley-face stickers that he was one step ahead of them, and his connection to Maggie was yet another way he could antagonize them.

"What do we think he's after? It's obviously not about big money. The senator's wife collects art, and Smiley didn't touch any of it. He ignored a half dozen pieces out in plain sight and made off with an older generation iPad, cash, and some Goddamn foie gras. It doesn't make sense."

Anthony cleared his throat and nodded his chin at the file in Jozlin's hand. "They think he's an egomaniac, sir. That he's stealing because he *can*. Maggie—Ms. Walker— has also indicated that he has a bit of an entitlement complex. Thinks he should have what other people have without working for it."

Jozlin slapped the folder on the table with a loud *whack*. "Still doesn't explain where he's staying. The guy isn't doing all of this so he can sleep on the streets. Let's dig deeper in his connections. Talk to his sister's babysitter's cousin, or the friend of a friend of his plumber. Check cameras in fancy hotels, see who's ordering extravagant room service—"

Anthony opened his mouth to protest that they were already doing that—had been doing it from the *second* Maggie gave them a list of every known relative, friend, and acquaintance, from the moment that...

Mandela shot him a *shut it* look before turning back to Jozlin. "Yes, sir. We're on it."

"Good," the taller man muttered. "Now what the hell to do about Senator Horton? I don't suppose he's issued a public apology yet for insulting us on the record?"

"Smiley stole the man's briefs, sir. And his wife's negligee. I don't suspect we'll be getting an apology anytime soon," Anthony said.

"This fucking fucker," Jozlin said, falling into his chair. "And we're sure it's Eddie Hansen we're looking for? We're not chasing the wrong guy?"

"The police sketch from the first and only witness matches photos of Mr. Hansen exactly. And even if the witness's eye account was off, we can also confirm that nobody has seen or heard from Eddie Hansen since the Smiley hits began. Everything fits."

"Allegedly," Jozlin said, steeling his hands over his trim stomach. "*Allegedly* nobody's heard from him. Because someone's got to be lying. And it's got to be one of the people Ms. Walker contacted," he mused. "Because obviously he knew where to find her."

Anthony nodded, hating the way Jozlin kept referring to *Ms. Walker* with the slightest sneer.

His superior's next words pissed him off even further. "How do we know it's not this Maggie that's in contact with him?"

"It's not," Anthony corrected quickly. Too quickly, because Mandela gave him a suspicious, considering look.

"What I mean is," Anthony said, calming his tone, "Ms. Walker's the one that connected us to Eddie Hansen in the first place. She also agreed to cooperate with the sting and to have officers watch her house, and when she saw him outside the diner, she called us immediately."

Jozlin's fingers tapped against each other. "Could she be conflicted? Wanting to do the right thing but subconsciously protecting him?"

"No—"

Mandela cut off Anthony's outraged rant. "We'll look into it, sir, although by all accounts, Ms. Walker's been playing it straight with us."

"Fine," Jozlin muttered. "And what about the note that Hansen left for her at that bungled sting? Did we look into the guy?"

There was a silence in the room.

Mandela finally spoke. "We don't know who he is."

Jozlin sat up straighter. "What do you mean you don't know? Who did Ms. Walker say it was?"

"She didn't. Just said that she didn't have a boyfriend, didn't know who Smiley might have seen her with. Said it could have been anyone from one of her co-workers who occasionally walks her to the subway station some nights or her cousin she recently grabbed dinner with."

"Yeah, I'm thinking her ex-husband doesn't care about her *cousin*," Jozlin said. "It's got to be a guy who Smiley thinks is interested in her. Find him. If Hansen's still hung up on her, we can use his jealousy. Draw him out that way."

Anthony felt his blood run cold.

The worst part of it was, Jozlin was absolutely right. If he spoke up, identified himself as "the him" in Maggie Walker's life, there was a chance—

"I believe it's one of the Moretti brothers, sir."

Anthony jolted, his attention turning toward Ray Mandela who gave him an apologetic look.

Jozlin looked thoughtful. "How's that?"

Mandela cleared his throat. "The Moretti family frequents the diner where Ms. Walker works. She's a family friend. And she actually saw the police sketch in the first place when Captain Moretti had it at the diner. And Luca Moretti is a frequent patron as well. So's the other one. The homicide detective. If Hansen's been watching her, he's undoubtedly seen her with any one of them at the diner."

Anthony relaxed. Slightly. Mandela knew only that Maggie was loosely connected with his family. Not that he'd slept in her bed, made her breakfast, walked her damn dog...

"It's possible," Jozlin mused. "Especially considering that Smiley's first note was sent to you. Right, Captain?"

"Correct," Anth said. "Sent to my brother Vincent, actually, but with my name on the envelope."

This time when Jozlin leaned back in his chair, his frustration had turned to speculation. "If Eddie's prone to jealousy and watching the diner, he could get the wrong idea about Ms. Walker's relationship with one of you. Mistakenly assume that there's something romantic there."

Mistakenly.

Ha.

Tell him. Speak up now.

But he couldn't. A relationship with an informant on an in-progress case was the ultimate career suicide. He'd taken enough risks as it is, going by her house late at night and then *staying* there.

He leaned his elbows on the desk, feeling unbearably weary.

He needed to put a stop to this thing with Maggie. Whatever it was. He could no longer tell himself it was just sex. Not when she was all he thought about. Not when he would—

Anthony's phone vibrated.

So did everybody else's.

Anthony stared at his phone for a split second and was already in motion before Jozlin spoke. "A hostage situation at the Darby Diner. Isn't that the same diner that—"

"Yeah," Anthony said, shoving open the door and all but running toward the exit.

Mandela was right behind him. "Think it's Smiley?"

"I know it is," Anth replied with grim certainty.

"Think he finally went after—"

"Yes," he said again, interrupting because he couldn't bear to hear Mandela say her name. Couldn't bear to even think it.

A dozen officers were swarming around him in seconds, as Anthony barked out questions that nobody had answers to.

How many hostages?

Did they have eyes on the suspect?

Was he armed?

And the most heartbreaking question...the one he couldn't bring himself to ask.

Was Maggie inside?

CHAPTER THIRTY

Margaret, baby. You don't look happy to see me."

Maggie's eyes flicked to the gun in Eddie's hand as he watched her with a Cheshire cat smile. The man she'd been married to had never been into guns that she was aware of.

But he looked comfortable with this one.

Too comfortable.

Maggie had always read about people in life-threatening situations whose minds went perfectly clear and focused.

But since Eddie had strolled into the diner, locked the door, and informed the occupants that he'd shoot anyone that moved, she'd waited for that moment of clarity.

It hadn't come.

Her mind felt completely blank with terror.

And not just that...she felt small.

Just seeing his face again felt like a time machine, and she went back to the place when she was quiet and meek and tired.

"I'm happy, Eddie," she said, hoping to keep *him* content.

Her eyes roamed around the restaurant for what felt like the hundredth time, making sure everyone was okay. Luckily he'd come in at a slow time. Only a handful of tables were occupied.

A couple of elderly men in the corner who came in every Wednesday for coffee and pie. A group of chatty women who'd each made about nine customizations to their order. A lone businessman on his laptop.

And worst of all, a mom and her little girl.

Gloria was the only other waitress working today, and she'd just gone out back to smoke. Maggie was the only server in the building, and judging from the silence in the kitchen, she was guessing the cooks had managed to get out the back door.

She was hoping so, anyway.

"The police are on their way, Eddie," she said quietly. "Might already be outside."

The mom and the businessman had called 911 within moments, before Eddie had demanded everyone hand over their cell phones.

He wiggled his eyebrows at her. "You know all about the police, don't you, baby?"

She closed her eyes. "You've been watching me."

"Mm-hmm." He lowered himself into one of the booths, watching her with an amused expression. "Watching you. Watching them watching you. It's been great fun."

She felt a surge of loathing as she looked down at his all-too-familiar form.

She'd touched him once. Loved him.

She wanted to throw up.

The worst part was, he'd never looked better. He'd always

had the haggard, dry look of someone who survived on whiskey and onion rings and bitterness, but he looked vibrant and alive.

Stealing had made him this way.

Except...

She looked closer. Something was off. There was a wildness to his eyes. He was radiating energy, yes, but a strange, manic kind of energy. As though he were high on something.

If Eddie had gotten into drugs—and she wouldn't be surprised—it would certainly explain the new changes in behavior.

Not to mention his creepy grin.

"Are you really doing these things? Stealing?" she asked.

"Of course," he said, studying the gun in his hand. "Who else could elude the cops for this long? Moretti in particular; I've heard he's sharp, but..." He shrugged, then grinned. "I outsmarted him, didn't I?"

"He'll find you," she said.

He snorted. "Well, of course. I all but delivered myself to him."

Maggie opened her mouth, then shut it, surprised by the truth of his statement.

"So you're here to turn yourself in?"

"God no. Why would I do that?"

"Then why are you here?"

His look was pitying. "Why do you think, Margaret?"

The terrified fuzz around her brain was starting to clear. "Me. You came for me."

"Correct." Now his smile was gentle, and even more creepy. "I did it all for you. I understand why you left, you know. Because I couldn't provide for you with everyone else keeping me down. It's why you changed your number and left home, abandoning your friends. And even your family. Your dad says hi, by the way."

Maggie put a hand to her jumpy stomach. "You talked to my dad?"

"Several times. Visited him when he got out of the hospital. He was all too happy to take me up on my offer to cover his bills after you couldn't."

Her hand moved to her mouth. She was going to be sick. *Eddie had gone to see her dad. Who hadn't said a word.*

"Have to take care of my people, and Charlie's still the closest thing to a dad. He called me son, you know."

Maggie's eyes closed. "Eddie…can you…will you let these people go?"

He glanced around. "No, I don't think so. Not until you agree."

"I agree," she said quickly, her eyes flitting to the little girl, eyes wide and confused as she rested against her mom's chest, just a tad too young to understand what was happening. "Whatever you want, I agree."

He studied her face before sighing. "No, you don't, Maggie. You don't understand yet."

"Then tell me," she said, slowly lowering to the seat across from him. "Because I've got to tell you, Eddie. You sound like a crazy person."

He stiffened, and over his shoulder, he saw the businessman give her an incredulous-warning look.

But she was acting on instinct now. Eddie clearly saw her as the same meek, pushover wife she'd been before, who'd be all too happy to do his bidding in exchange for even the merest thank-you.

She needed to establish that she wasn't that woman anymore. Never again. Needed to show that she wasn't Margaret

Hansen any longer. Margaret Hansen had been a people-pleasing fool, easily controlled by a guilt trip and the hope of praise.

Maggie Walker was...

Self-sufficient.

A writer. Waitress. A dog owner. A friend. Lover.

Maggie Walker was *whole*.

"Do you have any idea how pathetic a cop's salary is?" he asked, his expression returning to its neutral cheerfulness.

She frowned, confused at the change in topic.

"Even captains," he continued. "I mean, they can support themselves, but he'll never take you to Paris."

Paris? What the hell? She'd never had more than a passing interest in Paris. The way he was talking, it was like he was in some sort of fantasy world.

"Where have you been living?" she asked, trying to keep in control of the conversation before he could delve any further into his weird crazy place.

He laughed then, happily. "A hotel over on Fortieth, between Ninth and Tenth. Can you imagine? These fools have been bugging every one of our friends, checking security cameras in the fucking Plaza, and I've been living under their noses in a boring chain hotel just steps from Port Authority."

Eddie leaned forward then, his hair falling across his forehead boyishly. "Do you have any idea how many cops swarm around Port Authority? How many I walk by, looking them in the eye, who don't have a clue?"

He slumped back again laughing, having cracked himself up with his cleverness.

"You broke into a senator's house," she said.

He held up a finger at that. "Now, in my defense, I didn't

know it was a senator's house until I broke in. Saw a couple framed photos with the president and started to snoop through their mail—oh, speaking of mail, did you get my note?"

She pressed her lips together.

"I hoped the Morettis appreciated my effort on that one. Sending it to the surly homicide detective while making sure that Mr. Self-Important would get it."

"How do you know so much about the Morettis? Why do you care?"

He rolled his eyes. "Margaret, honestly. You used to understand me better. I care because you *care*. I've been coming by Sunday morning for a couple of months; watched the way you fawned over their tables. Watched you panic when you tried to not so subtly flirt with the captain by dropping bagels in his lap and whatnot. You did the same to me when I was courting you."

She frowned. "I did not—"

"The ketchup packet, remember?" His voice was earnest now.

"What are you—"

There was a flash of rage on his face. "Don't play coy with me, Margaret. I'm not in the mood. I know you remember."

She forced a smile. "Of course I remember."

She didn't.

He sat back, mollified, and to her relief, he didn't ask her to recount an incident for which she had no recollection. For all she knew, it had never happened. His grasp on reality was tenuous at best.

"Oh look," he said, glancing out the window. "The cavalry are here."

Her head turned, glancing out the window to see a barrage of cop cars. Her eyes skimmed for Anthony, but Eddie had already stood, jerking her arm and dragging her backward away from the windows.

"Eddie, please," she said, her voice pleading. "Let these people go. They haven't done anything, they're just—"

"Okay," he said simply, shocking her.

He waved his gun in the direction of the people seated at their tables, terrified eyes on every last one of them. "Outside. All of you. Don't try anything heroic; I'd hate for anyone to upset me and my gun here."

They all scrambled for the door. One of the elderly men looked at her, then straightened his shoulders and took a step toward Eddie, but Maggie caught his eye and gave a firm head shake.

He hesitated, his expression sad, before following his companion outside.

"You." Eddie stopped the mom carrying the little girl when she was steps away from the front door.

The woman and Maggie both tensed. *Please don't let him hurt these innocent people.*

"You go find Moretti—any Moretti—tell them that I'm taking her with me, one way or another. Make sure they understand that."

The woman nodded, and Maggie had a feeling she didn't understand, but Maggie did. She knew that Eddie was saying that if anything happened to him, he was taking Maggie with him. Dead or alive.

Who *was* this man? He'd always been possessive, maybe a little *off* toward the end of their marriage, but never violent toward her.

The door closed behind them, and Maggie breathed a sigh

of relief, just as Eddie gently pushed her toward the floor behind the counter. He followed her down so he was sitting across from her, cocky grin on his face, the gun stopping its haunting aim at her chest.

"Gotta avoid the window," he said. "Just in case their snipers are more competent than the rest of them," he added with a pleasant smile.

"How does this end, Eddie? If you wanted us to run away together, barging in here with a gun wasn't the way to do it."

"You know, I thought of that," he said. "Better to find a way to sneak you out from right under their very noses, disappear forever. I could do it, you know. Easily."

Yeah. Definitely off his rocker.

"So what's with the circus?" she asked, gesturing to his gun, to the likely ever-increasing police activity outside.

He pursed his lips, looking sulky. "I'm tired of being anonymous."

"Hasn't that been your entire point? You're Smiley. Your MO was a stupid *sticker*."

Eddie grinned, looking pleased. "I knew you'd like that."

Again with the nausea. "Tell me you didn't do this for me."

"Of course I did. Although it was just a game at first. A way of testing myself. And why shouldn't I have had what those people had? I only hit people that had plenty of extra."

"Yeah, you're a real Robin Hood."

His eyes flashed again, that deranged, angry look. "You know I've never cared for sarcasm, Margaret."

She pressed her lips together but refused to apologize. She was done apologizing.

"But then," he said, good humor returning. "*Then* I

started to watch the way he'd go to your house. *Stay* there. Saw the way you'd smile at him when he came to the diner. And then you went to his house…" Eddie clucked his tongue reprovingly. "You stayed the night, Margaret. Here I was busily outsmarting the police, and were you admiring me? No. You were choosing the loser in the match."

The terror was completely gone now, clarity setting in.

Eddie was crazy. Deluded. Jealous.

Armed. Definitely armed.

But he was careless too. His grip on the gun would loosen frequently. He hadn't tied her up. Didn't even seem to be watching her all that closely.

He underestimates me. It isn't occurring to him that I'll fight back.

"I needed you to see the real man in all of this, Margaret."

She lifted her eyebrows condescendingly. "So you corner yourself in a diner with two doors, both of which undoubtedly have dozens of officers on them right now?"

He blinked, as though surprised that she didn't get it. "None of that matters, Margaret."

"What *does* matter?"

Eddie leaned forward, his smile gentle. "That I *have* you. And that he sees that I have you. It's the checkmate he'll never see coming."

"Because he didn't even know there was a game," she said. "Anthony Moretti doesn't care about me. He's been trying to catch *you*."

Eddie blinked. "But—"

She leaned forward, her voice mocking. "I did stay over at his place, yes, but I slept on the couch. Did you bother noting that his sister was over at his place too? We watched movies, had too many glasses of wine—"

"He wants you!" Eddie barked. "I came here to show him that you'd always be mine."

"Wrong, Eddie. He wants *you*. And you walked right to him."

Eddie's look of outrage was priceless. But it wasn't nearly as satisfying as his look of complete shock when she grabbed the gun out of his slack hand and turned it on him.

"Margaret—" His hands went up.

"Don't bother, Eddie," she said, climbing to her feet, the gun trained on his chest. "Just one question. Have you *always* been this crazy?"

CHAPTER THIRTY-ONE

Where's the Goddamn negotiator?" Anthony bellowed, his voice turning several heads even amidst the chaos.

Sergeant Corvalis pointed. "Dorfman's over there being briefed by the fry chef. The cook was there, saw Hansen in person, so Dorfman wants to know his mental state."

"I don't want fucking Dorfman," Anthony growled. "Where's Evans?"

Christina Evans was the best damn hostage negotiator the bureau had.

"Evans just got married last week. She's on her honeymoon."

Anthony opened his mouth to snarl that someone needed to bring her *back* from her honeymoon.

That he needed her *here*, because Eddie Hansen had Maggie locked inside a diner.

With a gun.

He ran two hands over his face, only to realize that they were shaking.

Get a grip. She needs you.

"Anth."

He turned, saw his brothers and Jill, faces somber.

"We heard on the radio," Luc said. "Is Maggie—"

"In there," he said gruffly.

"Do we know it's Smiley?"

Anth jerked his chin in the direction of the distraught-looking chefs. "The cooks got out the back door, but one of them saw the guy. Description is a match for Hansen."

"Someone's coming out!"

They all turned toward the shout, guns drawn as the door slowly opened.

An elderly man stepped out, white as a sheet, hands over his head. Several others followed, each more terrified than the last.

Anthony's heart lurched when he saw a woman clutching a little girl. Christ, a *child* had been inside.

The cop in him mentally cataloged the wellness of each person coming out, saw as each person was promptly moved away from the diner.

The *man* in him continued to watch the door, which had slammed shut behind the mom and her child. His heart was thudding madly as he waited for the one face he needed to see.

But she didn't come.

"He's not going to let her out." Remarkably, his voice was calm. Steady.

It had to be. *He* had to be. For her.

An officer he didn't recognize approached. "You guys the Morettis?"

"What of it?" Vincent snarled.

Jill laid a hand on her partner's arm. "Yes. We are."

In another circumstance, Anthony might have smiled at the way Jill Henley quietly asserted herself as part of the family, but he was a long way from smiling now.

The officer jerked this thumb over his shoulder. "One of the hostages wants to talk to you."

It was the mother with the little girl.

Anthony moved over to where she was reassuring the paramedics that both she and her daughter were fine.

"Ma'am, I'm Captain Moretti."

She nodded, her eyes wide, probably still in shock, although her voice was steady. "That man...the one with the gun. He said to tell you that he was taking Margaret with him, one way or the other. I think Margaret must have been the other woman...the one he kept."

Anthony gave a terse nod. It was all he could manage before turning back to face the diner.

"Do you think he'll hurt her?" Luc asked.

His chest seized up at the very thought. He blew out a long, shuddering breath. "I don't know."

But if he does, I'll kill him.

"It doesn't make sense," Luc was saying. "The guy's been so...tepid up until now. What changed?"

"My guess?" Vin said, coming to stand on Anth's other side, both brothers flanking him. Supporting him. "This latest string of successful break-ins pushed his ego over the top. He thinks he's infallible. Invincible. He's probably a little nuts."

Anthony shook his head to clear it, trying to think of this the way he would any other hostage situation. One that didn't involve the woman he—

"He's got to know this doesn't have a good ending for him," he muttered. "What the hell are you up to, Eddie?"

"Moretti."

He turned, saw his boss moving toward him. "Snipers are a go if shit goes south. No sign of Hansen or the woman. Not since they were seated by the window when we first got there."

"Shoulda put a bullet between his eyes when we had the chance," Anth said savagely.

Mandela shook his head. "Without knowing for sure he was armed? Would have started a media firestorm."

Anthony jerked his head backward. "Yeah? And what do you call that?"

Mandela glanced over his shoulder at the ever-growing mass of the press. "Goddamn vultures."

"Do they know it's Smiley inside?"

"Not unless someone talked," Mandela said.

"So probably," Anthony said.

"Yeah. Probably."

Anthony pulled out his phone, dialed Maggie's phone for at least the twentieth time. Luc watched him with a sympathetic expression. "She's not answering, bro."

He let it ring all the way to voice mail anyway. Again.

"*Goddamn it*," he said, his voice almost breaking. "What the hell kind of idiot takes someone hostage, but doesn't make demands and doesn't even give us a damn way to talk to him."

"I'm guessing he doesn't want to talk to us," Vincent said. "This is all about *her*."

Anth didn't want to think about that. Didn't want to think of her at the hands of a madman who was high on his own assumed power.

"If he touches her—"

Then the diner door moved. Opened.

Anthony didn't know if the area actually fell completely silent, or if his ears just blocked out all sound, but he'd never known fear like he felt when he saw Eddie Hansen emerge from the diner.

Alone.

Unbidden images of Maggie lying in a puddle of blood flashed through his mind. Hansen wouldn't have gone through all this trouble only to walk away from Maggie...

"Hands up," someone shouted at Smiley.

Eddie ignored the order at first but then gave a quick snarl over his shoulder, and then slowly, incredibly, raised his hands over his head.

Seconds later, a woman in a bright orange waitress uniform emerged, gun pointed at Eddie's back, looking remarkably calm.

Maggie.

Everything happened fast then.

Eddie was pushed to his knees by a half dozen officers, then to his stomach on the ground, silent and sulky as he was cuffed.

Someone took the gun from Maggie, and incredibly she pointed at it and said something with a laugh.

A *laugh.*

She'd spent at least half an hour with an ex-husband and a gun, and she was laughing.

He didn't know if he wanted to hug her or shake her.

He couldn't move.

And then she saw him. Her eyes scanning the dozens of uniformed officers but finding him.

She smiled, wide and warm.

She was safe; it was over.

Vincent and Luc were already there, Luc wrapping Maggie in a bear hug, just seconds before Vincent did the same.

Anth wasn't sure who looked more surprised by the hug. Maggie, or Vincent himself.

And yet, Anthony's feet stood rooted to the ground.

"Captain." The impatient, confused tone of Mandela's voice told him it wasn't the first time his boss had said his name.

"Yeah."

Anth never took his eyes away from Maggie, who was now chatting animatedly with Jill, her hands gesturing wildly. No doubt adrenaline was still coursing through her body.

Later, she would crash. The reality would set in and he would need someone to hold her.

He wanted to be that person. Needed to be.

And yet...

"The press wants a statement," Mandela was saying. "I think it should be you."

He jerked in surprise. "Shouldn't it be you or Jozlin?"

"It's your case. Nobody's put in more time than you. You've earned it. And I've already told the guys you should be first to question Hansen. Figured you'd like that."

He did. Or he *should* like it.

Anth gave one look at Maggie. She was watching him, although her smile had dimmed. Her eyes hesitant and confused, no doubt completely baffled as to why he'd yet to take so much as a step toward her.

It was déjà vu all over again, and he was on the verge of making the same mistake he'd made then. Of not going to her.

But he *couldn't*. Knew that if he did, he couldn't be cool and professional. He'd pull her toward him and wouldn't let go, and there would be no doubt in *anyone's* mind that she was more than an informant.

More than a family friend.

More than—more than anyone had ever been to him, ever.

"Moretti. They're waiting," Mandela said, jerking his head toward the salivating reporters. "Go."

Here it was. He'd known it was coming. He'd felt it coming for months.

This was the fork in the road.

One path led toward Maggie.

The other toward recognition and crucial face time with the press. With as high a profile as this case had been, this statement would be all over the news, perhaps nationally.

It was a make-or-break moment for his career; the higher one rose in the NYPD, the more important camera skills were. This was his chance to show he had what it took to represent the department confidently, professionally.

He could turn toward Maggie...

...or he could turn toward his future.

He turned.

Faced the press. Walked toward the waiting microphones, the hungry reporters, the cameras, and the flashing lights.

Walked away from the woman who mattered. For her own sake.

Anthony told himself he didn't hear her heart break to pieces behind him. And that his own didn't break right along with hers.

CHAPTER THIRTY-TWO

Three weeks later

Y ou seem different, Bug."

She grabbed two more frozen dinners from her grocery bag, stacked them carefully in her father's freezer.

"*Maggie*," she said sharply.

"Huh?" her dad said around a belch.

"My name is Maggie."

"Sure, I know," Charlie Walker said. "Bug's just a nickname."

"One that I hate," she said, adding two more chicken dinners to the freezer.

"Since when?"

Maggie slammed the freezer door closed. "Since always. I've been telling you that for years."

"Huh." Then, "Get me a beer?"

They faced off in his grimy kitchen. It was the same kitchen she'd grown up in, done homework in, but it held no happy memories.

"You don't need a beer," she said.

He groaned and threw his head back. "Not this."

"Yes, *this*. You're in court-ordered AA."

"Only because the lawyer lady they gave me had her head up her ass. She actually looked relieved when they slapped me with the DUI. Told me I should just be happy I didn't have to go to jail. Can you imagine? Bitch."

"You *are* lucky you didn't have to go to jail, Dad. You wrapped your car around a light pole. The only thing they could salvage from your car was the fifth of Jim Beam rolling around under your seat."

"Christ," he muttered, reaching for his crutches. "Is this why you came all the way out here? To lecture me?"

"Yeah, you're welcome for the groceries," Maggie said, sweeping her arm to the table where she'd brought enough food to tide him over until he healed enough to go shopping for himself.

"Tossy was gonna do a store run. And she wouldn't have brought me this green shit." He swiped a bag of salad mix to the ground.

"Tossy?"

Who—or what—was Tossy?

"My new girl," he said, hobbling over to the card table against the wall, which apparently served as a makeshift bar because he poured a liberal amount of brown fluid into a dirty cup.

"Don't," she said quietly.

He turned around to meet her eyes, then deliberately took a long drink.

I can't stand you, she thought.

The thought was toxic and freeing all at once. *I can't stand the person you are—that you've let yourself become.*

They continued to stare at each other for several seconds before he took another sip of drink and moved back to the kitchen table, lowering himself carefully.

"So you landed your ex-hubby in jail, huh?"

Ah. So that's how it was going to be. He was going to be deliberately inflammatory now.

"I sure did," she said, refusing to let him get under her skin.

"Those fools on the TV seem to think you managed to unarm him." Her father let out a bark of laughter, as though the thought amused the hell out of him.

"I did," she said quietly.

"Eddie would never let you get the jump on him. He's clever, that boy."

"Did you know he was stealing?" she asked.

He looked away.

"When he came to see you," she pressed. "Did you know he was Smiley? That the money he gave you wasn't his?"

"At least he gave me the money! He wasn't even my son-in-law anymore after you got on your high horse and left him, but he helped me out. You never—"

"I've been 'helping you out' for years," she yelled, surprising them both with her shout. "I've given you *thousands* from a paltry waitress salary. All under the pretense of *therapy* or *rehab* or *counseling*. I replaced the living room window you broke while blitzed out of your mind, the TV you broke, also while blitzed out of your mind... and you know what you gave me in return? Not sobriety. Barely even a *thank-you*. No, the only thing I get from you is *more*. You always need *more*."

He had the decency, at least, to look guilty, but the look only lasted for a split second before he turned it around on her.

"We're family, Bug. You think I enjoyed taking care of you and your brother on my own for all those years? It's your turn to return the favor and help me out."

Maggie slowly sat in the chair across from him, in front of the food he probably wouldn't bother to eat because it wasn't fried or processed.

"I haven't been helping you, Dad." Her voice was tired now. "I've been enabling you."

He opened his mouth, but she held up a hand to stop him. "No, I have. I've been enabling you and it stops here. It stops *now*."

She could tell by the look on his face that he didn't believe her.

"Ah, Bug, come on—"

Maggie stood. "I love you, Dad. And I love Cory. But I'm done."

His mouth gaped, the whiskey, shockingly forgotten, although that wouldn't last long. "What do you mean, you're done?"

"I mean that if you want to call to talk, to see how I'm doing, or to spend a holiday together, I'd like that very much. But if you call me for money, I'll hang up the phone."

"Bug, what the hell? I love you, and I just—"

She picked up her purse from the kitchen counter and moved toward the front door. "Really? Because you only seem to *love* me when you need something. Same with Cory, who by the way, has stopped taking my phone calls because I've been asking him to pay me back on at least one of a half dozen loans."

"That's not my problem."

Maggie laughed. "You're right. It's not. It's mine, for surrounding myself with people who use me. I deserve better."

She walked out, pulling the door tightly shut behind her.

For a moment, she wanted to turn back. To rush back and tell her dad that she didn't mean it, that she'd always be there for him.

Instead, she straightened her shoulders and walked toward the train station, head held high.

Her decision hadn't been an easy one, but it was the right one. Maggie had meant what she'd said about enabling him; as long as she was his crutch, he'd continue to lean until he'd crippled them both.

Once seated on the train, she pulled out her phone. A picture message from Gabby with new pictures of the kids. A text from Elena, asking if Maggie had been getting her other texts, wondering if she wanted to grab dinner. An e-mail from one of her favorite stores that was having a massive blowout sale.

That one, she clicked on. She'd need a whole new wardrobe for the job she'd start on Monday.

Maggie had quit the diner the day after the incident.

Partially because she didn't think she could bear to be in there again without thinking of Eddie waving a gun in her face.

Partially because she'd had a bit of one of those quintessential life-or-death epiphanies in which she'd realized life was too short in a job that didn't feed her soul.

Partially because working at the diner would always mean *Anthony*. Seeing him, remembering him, pouring him freaking coffee...

She forced the thought from her mind, focusing instead on a couple of inexpensive blouses that looked like they'd be appropriate for an editorial assistant at a major publishing house.

Yes. Publishing house.

A *big* one.

Maggie still had to pinch herself when she thought about the job.

The fact that she'd even gotten the interview had been shocking enough. She was pretty sure it had been more a function of her brief brush with fame than it did her résumé, which had a whole lot of serving tables and not a whole lot of anything meeting their job requirements.

But she'd had one thing that all the other shiny recent college grads probably hadn't. An *insane* amount of knowledge about young adult fiction. The interview had lasted nearly three hours, with four different people, all of whom had seemed impressed by her passion for the genre.

The woman who'd be her boss—a recently promoted editor—had then taken Maggie out for drinks where they'd talked for two hours more about their favorite books, and even Maggie's own story.

The job offer had come the next day.

Life was looking up. *Way* up.

Not only had she finally managed to stand her ground with her family, but her wretched, slightly crazy ex was behind bars. Eddie had taken a plea bargain, but he'd still be in jail for a very, *very* long time.

Plus there was the not-so-minor fact that she'd never have to wear that bright orange Darby Diner uniform again, nor would she have to pinch her pennies quite so tightly.

The editorial assistant position pay wasn't great—at all— but it was a start. A career path that would hopefully teach her the tricks of the trade she needed to get her own book published someday.

To achieve the dream. *Her* dream.

Part of it, anyway.

Maggie turned her head, pressed her forehead against the cool window of the train.

Sometime in the past few months, her dream had shifted. Grown more complicated.

She still wanted to publish the book. Still longed for a day when she was good and truly living off a writer's income. Heck, she'd already started a second book while the first was out on query to agents.

But the dream felt...partial. It was a component of her dream life but not the heart of it.

And Maggie was very much afraid the *heart* of her dream was completely out of reach.

Anthony.

Anthony was at the center of her dream.

The strange thing was, she actually understood why he'd turned away from her that day. Even more strange, her happiness for his moment in the spotlight had overtaken her own shakiness, her own desire to be held.

She understood then what love was supposed to be. In its purest form, it was unselfish. It was wanting something for someone else because he wanted it, even though it would take him away from you.

And yet still, she'd thought—hoped—that once the Smiley case was put to rest, he'd finally understand.

Understand that he could have both, her *and* the job. That she would support his career, not take him away from it. That she understood its demands and wanted him anyway.

Except you never told him that, did you?

Maggie sat up, pulling her face away from the window as the thought seeped beneath her skin. Repeated. *You never told him you loved him.*

For three weeks, Maggie had been waiting for him to call. Waiting for him to see the light.

Like she was one of the immature high school characters from her book.

Old Maggie waited. *Old* Maggie let life happen around her.

New Maggie...

New Maggie fought for what she wanted.

And she wanted Anthony Moretti.

CHAPTER THIRTY-THREE

His siblings had forsaken him. All three had said they'd "probably" be headed to Staten Island for dinner.

All three had bailed on him, leaving him to a lonely ferry ride out to his parents.

Also? All three siblings cited the same reason for skipping dinner:

You're awful company.

Adding insult to injury, even his *own* mother didn't look particularly pleased when he'd let himself into the house.

"Your mood better have improved since brunch," she said on a sigh.

He set down the bottle of wine he'd brought with him on the counter and frowned. "You're my mother. Aren't you supposed to ask me how I am?"

"I already know how you are. You're miserable."

He shrugged. Couldn't argue with that. "Dad around?"

"Tinkering with the gas grill out back. Don't know why since we're heading toward winter, but you know how he gets. He drives me and himself out of his mind unless he has something to do."

Anthony was barely listening as he blindly watched his mother stir something around and around on the stove, snapping out of it only when her wooden spoon clattered loudly against the homemade spoon rest one of the kids had made her in kindergarten.

"Is your rotten mood because Maggie quit the diner?" she asked.

His eyes snapped up, drilling into her, outraged. *Nobody* in his family had dared to mention her name to him since he'd practically ripped Vincent's head off for calling him an idiot a couple weeks back.

"Glare all you want, dear," Maria said mildly. "I've seen far worse from your father. And you may be able to muzzle your brothers and sister with that snarl, but we mothers are made of firmer stuff."

"Grandmothers too," Nonna said, wandering into the kitchen while smearing on a tomato-colored lipstick and smacking her lips noisily. She blew him a kiss.

"Hey, Nonna," he said dutifully. "Didn't know you were here."

"Been staying here for days," she said. "Not surprised you didn't notice, what with the burying yourself in your office and all around having your head up your—"

"Nonna," his mother said.

"What? If his grandmother won't be straight with him, who will—"

"I was *trying* to, before you came and barged in here—" Maria said, getting riled up in only a way that Anthony's grandmother could manage to achieve. She took a deep breath. "We'll tell him together."

Nonna nodded, a rare moment of quick agreement between the two women, and then they both turned to face him, speaking at the same time.

"You made the wrong decision." (His mother)

"Dry rigatoni has more brains than you." (Nonna)

He glanced between them. "That's nice. Thanks."

His mother sighed, gave whatever was in the pot one last stir, and then pointed to the kitchen table.

"Sit."

He did, mostly out of habit from his mother making that very same gesture with that very same tone at least a million times throughout his childhood, usually after bombing a spelling test, or putting a spider on Elena's pillow, or telling a very young, gullible Luc that he could fly off the back of the couch if he hummed Michael Jackson songs at the same time.

"Sweetie, what we want to know is why, if you're missing Maggie so much, you don't go to her?" His mom patted his hand.

"Also, if you make amends, maybe she'll come back to the diner, and we can all get extra bacon again." Nonna patted his hand as well.

"I don't want her to come back to the diner," he growled.

And he meant it, although perhaps not for the reasons they thought. On one hand, he'd give anything to see her again. Just once. To have her spill eggs, or a sandwich, or, hell, even scalding hot coffee on him again, the way she had back when things were simple and he could satisfy himself— mostly—on the warmth of her smile.

But on the other hand, the diner wasn't where Maggie belonged. It was a quaint, small place, for quaint, small minds, and Maggie was...

Maggie was a dreamer. Who dreamed big dreams and thought big thoughts and wanted big love.

Not just for herself but for everyone else, which made her even more remarkable.

What does your dream feel like? she'd asked.

She hadn't told him his priorities were out of whack. Hadn't condescended to his dream of being police commissioner. She'd only supported. Lifted him.

And he'd done the same for her.

By leaving her.

"Did she break up with you?" Nonna asked bluntly. "I break up with my fellas all the time when they stay moody for too long."

"No," he said quietly. "I let her go."

"Oh Lord," Maria said. She never used the Lord's name in vain, which meant this was a desperate prayer, perhaps for patience, and Anth resisted the urge to squirm in his seat.

"You didn't fall into that ridiculous, 'it's for her own good' nonsense, did you?" his mother asked.

He remained silent.

"Oh, Anth." It came out on a sigh. A tired sigh.

Nonna giggled gleefully. "Oh, you're gonna get it now! That's the preamble to a lecture if I've ever heard one."

"With all due respect," he began, "I don't think either of you understand—"

"Probably because it's silly, but go ahead, dear, explain it to us," Maria said, setting her chin on her hand.

He eyed her warily. "Well. Um, okay. It's just... you both know that I want to be the police commissioner someday. That if I play my cards right, I'm on my path to get there.

That everyone expects it of me. That I want it. Really truly *want* it."

They both nodded.

He fell silent.

They too were silent, waiting for more.

"That's sort of it," he said awkwardly.

His mother's mouth dropped open. "Wait, that's *it*? That's your big reason? Did she not support your choices?"

Nonna wagged her finger. "I like Maggie, but if you tell me she's one of those pansy girls who gets all faint at the notion of her man having a dangerous job, I'd be happy to go shake some sense into her."

"No—" he held up a hand. "She was...she understood. She more than understood, she wanted it for me."

"So then what's the problem?" his mom asked, relaxing slightly.

"I can't have both."

"Well, that's just silly," Nonna said, her voice uncharacteristically gentle. "Of course you can have both. You *should* have both."

He looked at his hands folded on top of the table. "You saw what happened with Vannah. I never took her on a date. Stood her up more times than I can count when she tried to plan something. I missed dinners she'd cooked, outings she'd planned...I forgot her birthday..."

"So your job came first with Vannah," his mom said with the smallest of shrugs. "That doesn't mean that it would be that way with Maggie."

"But it *would* be that way. It already is that way. Look at the way the Smiley case worked out. Had I been her boyfriend, I could have comforted her...*been there*. Stayed at her place, made her feel safe. I could have hugged her after she was held at gunpoint. But I didn't get to be Anthony. I had to be Captain Moretti."

I had to choose.

His mother's hand rested over both of his, squeezing. "Those were exceptional circumstances. I'm certain that Maggie understood that."

He felt a little flare of hope ignite in his chest, but he stamped it out. "But there will be other times—"

"Other times when your work comes first, yes, but sweetheart, that's true of all jobs. Anyone with *any* career is going to have to work late sometimes, or leave early sometimes. When you have children you may even miss the occasional ballet recital or soccer game because of it. But that doesn't mean you'll have to miss *all* of them. You just... you do the best you can."

"What your mother is trying to say is that you're smelling a wee bit high-and-mighty, aren't you? Thinking your job's more important than other boyfriends and husbands and fathers."

He opened his mouth to argue, but Nonna charged forward. "And you of all people should know that it is possible to have both. You had your father."

"Who frequently missed dinners," Anthony was quick to add. "And who missed more than a handful of soccer games. Who made Mom cry on more than one occasion when he had to reschedule an anniversary dinner."

"Yes, there were occasional hiccups and tears. But you think Gloria and Bruce Varni next door didn't have those very same issues? That anniversaries and piano recitals weren't missed occasionally?"

Anthony chewed the inside of his cheek. The Varnis owned a small specialty food store, and he immediately understood the point his mother was trying to make. *Cops aren't the only ones who struggle with work/life balance.*

"And more important," she said, squeezing his hand once more. "In spite of everything you just mentioned about your father working, you grew up wanting to be just like him. *Just like him*, Anthony. Had it been so bad for you kids—*or* for me—I don't think four out of four sons would have followed in his footsteps."

He pulled his hands away, running them over his face. Considering. "I need to think."

"Okay," his mom said softly. "But one other thing…"

"God, there's more?" he muttered.

"Definitely," Nonna chimed in, her expression gleeful. "Can I be the one to tell him?"

"Tell me what?"

"That none of what we just said is really the point."

"It's not." His voice was flat. Confused.

"Nope," Nonna crowed, and tapped her temple. "That's all head stuff. Logistics. What you really need to figure out, what will really matter at the end… is *do you love her?*"

Anthony stared at his grandmother, then his mother, who shrugged. "Your grandmother's quite right for once, darling. Either you can live happily without Maggie, or you can't. Decide *that*, and everything else will fall into place."

Love.

The word buzzed in his ears. Toyed with the edges of his mind. Settled in his heart, only to realize…

It was already there.

He loved her. He loved Maggie.

And the women of his family were right. It was all that mattered. It was all that mattered all along.

If someone told him right now that he couldn't be a cop

tomorrow, he'd be crushed, devastated. But he'd get over it. Eventually.

But when it came to Maggie, there was no getting over her. *Ever.*

The back door slammed shut as his father came back inside, skidding to a halt when he saw the three of them at the table. "Whoa, what did I miss?"

Tony walked to the sink to wash his hands.

"Your son just had a revelation," Maria said, sounding quite pleased with herself as she stood and resumed her usual position by the stove.

"Oh yeah?" Tony asked, turning to give his son a steady look. "What about?"

"Maggie," Nonna said, her voice even more blatantly smug than his mother's had been.

"Ah," his dad said, grabbing a towel and drying his hands. "That's good to hear."

"It is?" Anthony asked skeptically.

He'd been prepared for his father to have some dark words about the dangers of getting involved with an informant when he should have been focused on his work, and that women would come and go, but the NYPD was forever, and blah blah blah.

"Definitely," Tony said. "That means you won't bite my head off when you find out I invited her over for dinner tonight."

Anthony's spine slowly straightened, and all the nerve endings that had felt deadened for weeks slowly came back alive. "Say that again."

"Maggie," his father said, pouring himself a glass of wine. "I invited her over for dinner tonight. *Someone* had to take action."

Anthony stared at his father before transferring his gaze to his mother who looked...not shocked. "You knew about this."

"Of course, darling. Now why don't you do something useful and go fetch your girl from the ferry dock. Oh, and ask her if she likes lamb. Oh, and—"

But Anthony wasn't listening.

He was already out the door.

CHAPTER THIRTY-FOUR

It hadn't been exactly like she'd envisioned it. And she'd been doing a *lot* of envisioning on how to win Anthony Moretti's heart.

Everything from the classics (showing up on his doorstep with naught but a trench coat and high heels) to the more modern (declaration on Twitter) to the truly iffy (getting ahold of a police radio) had crossed her mind, but nothing had felt right.

In the end, she'd settled on simply calling him. Asking if they could talk.

But before she could get there, Tony Moretti had called *her*.

Invited her to family dinner. Actually, *invite* was a gentle, inadequate word. Her presence had been demanded.

So here she was, standing on a Staten Island ferry dock, wearing the best of her new dresses, a pretty blue wrap-dress thing with her new boots, and...no sign of Anthony. Or any Moretti.

Tony had told her all she had to do was make it onto the Staten Island ferry and someone would be there to meet her.

And she'd hoped—*oh, how she'd hoped*—that that someone might be Anth.

Only, Maggie wasn't entirely sure Anthony knew about his father's invitation. Tony had been particularly vague about that, which would have made the old Maggie chicken out.

But new Maggie almost hoped he didn't know. Hoped that surprise would work in her favor, would jolt him into realizing what was right in front of him, and—

And then *he* was right in front of *her*.

Walking toward her, his stride slow but purposeful.

Maggie sucked in a long breath, letting herself relish the sight of him. He was wearing jeans and boots and a long-sleeved white shirt. His hands were shoved into the pockets of his down vest, and he looked wonderfully, boyishly handsome.

She didn't move toward him. Couldn't make her feet move. Or her brain either, for that matter.

Maggie had spent the past several days trying to figure out what she'd tell him when she saw him again. She had whole speeches prepared on how she wouldn't stand in the way of his career, and how she wanted to be his partner, and now she couldn't remember a single word.

He stopped in front of her.

"Hi," she said softly.

He said nothing. Didn't smile, just stared down at her with that familiar, unreadable expression.

"I, um...your dad invited me to dinner? Which, I'm thinking maybe from the scowl, you didn't know."

Still nothing. Not even a hint of a smile.

Maggie rubbed her hands over the sides of her jacket. Darn sweaty palms.

"If you don't want me here, I can leave," she said quietly. "I don't want to leave, but I will. Because while I adore your family, and your dad is sweet, I didn't come for them. I came for *you*, and to tell you—"

His hands found her face seconds before he tilted her head up, his lips hovering above hers just briefly before he kissed her sweetly. Tentatively.

It was a kiss that spoke volumes, but not as much as the look in his eyes when he pulled back slightly. They were softer than she'd ever seen them.

"Oh," she breathed slightly.

He smiled then, slow and sexy before he lowered his mouth to hers again, one arm wrapping around her back while the other cupped the back of her head.

Someone passing them whistled, and another grumbled about getting a room, but Maggie barely heard them. She was too busy wrapping herself around the love of her life.

They kissed endlessly, and when he finally pulled back they were both out of breath.

His fingers brushed along her temple, a little line between his brows. "I'm not good at speeches, Maggie. I don't know . . . I've never known what to say in these situations—"

"I know, I—"

"—but I know I love you."

Oh. *Oh*. She hadn't known it would feel this good to hear it. She thought *nothing* would ever feel as good as loving him, but knowing he loved her back? *That* was better.

"I think you're supposed to say something," he grumbled.

"I was supposed to say it first, you insanely bossy man," she said, her palms resting against his chest. "And I'm not sure I want to say it second."

"Say it anyway," he said, a little desperate. He bent his knees so they were eye-level, his gaze pleading. "Say it, Maggie. Say—"

"I love you too."

Anthony Moretti's grin was gorgeous and Maggie was pretty sure she fell in love all over again at the sight of it.

"You should smile like that more often," she said, her fingers finding his lips. "Or on second thought, don't. Save them all for me. Just for me."

He kissed her again, then trailed his lips over her cheek to her ears, and he kissed her there too. "You'll always come first. You're *everything*. You know that, right?"

"I do. But I'll *never* make you choose, I swear it. I'll be your biggest fan."

He pulled back, his grin wicked. "Could you also be my nakedest fan?"

"Um, I better be your *only* naked fan."

He laughed and the sound was wonderful. Then he reached for her hand, and that was wonderful too.

"I'm supposed to ask you if you like lamb. Or maybe chicken," he said as they walked hand in hand toward his family's house. "I can't remember."

"I'm sure I'll like anything your mother cooks. Do you think she'll let me help serve? Maybe I can dump something in your lap for old times' sake, and then you can scowl at me for old times' sake."

"I think you *like* the scowl."

"I'm on the fence," she said as they crossed the street. "It may take me a couple months to decide. Years even…"

He pulled her to a stop then, spinning her around to face him. "Years, huh? How many?"

Maggie pretended to consider it. "At least one. Probably closer to two."

"I can do a hell of a lot better than that," he said, pulling her in for another of those melting kisses.

"Yeah?"

"Yeah," he said gruffly. "Because the thing is, Maggie..."

She held her breath, watched as he paused, looking unbearably shy before his eyes met hers once more.

"I was kind of planning on giving you forever."

EPILOGUE

V incent, damn you, you've gone and gotten champagne all over my new shoes!" Jill said, swiping at her purple suede heels with a napkin.

"Uh-oh," Elena said, nudging Maggie. "Looks like someone forgot to tell Vin that you've cornered the market on spilling things on people."

"This has a nice symmetry to it though, doesn't it?" Jill asked, glancing up from where she swiped at her shoes. "Maggie spilled iced tea on Anth's shoes at his celebration party, and now Vincent's trying to flood Elena's place with champagne on Maggie's celebration! But honestly, Vincent, you fool, look at my shoes!"

Vincent glanced down at Jill's shoes and shrugged. "So? Buy new ones."

Jill's jaw dropped as she turned to Maggie, Ava, and Elena. "Tell me he did not just say that. Is there no respect—"

"No, none," Elena said, holding out her champagne flute so her brother could refill it. "The sooner you accept this, the more peaceful your life will be."

"Peaceful is not in my future. I'm a homicide detective in New York, and don't tell your parents, but I'm pretty sure there was a mix-up at the hospital and my partner is actually the biological son of the Grinch..."

"Who's the Grinch?" Vincent asked as he poured champagne into Jill's glass.

"I can't even," she muttered. "Fill up our glasses and then scram. We need girl talk."

He shook his head and met Maggie's eyes. "Is this what it was like when you had to serve us at the diner? Horrible?"

Maggie narrowed her eyes. "Hmm, it's hard to know if you're getting the full experience if you're not wearing the orange uniform. I think I still have mine, if you want to—"

"And I'm out," Vin grumbled, grabbing another bottle of wine from the bucket and heading over to his brothers.

Maggie followed his progress and found Anthony watching her. She smiled, and he didn't smile back—not quite—but his eyes were adoring.

She gave a happy sigh.

Ava made a hooting sound. "Girl, you have it so bad."

"Oh, because you and Luc are so much better," Elena grumbled. "Don't think I didn't see that you both came out of my bathroom at the same time and that I had to remind you to pull the back of your dress out of your thong."

Ava gave a smug, sorry-not-sorry smile.

"Thanks again for hosting us all tonight," Maggie said to Elena. "Your new place is gorgeous."

"Isn't it?" she said happily.

Anthony's sister had recently moved into a gorgeous midtown high-rise with a view of the Empire State Building. It was a tight fit with all of the Morettis, plus Vincent's and Luc's partners, and a few of Maggie's friends from the diner, but it was a *wonderful* kind of crowded.

The loving, happy kind of full.

"Is it too early to toast Maggie?" Jill asked, raising her glass.

"Hell no. I've been toasting myself all week!"

"Are you making Anth address you as Published Author?" Elena asked. "If not, you must implement this plan immediately."

"No," Maggie admitted. "But I have started practicing my signature on every scrap of paper that crosses my path. A little premature considering the book hasn't even been printed yet, and book signings are a long—"

"Oh stop," Ava said, clinking her glass against Maggie's. "None of that. You've sold a book. A *book*. That's huge. Beyond huge. Tonight is about *you*, you fabulous published author."

Maggie couldn't stop the goofy grin.

She hadn't gotten tired of hearing it. Hadn't gotten tired of *thinking* about it. It had been a long road; eight months of rejection after rejection and false hope after false hope, but she'd gotten the call last week.

A New York publishing house wanted to publish her book.

Her book.

She felt a warm hand on the back of her neck and smiled as she smelled Anth's spicy cologne.

"Ladies," he said in his deep voice. "How about you share the guest of honor, hmm?"

"Please, like *you* share her," Jill said. "You hardly let her

out of the apartment for the first three months after you finally came to your senses—"

"Hey, Henley," he interrupted. "I believe your shoes are
bleeding purple all over Elena's new hardwood floor."

Jill shrieked. Elena shrieked. Ava rolled her eyes at both
of them and grabbed a roll of paper towels, and Anthony
pulled Maggie in for a kiss.

"They're right, you know," she murmured against his
mouth. "You have been hogging all of my attention."

"Yeah? Strange, I don't remember you uttering any
protest."

She held her champagne, still not drinking, her eyes taking in the room. Taking in the people that had come for her.

She'd invited her father and Cory. Neither had responded,
much less shown up.

But that was okay.

Because she had a new family now. One that was warm
and loving and who brought copious amounts of champagne
to celebrate her accomplishment.

"This is real, isn't it?" she said quietly. "I'm not dreaming
it?"

"Well it *is* real," he said, touching a gentle fingertip to her
cheekbone. "But it's a dream too. Your dream."

"True," she said, snuggling closer. "But I've had a little
epiphany about that dream lately. An addition."

He lifted his eyebrows. "Did you now? Not sure that's allowed."

"It is," she said confidently.

"Okay then. Tell me about this new and improved
dream."

"Well, I'm still a published author and I still get to wake
up each morning and write books. But there's also more. A

tall, *gorgeous* man, who is short on smiles but had this way of looking at me that turns me to mush…"

His eyes were tender as he listened.

"And there's Duchess, of course," she continued.

"Of course." Duchess was now officially Anthony's dog. Maggie was lucky to get a pet in.

She took a deep breath. Took a chance. "And there's a baby," she said in a rush, her voice quiet. "Who cries every time I finally sit down to write, but it's okay because I love him or her so much—"

Anthony's fingers wrapped around her bicep, his expression stunned. "Maggie, are you—are we—"

She smiled. "I think so. I mean, I'm not a hundred percent sure, but I took, like, five tests. All positive."

He stared down at her. Stunned. And Maggie felt a little stab of nervousness. "Is this okay? I know we didn't plan it, but—"

He put a hand over her mouth. "I have something to tell you too."

She nodded and he removed his hand, replacing it with his mouth, kissing her softly before he moved his mouth to her ear, drawing her close. "*My* dream has evolved over the past few months too. And you just made it come true."

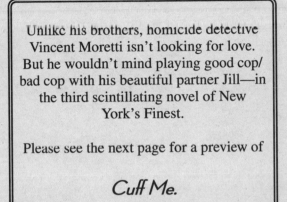

Unlike his brothers, homicide detective
Vincent Moretti isn't looking for love.
But he wouldn't mind playing good cop/
bad cop with his beautiful partner Jill—in
the third scintillating novel of New
York's Finest.

Please see the next page for a preview of

Cuff Me.

CHAPTER ONE

here's something wrong with a man that grins like that at a crime scene."

Detective Vincent Moretti glanced up from where he'd been studying the gunshot wound of the vic and glared at the officer who'd been shadowing him for the past three months.

"I wasn't grinning."

Detective Tyler Dansen never paused in scribbling in the black notebook he carried everywhere. "You were definitely grinning."

"Nope."

Dansen glanced up. "Fine. Maybe not grinning. But I'm one hundred percent sure I saw you smile."

"How about you be one hundred percent sure about who shot this guy instead?" Vincent said irritably.

Dansen returned his attention to his damn notebook, but he didn't look particularly chagrined by Vin's reprimand.

Oh what Vin wouldn't give to go back to those early days

when all he'd had to do was *look* at Dansen and the kid practically dropped in a deferential bow.

Three months of spending every workday in each other's company had the newly minted detective acting nearly as impudent as Vincent's *real* partner.

Nearly being an important distinction, because Vincent didn't think they made 'em sassier, more stubborn, or more annoying than Detective Jill Henley.

And he would know. They'd been partners for six long years, and their pairing up as partners was proof of God's sense of humor.

Jill Henley was Vincent's opposite in every way.

Jill was chipper, charming, and smiley.

Vincent was . . . none of those things.

Especially not the last one. Although, if he was being really honest with himself, Dansen may have been right about Vincent cracking a smile earlier.

It's not that Vin was immune to death. There was absolutely nothing humorous about a man lying cold in his own blood and guts, dead from a gunshot wound to the stomach.

But after six years as a homicide DT for the NYPD, one learned to compartmentalize. To let the brain occasionally go somewhere else other than death even as you were staring straight at it.

It was the only way to survive. Otherwise it was nothing but puking and nightmares.

And speaking of puking . . .

Vincent stood and gave Officer Dansen a once-over. "If you're gonna barf, do it outside," he said, just to needle the younger man.

Dansen threw his arms up in exasperation. "That was one

time. One time! And I hear it happens to everyone on their first day."

"Didn't happen to me."

"That's because you're a machine," Dansen muttered under his breath.

Vincent didn't respond to this. It was nothing he hadn't heard before. *Robot. Machine. Automaton.*

He just didn't know what people expected him to do about it.

In the movies, there was always some reason for the semi-mechanical, unfeeling action hero.

Either a dead wife or an abusive past or some other sort of jacked-up emotional history. But Vincent had always sort of figured he'd been born this way. Quiet. Reserved. Broody.

It's not that he didn't feel. Of course he did. He just didn't feel *out loud*.

He wasn't sure that he really knew how to. Wasn't sure he wanted to learn.

But in Dansen's defense on the puking thing, the kid's first crime scene as a homicide DT had been a rough one. A sixteen-year-old girl sliced to pieces and then tossed in the Dumpster behind a one-dollar-slice pizza joint in Queens.

Vincent's fists clenched at the memory.

It had taken them three days to find the guy who'd done that to her—a real sicko who'd claimed he'd done it because he was "bored."

That was one son of a bitch he hoped prison was *really* rough for.

"Let's move out," Vin growled at Dansen.

He headed toward the door of the hotel room where the body was found, and Dansen fell into step beside him, flipping through his notebook. "Okay, so here's what I'm thinking. The wife is the one who found the body and called it in, but—"

"She also shot him," Vincent said, impatiently punching at the down button for the elevator.

Dansen huffed in exasperation. "I was getting to that."

"Get there faster," Vincent said as they stepped into the elevator.

"So, can I—"

"Bring her in for questioning?" Vincent finished for him as he pulled out his cell phone. "Do it. And don't go easy on her. She'll slip up within minutes, all tangled up in her own guilt."

The younger man snapped his notebook shut. "It's really annoying when you do that. Finishing other people's sentences."

"'Kay," Vincent said distractedly, already striding off the elevator.

The lobby was crawling with reporters, and Vincent glared at Dansen, who held up his hands in surrender. "Don't look at me. I didn't call them."

Vincent gritted his teeth. He *hated* hotel cases. There always some bellhop or housekeeper who couldn't keep his or her damn mouth shut, and the result was a media circus that made the police work a thousand times more complicated than it needed to be.

Not that it really mattered in this particular case. There wasn't a doubt in his mind that the wife had pulled the trigger. He'd bet his pension on it. Vin had been doing this too long not to see the signs immediately. The too-fast way of speaking. The awkwardly forced eye contact in a conscious effort to minimize nervous blinking. Fidgeting hands.

The vic's wife had all of the above. This murder was practically the definition of open-and-shut case.

"You care if I leave you to finish this one up on your own?" he asked Dansen as they headed toward Vincent's unmarked patrol car.

Dansen skidded to a halt. "Seriously? You even have to ask? I've been begging you for *three months* to let me take point, and—"

"All right, calm down," Vincent said, jerking open the door of the driver's seat. He hesitated before getting in, realizing that there were things to be said.

He rested an arm on the roof of the car and glanced at Dansen who was...

Smirking.

"Wipe that shit smile off your face," Vincent said without any real heat.

"You're gonna miss me," Dansen taunted.

Vin narrowed his eyes. "Don't push it, kid."

"Kid? I'm thirty-one."

"Exactly."

Dansen gave an incredulous laugh. "You're thirty-three. One year's difference hardly makes you my senior."

Not in years, maybe. But in experience...

It wasn't about who was youngest or oldest. It was about who was best.

And Vin was confident that was *him*.

Vincent was damn good at his job. It was why he'd been assigned a trainee during Jill's leave of absence despite the fact that his lack of people skills was as legendary as his ability to sniff out even the most clever of murderers.

In truth, Vincent had been dreading his three months with the near-rookie, but it had been less painful than expected. Dansen was a good cop. A little green. When Dansen was assigned his new partner tomorrow, Vin had no doubts that the guy would be able to handle whatever came his way.

And then Vincent's life would finally get back to normal.

Not that these three weeks without Jill had been abnormal, precisely.

He still worked the same four-week days.

Still saw death on most all of those days.

Still went to breakfast with his family after Mass every Sunday, and argued with his brothers and occasionally with his sister during said breakfast.

He still watched baseball most evenings, still worked out most mornings.

So really, his life wasn't different without Jill at all.

Except that it was.

He glanced at his watch. Ninety minutes. An hour and a half until her plane landed. Not that he was counting.

"Hey, Detective Moretti." Dansen cleared his throat from across the hood of the car, and Vin tensed, knowing what was coming.

God, he hated shit like this.

"You can drop the 'Detective,'" Vincent said roughly. "Just call me Moretti. Or Vin. Whatever."

Dansen's smile flashed white across his dark face. "Do you know how many cops dream of the day when they're given permission to call one of the members of the royal family by their first name?"

"Oh Jesus. Don't start that again."

For the most part, Dansen had done a remarkable job of not getting on Vincent's nerves over the past couple months. But Dansen's ridiculous hero worship of Vincent's last name grated on his nerves. Yet another reason he couldn't wait for Jill to get back.

Jill, who'd never cared that Vincent's father was the recently retired police commissioner. Or that his older brother was a captain. Or that his younger brother was the NYPD's most famous officer.

Or that his grandfather had been a cop, and his mother had been a police dispatcher...

Okay, so maybe Vincent could *sort of* understand where Dansen was coming from. The Morettis were kind of NYPD royalty.

And Vincent was proud to be a part of it. Proud to carry on the legacy.

He just got damn tired of the ass-kissing.

"Seriously though, thanks," Dansen said. "Couldn't have asked for a better detective to show me the ropes. A nicer one, sure. A better-looking one, definitely. And you can be a real—"

"Asshole, I know," Vincent said.

Dansen held up a finger. "Not what I was going to say. I think that's the first time you've tried to finish my sentence and gotten it wrong."

"I'm never wrong," Vin said out of habit.

"Fine." Dansen rolled his eyes. "You are an asshole. Happy?"

Vin didn't bother responding, just lifted his hand in a final farewell to Dansen before the younger man could say whatever it was he'd wanted to say, and lowered himself into the car.

Vincent slid on his aviator sunglasses as he fastened his seatbelt.

He kept his face perfectly blank until he'd pulled away from the curb and merged into traffic.

Only then, only out of sight of prying eyes, did he let a smile overtake his face. A smile that quickly became a grin as he headed toward the airport to pick up his long-lost partner.

It was possible he'd missed Jill. A little.

Not that he'd be telling *her* that.

Fall in Love with Forever Romance

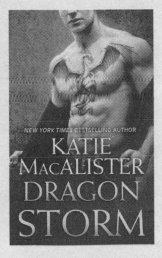

DRAGON STORM
by Katie MacAlister

In *New York Times* bestselling author Katie MacAlister's *Dragon Storm*, Constantine must choose: save his fellow dragons or the mortal woman he's grown to love.

HIS ALL NIGHT
by Elle Wright

In relationships, Calisa Harper has clear rules: no expectations, no commitments, no one gets hurt. She doesn't need a diamond ring to bring her happiness. She just needs Jared. Fine, fit, and ferocious in bed, Jared is Calisa's ideal combination of friend and lover. But the no-strings status they've shared for years is about to get very tangled...

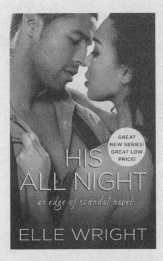

Fall in Love with Forever Romance

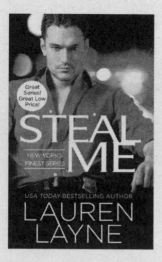

STEAL ME
by Lauren Layne

Faster than a New York minute, homicide detective Anthony Moretti and waitress Maggie Walker find themselves in a perilous pursuit that only gets hotter with each and every rule-breaking kiss.

A BILLIONAIRE
BETWEEN THE SHEETS
by Katie Lane

A commanding presence in the boardroom and the bedroom, Deacon Beaumont has come to save the failing company French Kiss. But one bold and beautiful woman dares to question his authority and everything he knows about love.

Fall in Love with Forever Romance

DUKES ARE FOREVER
by Anna Harrington

When Edward Westover takes possession of his rival's estate, everything that villain held dear—even his beautiful daughter—belongs to Edward. Will Kate Benton fall for the man who now owns everything she has come to know and love—including herself? Fans of Elizabeth Hoyt, Grace Burrowes, and Madeline Hunter will love this Regency–era romance.

Find out more about Forever Romance!

Visit us at
www.hachettebookgroup.com/publishing_forever.aspx

Find us on Facebook
http://www.facebook.com/ForeverRomance

Follow us on Twitter
http://twitter.com/ForeverRomance

NEW AND UPCOMING TITLES

Each month we feature our new titles
and reader favorites.

CONTESTS AND GIVEAWAYS

We give away galleys, autographed copies,
and all kinds of exclusive items.

AUTHOR INFO

You'll find bios, articles, and links to personal websites
for all your favorite authors—and so much more.

GET SOCIAL

Connect with your favorite authors, editors, and
other Forever fans, and share what's important to you.

THE BUZZ

Sign up for our monthly romance newsletter,
and be the first to read all about it.

VISIT US ONLINE AT

WWW.HACHETTEBOOKGROUP.COM

FEATURES:

OPENBOOK BROWSE AND SEARCH EXCERPTS

•

AUDIOBOOK EXCERPTS AND PODCASTS

•

AUTHOR ARTICLES AND INTERVIEWS

•

BESTSELLER AND PUBLISHING GROUP NEWS

•

SIGN UP FOR E-NEWSLETTERS

•

AUTHOR APPEARANCES AND TOUR INFORMATION

•

SOCIAL MEDIA FEEDS AND WIDGETS

•

DOWNLOAD FREE APPS

BOOKMARK HACHETTE BOOK GROUP @ WWW.HACHETTEBOOKGROUP.COM